DADDY'S BOY

MICHAEL DAVID WILSON

PRAISE FOR DADDY'S BOY

"A delirious ride through mundane absurdity and surreal brutality, *Daddy's Boy* perfectly captures the feeling of reconnecting with a loved one, only to find out they're a filthy, out-of-control chaos gremlin."

JASON PARGIN, AUTHOR OF *JOHN DIES AT THE END*

"Dripping with wit and nastiness, Michael David Wilson's *Daddy's Boy* is a gem of a dark comedy thriller. As always, Wilson's prose is fiery and provocative. This excellent novel took me by the throat on the first page and truly surprised me until the bitter end."

ERIC LAROCCA, AUTHOR OF *THINGS HAVE GOTTEN WORSE SINCE WE LAST SPOKE*

"*Daddy's Boy* is a profanity-laced cocktail of blood, guts, and every other bodily secretion you can think of. If you're squeamish or a prude, don't pick it up. But if you're in the mood for a wild, no-holds-barred, unpredictably violent family comedy, then this is the book for you. I loved every disgusting second of it."

DAVID MOODY, AUTHOR OF *HATER*

"Delightfully deranged and bursting with pure British humor, *Daddy's Boy* is an addicting sprint of twists and turns you'll never see coming. Contains one of the most emotionally significant dick pic scenes captured in literature. Read it."

MAX BOOTH III, AUTHOR OF *WE NEED TO DO SOMETHING*

"A madcap slice of slacker noir. Michael David Wilson's the kind of magician who can make a switchblade dance across his fingertips, then a moment later it's sticking out of your gut. A funny, wild tale you won't want to miss!"

BRIAN ASMAN, AUTHOR OF *MAN, FUCK THIS HOUSE*

"Starts out as a fast-talking crime caper but soon takes a hard left into all-out WTFery. I never knew what was coming next. *Daddy's Boy* is exciting, weird, violent, hilarious, harrowing, original, and a helluva lotta fun. Exactly my kind of jam."

DANGER SLATER, AUTHOR OF *I WILL ROT WITHOUT YOU*

"With humour so black no light can escape it and a plot with more twists than a tourniquet in an auto-asphyxiation, this novel knows where all the bodies are buried. Read it with caution, it might just make Daddy's Boys of us all!"

JASPER BARK, AUTHOR OF *STUCK ON YOU*

A This Is Horror Publication
www.thisishorror.co.uk

ISBN: 978-1-910471-07-4 (paperback)
ISBN: 978-1-910471-08-1 (ebook)

First published in 2025 by This Is Horror

Editor: John Thomas
Cover Art: Vincent Chong

For Jeremy Corbyn, Anna Richardson, and John Crinan

1

So, there I was, queueing up outside NatWest bank, in the red figuratively and now literally, thanks to the botched suicide attempt. The red rope burns around my neck concealed by a loose linen summer scarf. My cat kidnapped, my money non-existent, and my landlord so on my back I was practically a camel. To the left of me stood a Subway sandwich shop, outside two young lasses were physically fighting over a footlong meatball marinara. And to the right, in front of Pandora jewellery, a tracksuited twenty-something voiced aloud the pros and cons of robbing the place to his teenaged protégé.

Kidderminster is one hell of a drug.

It's moments like these, you wonder if you've reached the bottom, but something always comes along to humble you. On this occasion, it was a one-legged pigeon. Now, why it hobbled towards me and not the girls spilling crumbs and marinara sauce all over the concrete, I couldn't tell you, but so it goes. At first, I felt sorry for the little guy. One leg, all out of food, and living in Kiddy. We had a kind of pitiful kinship.

"How you doing, little fella?" I said.

The pigeon didn't say anything to that, obviously, on account of it being a pigeon. But there was something in its big, dumb reddish eyes that said it understood. Then, as if in answer, it flew up into the air—which, by the way, I didn't know one-legged pigeons could do with such ease—and flew off in the direction of the British Heart Foundation charity shop. Fair enough, perhaps it was looking for a ratty cardigan or a yellowed Enid Blyton book. Who was I to judge? One minute later, when it came limply flying back, I thought one of the Subway sandwich fighters had flicked mayonnaise at me, but nope—you guessed it—it was pigeon shit.

You see? You can always fall a little bit further.

Thanks, pigeon, you ugly little flying shithouse.

But sometimes you're offered a lifeline. These gifts come in the strangest of forms. And on that day, about half an hour before lunch, it traipsed towards me in the shape of a man with grey shoulder length hair, wearing an 'I was on *Naked Attraction*' t-shirt, a denim jacket, blue-rinse jeans, a tattered rucksack, and scuffed Reeboks.

At first, he just stood at my side, less than a metre away. Snatching glances at me and trying his best not to make it obvious. Though, given his proximity and the exaggerated nature of his jumpy movements, how could it not be obvious? He scratched the back of his wrist vigorously, flaking skin to the floor. He mumbled something to himself, took a hipflask from his inner jacket pocket, and enjoyed a cheeky swig which apparently gave him some confidence because the next thing I knew he was patting me on the shoulder, smelling of hard liquor and old tobacco.

"What you in for then?" It sounded more like we were serving prison time than standing outside a bank, though in Kiddy the likening fit.

"A loan," I told him.

"Loans are bollocks." He was skittish, swaying back and

forth, and playing with his hands. "What you want is honest money for an honest job."

"I already have two jobs, but they aren't enough to pay my lawyer or the rent."

"Solicitors and landlords," he said. "Thieving bastards, the lot of them."

A woman with blue rinse hair and a patterned cardigan, further ahead in the queue, tutted, though whether it was because of the profanity or the man's assessment of solicitors and landlords, I couldn't tell.

"Word to the wise," the man said. "Don't bother with solicitors. Get a public defender instead. Much cheaper. That's what I got. Didn't end up doing any time either. Though if you'd seen the state of the other guy, I probably should have, know what I mean?"

I looked forward, careful not to give the man much eye contact.

"Public defenders," he said again. "They're well good. Little bit of legal aid. That's what you need, boy."

"Not for this," I said. "A different type of business."

"Ah, Jesus, you're not seeing a solicitor about a will, are you? Don't bother with any of that. You can get a template off Google for that kind of shit."

"That's what you did? You made a will based on a template from Google?"

He scratched the back of his neck. "That's what I *would* do."

"And it's legally binding?"

"It's good enough. End of."

"Well, thanks for the advice." I moved forward in the queue, hoping my newly acquired human shadow wouldn't follow, but of course he did.

"You can have that one for free," the man said. "But anymore and I'll start charging, know what I mean?"

He grinned.

I didn't.

"Anyway, that's not why I'm seeing a lawyer," I said. "Nothing to do with wills."

"Oh. Then what?"

"The lawyer—"

"Solicitor," he corrected. "You ain't a bloody yank by the sounds of you, so I don't know why you're acting like it. Watched too many reruns of *Friends*, have you? Bit of a *Frasier*-holic?"

The queue shuffled further forward. We were almost in the bank. So close I could hear generic music on tinny speakers.

"Well, whatever's going on with you, I guess you need a lot of money, huh?" the man said.

I didn't respond.

The man continued to keep pace with me, moving forward as I did.

"How much you hoping to borrow then?"

"Seeing as we've only just met, I'd rather not discuss that."

"*Only just met* ..." The man sniggered as if it were funny. "Nah, that's fair enough, that is." He nervously patted the cigarette packet in his trouser pocket. "Anyway, what if I said I could give you an easy job for a million pounds?"

I turned to look at him head-on for the first time. I know it's not right to judge people by appearances but this bloke looked like he'd be hard pressed to offer me a job for five pounds let alone a million. It was my turn to snigger.

"Well, boy," he pressed, "a job for a million pounds, what would you say?"

I swallowed, unsure why I was about to indulge him, but it wasn't as if I had anything better to do. "If you were serious, I'd consider it."

"Consider it? You'd more than consider it. You'd bite my

hand off like a wild crocodile—snappity snap snap." He mimicked the actions of a crocodile with his teeth. "Consider an honest job for a million pounds? Come off it!"

"Honest?"

The man checked over his shoulder, lowered his voice to an almost whisper. "Sure. Why not?"

"Wait. Is this actually real?" I said. "Is that what's happening here? Are you offering me a job?"

"Yeah," he said, but he didn't sound so sure.

I scratched underneath my scarf. Pain burned from where the rope had pinched before breaking. I'd told Amanda it had been an autoerotic asphyxiation wank gone wrong, but the sadness in her eyes told me she hadn't bought it. Christ, I needed to sort myself out.

"If only it *were* real," I whispered, more to myself than the geezer.

He must have heard, cos the next thing I know he went, "Oh, but it is."

It wasn't. It couldn't be. People like me didn't win a tenner on The National Lottery, let alone get handed a fortune. But, on the other hand, what was there to lose, I hadn't already lost?

"It *really* is," the bloke said again.

"If you're serious, then I guess I'm interested."

"That's the spirit! Well, heck, what are we still doing in line at this wreck of a bank? Come with me, boy."

"I need to get this loan now. I can't just follow you based on a hypothetical."

"Haven't you been paying attention? Nothing hypothetical about it. In three seconds, I'm leaving. You follow me and your life will change forever, or you stay here and ask yourself, *what if?*"

I appraised the guy. Everything about him and the situation screamed 'bullshit'. But he was right about one thing, if I didn't follow this probable waster, there would always be a part of me that asked *what if?* And if—no, *when*—it inevitably turned out to be bullshit, I could simply return to NatWest and apply for the loan or alternatively jump off the Galton Bridge depending on my mood.

The man headed away and up the high street. I took a deep breath, counted to five, then jogged after him.

He turned his head slightly, grinning cigarette-yellowed teeth at me. We passed the two Subway sandwich fighters, now sidled up closely next to each other on a graffiti-kissed bench, chatting as if nothing had happened, covered in the saucy aftermath of their battle.

"A million pounds," I said. "How do I know you're not full of shit?"

"For starters, I'll give you a grand right now. There's an ATM up ahead."

"You could have just used the one outside NatWest."

"Ha! After what we'd been talking about? I'm no idiot, boy. You want me to get jumped? All those fuckers know I'm loaded. I'm surprised no one pulled a gun on us." He glanced around, checking the coast was clear. "Bloody parasites, they'll do anything for a few extra quid in this town."

"It's mostly just OAPs and mothers."

"Them's the worst. They look innocent enough, which is how they get you." He scraped his hair back, parted it in such a way to reveal a scar on the left side of his head. "You see that, boy? Tyre iron. And who'd you think was responsible? A pregnant cherry up at the Horse Fair."

"Isn't a cherry a virgin?"

"Well, this one obviously weren't, given she was up the duff something proper. Come on, boy, use your smarts." The man inserted his debit card into the ATM, got his pin wrong, then slammed his fist into the front of the thing. "Bollocks! You have to put your PIN in quickly, you know. They might have a camera, so you don't want them to catch your deets."

"Why not shield your pin with your other hand or wallet? That's what I do."

He raised an eyebrow. "Not a bad idea, but if you do it quickly, it's just as good. They call me Ninja Fingers. And not just cos of this, if you know what I mean." He winked. "Also cos—"

"Nah, think about it. If someone's installed a camera, they could just slow the video down when they play it back, then they'll catch everything. So you really should use your other hand as a shield."

He shrugged. "Whatever. I have my method. You have yours. If one of us gets caught out, we'll know who's smarter, but until then ..." He tapped his pin in with speed, as if touch typing. It was accepted. "You see? Ninja Fingers. Now, let's get you your thousand quid, yeah?"

He went to withdraw a grand, but the machine soon informed him his daily limit was £300.

"Ah, crap," he said. "Listen, I'm really sorry about this, boy, but I tell you what, I'll give you three hundred from this card and another three hundred from the Nationwide account. How's that sound?"

"It sounds as if I'll be four hundred pounds poorer than I thought I was gonna be five seconds ago."

He shook his head. "Bloody hell, you really are one of those glass half empty types, ain't ya? Four hundred pounds poorer than five seconds ago? More like six hundred quid richer than two minutes ago."

He shoved the first £300 into my hand, which I swiftly deposited into my own wallet, then he inserted the second debit card into the ATM.

"No need to mope, boy. By the end of the day, you'll have a million pounds, so who cares if we run into a few obstacles along the way."

"You'll pay me that soon?"

He shrugged. "I mean, not literally. It's just a phrase, innit?"

"I'm fairly sure it's not just a phrase. If you say you'll—"

He stamped a Reebok into the ground. "Give over, would you? You're getting paid. You need to relax more and worry less. Here." He handed me another wad of cash. "Now let's get out of here and to the task at hand."

The town was a gaping wound with the plaster half-off. We passed charity shops, bookies, and discount outlets with names like MegaValue.com. Soon, we were walking amongst the ghosts of yesteryear. A retail paradise in the nineties, buildings that had once housed shops such as Woolworths, Index, and Tandy were all boarded up and covered in 'For Sale' signs. But let's face it, nobody was buying a place like that in a town like this. Broken Britain was fast becoming comatose Britain, do not resuscitate Britain, off to the morgue in five Britain.

"The high street of broken dreams," the man said. "Not like me, boy. I've got dreams. Wild dreams. Dreams that stretch from here to … Well, a darn sight further than here. Somewhere a long way away … Like Bromsgrove."

"Bromsgrove? It's only twenty minutes away, tops."

"Not if you walk it. Suddenly it's a long way away. Another land …"

"It's about nine miles, give or take. So you could do it in what? Three hours."

"I don't have three hours to walk to Bromsgrove!"

We headed up a set of concrete stairs to a more secluded area, out of the town. Brick walls were punctuated with graffiti declaring things like 'Gazza woz ere' and 'Eddie got fingered'. The latter sounded like a rip-off of a Tom Green movie.

"What's the job?" I said.

"I need you to drive me somewhere."

My cheeks warmed—this was gonna be awkward. "So, the thing is … I don't have my car here."

"Hmm … But you can drive, right?"

"Had my license for over ten years."

"Then there isn't a problem."

The man scanned the vicinity. The backstreets were secluded. Filled with soiled carrier bags, empty crisp packets, and crumpled beer cans. Cars that had seen better days were parked along the kerb. He approached a half-rusted orange shit-heap of a car, fresh out of the eighties, then looked around before smashing the driver's side window with his elbow.

"What the fuck are you—"

"Shh, boy. Shh. I'm solving a problem." He reached his hand through the broken glass, unlocked, then opened the door. "Give me a moment and we'll have her up and running in a jiffy." He brushed glass fragments from the front seat onto the pavement, shards sticking to and sparkling on his skin, then took a screwdriver from his rucksack and started unscrewing the steering column. His hand began to bleed, but he continued, unperturbed. He looked up. "Don't just gawk at me, boy. Keep a lookout. If you see anyone angry-looking coming towards the car, I might have to use my judo."

I gazed up and down the street. It was empty. As grey and lifeless as the town itself. My heart thumped in my chest.

What the hell was I now part of? Could I leg it before I became an accessory to a crime or was I already in too deep? Knowing my luck, he'd use his judo on me if I backed out. Assuming he even knew judo. Plus, I'd have to give him the six hundred quid back and wouldn't see a penny more.

The radio began to play, interrupting my internal panic—some pop tune as old as the car itself.

The man got out of the car and beamed at me proudly. "All right, get in the driver's seat."

He hastily made his way to the passenger side. I was still

stood there contemplating my options by the time he got in the car, which apparently wasn't a good look because the man soon screamed, "Come on, come on. We haven't got all day, boy. Get your arse in the bloody car already."

I felt and heard the crunch of old glass underneath my rear as I plonked myself down in the driver's seat. The man switched the radio off and sparked the starter wire against the battery wire and the car started.

"Go on, boy. Rev the engine something proper."

I did as instructed and the old shit-heap roared to life.

"You sure we should be doing this?"

"Doing this?" he said. "We've bloody done it, boy. We're off to the races. Or at least we will be, once you put your foot down."

"I mean, if it isn't too late, perhaps we could just get a taxi and—"

"This is time sensitive. 'Isn't too late'." He scoffed. "We've done the window in for god's sake. And look at your arse! Covered in more glass than the Crystal Palace. If the glass was a prostitute and you bailed after that much contact, you'd still have to pay a pretty penny."

A scream echoed from behind us.

I looked in the rear-view and saw a couple of men in Wolverhampton Wanderers football shirts dashing towards us.

And from the looks on their out-of-breath, raging-red, too many Carlings before eleven a.m. puffy faces, the lads weren't happy.

"Oi, wanker!" one of them yelled.

That settled things. No time to worry about the repercussions of stealing a car—we were well and truly in it.

I stepped on the accelerator and got us the hell out of there. One of the football lads picked up a rock, which he threw towards the car. It conked the bumper and rolled away. Dribbles of sweat trickled down my forehead.

"We showed them. Bunch of pussies!" the man said.

"It's no laughing matter. What if they call the police?"

"I'd imagine they will, given we nabbed their motor. So no pissing around. Treat the accelerator like a StairMaster and step on it."

"Oh god! Oh god!" I was close to hyperventilating.

I'd done some questionable things before but not like this and not so spontaneously. Then again, after so many dalliances with death and suicidal ideation playing more frequently than 'Last Christmas' by Wham in December, the rules had changed.

I should have texted Amanda. Let her know what was going on, just in case. But my phone was wedged deep in my pocket, and I didn't want to lose control of the vehicle and add further charges to my future rap sheet.

The man scratched his blackhead dotted nose. "Ah relax," he said, picking up on my panic. "They might not even call the pigs. Round here, a couple of cunts like that could be just as likely to take things into their own hands. Especially if they've had a few tinnies. Police don't exactly do much in these parts and it's more fun to give someone a good kicking, know what I mean?"

I knew precisely what he meant, and it didn't make me feel easier about anything I'd done since meeting this oddball. My life consisted of drawing as little attention to myself as possible post-breakup with Amy. What most certainly was not part of the plan was starting beef with any of the local football hooligans.

We neared the ring road up by the train station. The Wolves lads long out of sight. My heart rate slowly returning to normal.

"So, where exactly do you want me to drive us?" I asked.

"New Wood Lane, Blakedown."

"That's the posh part of town, right?"

"Course it's the posh part of town. I'm giving you a

million, aren't I?" He cleared his throat. "I'm bloody loaded, boy. They call me Big Load Brian."

"Your name's Brian?"

"Nope. It's Norman, but Big Load Norm don't sound as good."

"I thought you said people called you Ninja Fingers."

He grinned. "Yeah. That, too. You've got a nice memory, boy."

"Big Load Brian doesn't sound like it's about money. Sounds like it's—"

"About how much jizz I can shoot out the end of my lunch box?" he said, smirking. "Popular misconception. Anyway, make no mistake about it, I'm more minted than a bottle of Listerine."

I noted the ketchup stain on Norman's *Naked Attraction* t-shirt, the weathered fade and tears up his jeans—stringy sections of loose fabric no clothes designer would ever have sanctioned—and scuffed Reeboks so worn, I could practically smell the sweat-seasoned mildew with my eyes. Those trainers had been abused so badly they could have taken Norman to court. If he'd told me the soles had gangrene, I'd have believed him. Now, granted, I supposed the richest in society didn't have to dress up or prove anything. Look at how Steve Jobs dressed or Mark Zuckerberg. But something told me Norman wasn't amongst the elite. Less Steve Jobs, more Steve outside the Jobcentre in Stourport.

I checked the rear-view extra hard. Still no sign of the footie lads whose car we'd nicked, and no sign of the police either. But how long would it last? As soon as it was called in, the Old Bill would be onto us faster than a mould problem in a tower block apartment at the height of winter. And stealing an orange car from the eighties? As subtle as a brick in the dick.

We eventually pulled up outside a pair of tall open gates

to a large Tudor house with a luxurious garden so well maintained it could have passed for an English Heritage site.

"Ha! Gate's already open," Norman said. "Your million is so close I can smell it."

Norman sniffed the air, but I reckoned the only thing he could smell were the acrid fumes wafting off his Stilton shoes.

He slapped me on the back. "You look nervous, boy."

Of course I *looked nervous*. I was nervous. Why wouldn't I be nervous after all he'd put me through?

It was supposed to be a quiet morning. An easy day off. Apply for and receive a loan from NatWest. A jacket potato with cheese and beans for lunch. A cheeky wank in the afternoon. Tarantino movie on the box—*after* not during the wank. Homemade curry for dinner with keema naan, followed by a game of FIFA on the PlayStation. The most taxing decision I was supposed to make all day was the starting line-up for the said game of FIFA. Next game was against an in-form Liverpool who'd just won five games on the trot. Hell, the planned day off would only have been topped if Amanda had popped round in the evening, but she was working a late which meant no Amanda and probably another more indulgent wank before bed. Might even use the Nivea intensive moisture hand cream if I was feeling particularly extravagant and could keep the suicidal ideation at bay long enough to get it up.

"It's still not too late to back out of this," Norman said, snapping me out of my imaginings.

And frankly, that was incredible because he hadn't given me a chance to back out when he'd smashed in the car window or demanded I get my arse in the car and hightail it out of there. Still, a lifeline was a lifeline. Better late than never.

"Get out of what, exactly?" I said, making sure I understood him.

"This." He pointed to the Tudor House as if it explained

everything. It did not. "Then again, if you want your million, you drive through them gates. But once you do, there's no going back. Ever."

His vagueness, aura of stupidity, and track record thus far should have been enough for me to get out of the car and say: "You're on your own, pal. I'm done."

But I guess Norman's stupidity was contagious because instead I eased off the brake and drove towards the house.

No going back.

2

THE TUDOR HOUSE was something else entirely. Hedges pruned to resemble woodland animals, flowers from all colours of the rainbow, and a fountain with so many layers it could have formed the centrepiece of an evening illumination show. This was a different world from Kidderminster. Even the birds sang a more sophisticated song from the town centre pigeons that drunkenly stumbled around, belly-first, bleating out coos and grunts if you looked at them funny.

Norman unstrapped his seatbelt. "Right. You just stay put and I'll be out in a jiffy. Then you'll get your money. You hear me, boy?"

He got out of the car and proceeded to the front of the property, but instead of going through the front door, he went around the left side of the building, disappearing out of sight.

I wound the driver's window down. All I could hear was the petrol-hungry engine of the stolen motor and some enthusiastic birds tweeting louder than Donald Trump in 2017. I gazed up at the sky, which appeared bluer in Blakedown, as if the rich had access to better weather. I put an arm out the window and switched the radio on. When a One Direction song came on, I shut it off and fiddled with my phone. I toyed with sending Amanda a text to let her know about my current predicament. A kind of insurance so that somebody knew where I was and what I was doing if shit went south. But what could I say? *I've traipsed across Kiddy with some old waster in a* Naked Attraction *shirt because there's a slim chance he might make me a millionaire?* She'd think I was higher than the time I'd thought my potted plant collection on the windowsill was all seven of Snow White's dwarves and they were plotting to kill me.

Raucous shouts reverberated from inside the Tudor House, snapping me to attention.

"And if you don't, I'll stuff your dismembered dick up your withered cornhole, you filthy cunt!" A woman yelled.

Norman bolted out of the place, running faster and more chaotically than a naked toddler covered in shit.

"Go! Go! Go!" he shouted, waving his hands at me and jumping into the passenger seat.

I went to ask but he got there first, saying, "No time to explain. Just put your foot down, boy."

A couple of thickset men with no necks barrelled out of the house and towards the car. They wore black suits, no tie, top button undone, and resembled bouncers whose gym membership had lapsed and takeaway orders had gone through the roof.

I wasn't sticking around to find out anything further. I hit the accelerator, swinging the car round so it faced the long driveway out of there. In the rear-view, a short athletic woman with pillar box red hair, and wielding what looked like a samurai sword, rushed out of the house, her face Vinnie Jones-angry yet oddly attractive. Like a sleep-deprived Emma Stone, running on cocaine and repressed rage.

Norman screamed, "Get us the hell out of here!"

I hightailed it out of the still open gates to the Tudor House, nearly colliding with a white Mercedes SUV. An angry Southeast Asian woman with glossy hair and stylish glasses sounded her horn and flipped me the bird. I sped away, leaving the Merc, two no-necks, and one coked-up Emma Stone samurai, seething beyond the car exhaust fumes and standing at the Tudor House's front gate.

We rode the next few minutes in silence, aside from Norman's asthmatic wheezing. I drove in a stunned state of shock, a focussed trance in which all I could do was concentrate on the task at hand: getting the absolute hell out of there and away from the danger.

When Norman had got his breathing under control, he said, "Things went very wrong."

And did this guy ever *not* state the obvious?

"Oh, that was things going wrong, was it? Because I'd assumed everything went off without a hitch and you now had the million plus in your possession and we were going to celebrate with a nice pub lunch at Toby fucking Carvery."

"All right, all right. Keep your head on, boy. I'm the one calling the shots here."

"What shots? You nearly got *your head* sliced off by some mad cow with a samurai sword, you fucking moron."

"That probably weren't even a real sword. Now less of the lip and drive us to Worcester."

"Why the hell should I? You almost got us killed."

"And you *will* get us killed if you don't do exactly as I say."

"Oh, fuck off."

"You don't have a clue who we're dealing with, boy."

"So tell me."

"To Worcester. Now. I mean it. I'm not fucking about." He slammed his fist against the glovebox so hard, I veered the steering wheel to the right, nearly swerving into oncoming traffic. I went to reprimand him but before the words came out, he delivered a flurry of rights and lefts to the progressively more damaged glovebox. He didn't stop swinging until his knuckles were red, raw, and bloodied.

"Fuuuuuck!" Norman's scream was so loud it set off my tinnitus. He took a deep breath, retrieved the hipflask from his jacket pocket, and guzzled. "Fucking Swain. He stitched me up, good and proper this time ... Come on, put your foot down. Why are you slowing down?"

"There are sometimes police on the bridge up ahead. They wait around and—"

"You know what's worse than police with speed cameras? Big bastards who want to kill you. And raving lunatics with swords."

"So it was a real sword?"

"I mean, her nickname's the Slicer but ..." He waved a hand dismissively. "Forget it for now. Them boys from inside the house will be on our tail in no time, so we need to get as far away as possible before they get us gone permanently, know what I mean?" He shook his head. "Concerned about a speeding ticket? Bloody hell, boy."

"It's not a speeding ticket I'm worried about, you thick log of shit. More like the whole driving a stolen vehicle thing."

Norman drank from his hipflask, alcohol perfuming the air.

"I dunno why you're being so bloody rude all of a sudden," he muttered, reaching into his trouser pocket and pulling out a packet of cigarettes.

Norman sparked up. After his first pull, his scowl softened.

He thrust the cigarettes in my direction. "You want one?"

"I'll be all right."

"A drag for the road?"

"I said, I'll be all fucking right."

"Jesus. You sound more stressed than I am. I reckon you need a fag more than you think."

"Gee, I wonder why the fuck I'm stressed, Norman? You any idea why that could be?"

"Anger management issues? Unresolved childhood trauma?"

"Just shut the fuck up and let me drive."

Norman laughed, reclining his seat back, and puffing his cigarette. "I kind of like this side to you, boy. You were such a wet fucking fish before, but now you're showing a bit of attitude. That'll serve you well if we have to fight the lads, innit?"

"Seriously, what is wrong with you? One minute you're beating the shit out of an inanimate object until you're bleeding, the next you're laughing as if this is all one big joke."

"Trust me, none of this is a joke."

"You can't blow hot and cold like that. There's something wrong with you."

"Oh, believe me, I know. There's been something wrong with me for a long time." Norman finished his cigarette, then lobbed it out of the window.

We were quiet for a moment, save for the encroaching rumble of a motorbike. Norman jolted so fast it was as if he'd woken from a night terror to a house fire. "Next exit, next exit!"

"But that isn't the way to Worces—"

"Take the left. Now!"

I hard-turned, tyres screeching—an assortment of car horns blaring as I narrowly avoided missing the turn and smashing into the side of a pink Peugeot 206.

The motorbike boomed past, long fiery hair spilling out the back of the helmet and dancing in the wind.

Heart pounding and hands trembling after nearly killing us and a car full of people in the Peugeot, I eased the car into the parking area of …

"Driver and Vehicle Standards Agency," I said, reading the sign. "Isn't this literally the worst place to show up with an uninsured stolen vehicle?"

Norman howled "woo" louder and more energetically than The Nature Boy Ric Flair.

Norman flung his arms over his head. "Boy, oh boy, what a bloody day, huh?"

"You nearly got us killed, you cockwomble," I shouted.

"No, I just got us saved." He sipped from the hipflask, unaffected by my rage. "That motorbike that came zipping past like it was fresh out of *Road Rash* only happened to be ridden by the sword-swinging loon from the Tudor House. So, you know, you're welcome."

"How the hell didn't she see us? This car is hardly inconspicuous."

"Who's to say she didn't? But the way you took that turn, she'd have face-planted the concrete if she'd followed suit. Guess she decided to live another day."

"Wait, if she saw us, then she'll just take the ring road and go back on herself, so …" I stepped on the accelerator.

"Easy does it, boy. We've got to take the back roads for now. Be more discreet."

"Says the guy who saw a bright orange retro-mobile and decided it was a better bet to nick than an average grey hatchback."

"An average grey hatchback with a modern immobiliser and fancy alarm system. I'm not as thick as you make me out to be. Now, let's press on. Trust me, if any of that lot catch up with us, you'll be wishing we'd been pulled over by the police."

"Who *are* that lot?"

"I'll explain in good time. But for now, we just need to concentrate on getting to Worcester. You've got to trust me on this one."

Nothing Norman said commanded trust or reassured me, but turning back towards Kiddy seemed riskier than continuing to Worcester. I'd go along with Norman until I landed upon a better way out of this mess.

We rode much of the remainder of the journey in silence, which was preferable to both Norman's bullshit and One Direction's music. We never saw the motorbike again, though I felt my hands getting clammier anytime I saw or even heard the roar of a bike's engine. I even did a double take when I saw an old woman in a straw summer hat on a bicycle.

As we neared a retail park, Norman gestured to a hardware store. "Stop off there, would you? I need to get some things."

The last time he'd asked me to take a turn it had arguably saved our lives—though had almost taken the lives of a woman and a bunch of kids in a Peugeot 206. Still, I did as instructed and pulled into the car park. "What you after?"

"Lighter fluid and a bottle of piss."

"I don't think they sell bottles of piss, mate," I said.

My laughter at his slip-up bringing slight relief.

But apparently his wording hadn't been a slip-up, cos he went, "Oh, but they kind of do."

Norman exited the car, slamming the door, and for the second time that day I was left waiting on this malfunction of a human being as if I were his personal chauffeur, which I was fast becoming.

The place I was parked outside was called 'Ronnie's Hardware', according to the sign. No points for imagination, but at least you knew what you were getting. As long as Norman didn't get chased out of the fucking place by security, it would be more successful than the last time I'd waited for him. I hoped he had some cash in his wallet. Didn't want to add "bottle of piss theft" to the charges against us.

A security camera overlooked the car park. I stared into my lap, scratching a dry fleck of dirt off my jeans. If that camera was on and the police caught onto our whereabouts, we were ruined. Come to think of it, how many other cameras had we passed during this little escapade? Perhaps I could get out of the situation now before it was too late. Just abandon the car and leave Norman to deal with the aftermath of whatever it was he was doing. The guy was clearly a grade-A idiot—probably the first time he'd scored an A in anything—and I should have known better than to have got involved with him from the start. But the deeper this got—whatever the hell *this* was—the more we were tied together. And the more I was implicated.

I tapped my fingers against the steering wheel.

I should definitely abandon the car. It was the strongest thing tying me to things. Norman had been the one who everyone had seen. I doubted anyone in the Tudor House had so much as glimpsed my face, the way we'd sped out of there. Then again, that camera was looking dead at me. If I left the vehicle, I was Jeremy Beadled, aka well and truly caught on video. You've been framed. Framed by a waster with a penchant for *Naked Attraction*.

The car door opened suddenly. I jumped, half-expecting to be lynched, but it was just Norman, with a large carton of lighter fluid and a bottle of vodka.

"This doesn't look good," I said, eyeing his shopping and trying to keep calm.

"Nothing to worry about, my boy," he said, which seemed precisely the thing he would say if there was absolutely something to worry about. "Now, I need you to drive over to Chedworth Drive."

"Where's that?"

"You don't know Chedworth Drive?"

"That's pretty much what I just said."

"I suppose. It's just … well, who the hell doesn't know Chedworth Drive?"

"Me. I don't know Chedworth fucking Drive, you dimwit." So much for keeping calm.

"All right, all right. Less of the attitude. I'll show you the way."

Reluctantly, I turned out of the car park, nodding at the parking attendant on the way out. It was supposed to be a friendly nod, a clear sign we were just two regular and definitely innocent guys, should the police poke around asking questions. Though, in reality, it was giving the attendant a reason to remember and positively ID me. Not least given the feverish prick in the passenger seat, who was clutching the vodka and lighter fluid as if they were sacred treasures. Norman's stupidity was infecting me.

Time to make amends.

"I'm not taking you to Chedworth Drive if you're about to torch the place," I said.

Norman laughed. "You're a sick little bastard, ain't ya? I'm no pyro, boy. Now continue straight down this road, yeah?"

"You bought a bottle of vodka and lighter fluid. Pretty flammable, so …"

"Yeah and? So is my dad's deodorant, my mum's hairspray, and your wrinkled old gran's soiled mattress, but it don't mean they're starting house fires, does it?" Norman uncapped the bottle of vodka and started chugging it back. "Ugh, rough as a dog's arse on a Sunday morning. Take a left here, boy." He winced, then necked some more. "You know, doesn't matter how many times I do this, it doesn't get any easier."

"If you don't like drinking, then why do it?"

He laughed, motioned towards the next left, directing me with one hand and holding the vodka bottle with the other. "This ain't about drinking. This is about prep." He thrust the bottle towards me. "Here. Help me out, would you?"

I kept my hands on the steering wheel and eyes on the road.

Norman moved the vodka bottle away from me and downed some more, sputtering then coughing half of it back into his lap. He pushed the bottle towards me again. "Come on, boy, we're getting close. You've got to help me finish this."

"I can't. I have a drinking problem."

"The problem is you're not bloody drinking."

The bottle lingered in my peripheral vision. I swatted it away as if a fly. Norman groaned before finishing the lot himself.

"Second exit at the mini roundabout. Not much further now."

Norman unzipped something.

I glanced over.

Oh Christ! His little man-pecker was out. He pulled his foreskin back and aimed his piss-gun towards the small mouth of the now empty vodka bottle, firing his yellow cable. He wasn't a good aim—splashes of urine wet his trousers and the car upholstery.

"Jesus, you're pissing on the seat," I shouted.

"Cos you're driving too fast! Taking those mini speed bumps like a madman. This is a residential area for fuck's sake, not *Fury Road*. You can't expect me to get it all in the bottle if you drive like a loon."

"You're ruining the car!"

"Yeah *and?* It isn't your car, so no need to get your knickers in a twist."

"Stop pissing! What are you doing, man?"

"I can't. Once it gets going, I have trouble turning it off— it's like a broken tap. When you get to my age, you'll understand. Now, I need you to pull over here."

I took a hard left—piss sloshed out of the bottle—and pulled the car up on the kerb. Norman swung the door open and bolted out onto the street in a bizarre half-squat-shuffle, holding his dick in one hand and the vodka bottle in the other —his human super soaker spraying golden fireworks as he mostly missed the bottle. A dog walker, wearing so much Adidas she might as well have been sponsored by them, gave Norman a strong disapproving glare and a stronger tut. He took his hand off his dick to flip her off, and she promptly crossed the road. Once Norman was done pissing, he fixed the screw cap onto the now full bottle of human lemonade, let out a sigh, then sorted his jeans.

"Fuck me, that was quite the ordeal, but we got there in the end," he said.

I could smell his garlic-infused pee from the driver's seat, which made sense given his trousers were two-thirds drenched and there was a literal piss puddle in the footwell.

"You're a disgrace. What the hell is wrong with you?" I said.

"If you'd helped me drink the sodding thing, this wouldn't have happened. I've got a weak bladder. You can't expect me to drink it all without consequences." He shuffled back inside the car, clasping his hands around the piss bottle protectively as if it contained his mother's ashes. "Anyway, keep driving. We're almost here, but I think you know that."

"Haven't a clue."

"You really don't know Chedworth Drive? It's kind of infamous around these parts. Did you hear about the drugs raid with the thirteen-year-old boy who had a bag of skag and gak stuffed up his jacksie? *That* was Chedworth Drive. Speaking of which, we're here. Pull up behind the van with the penis graffiti, would you?"

Once I was parked up, Norman opened the passenger side door, still clutching the bottle of piss, and stumbled outside. "Be back in a jiffy, like."

"Are you sure that's a—"

Before I could finish my sentence, Norman was skipping up a short driveway to a house in such disrepair even squatters would have given it a wide berth. Next thing I knew, Norman was slamming his fist against the front door with such urgency, you'd think he was being pursued by Michael Myers.

On the plus side, he was out of the car, which presented me with yet another opportunity to get out of there and away from Norman. Though, of course, I didn't leave. Whether it was optimism, nihilism, apathy, pure stupidity, or a combination of the four, I stayed put and watched.

Seconds later, Norman lobbed the bottle of piss towards the house. Yellow fireworks crashed through the downstairs window of the dilapidated house. It was like giving a paper cut to someone who'd been shot in the face—it added further damage, but would anyone notice? What people within a mile absolutely would register was the window shattering. A harsh cacophony of noise, blasting my eardrums and inflicting a lingering pain—sharp and targeted—as the noise whirred around my head.

Norman legged it towards me, yanking at the passenger door as if trying to pull the fucking handle off. He threw himself into the car, my head and ears still ringing—a migraine imminent.

"Step on it then!" Norman shouted—locking his door, overgrown fingernails nervously scratching the back of his left wrist, all pale where a watch once lay. "Come on. Come on! What are you doing, boy?"

For the second time that day, someone came running out of a building and towards Norman. This time it was a fifty-something in a red and white dressing gown.

I put my foot to the floor, alarmed tyres screeching.

The pursuer hobbled after the car—knobbly knees and rubbery chicken neck—but he was quick to give up. At his pace, he'd have struggled to win a race against a sloth in a leg brace. Defeated, his gown flapped open in the wind, revealing his shrivelled body, low hanging testicles bouncing around like a couple of golf balls in a long sock. He shook a fist at us as he faded into a silhouette.

"Ha! We showed him," Norman said. "Take that Swain, you chav cunt!"

"What the fuck is going on here?"

"That wrinkly little prick stitched us the hell up. That's

why everything went so bloody wrong at the Tudor House. Now head to the station."

"Why?"

"Cos it's part of the plan."

"What plan? You've told me nothing. You just do shit and expect me to go along with it. Well, frankly, I'm sick of this."

"Oi! What do you think I'm paying you for?"

"An honest and easy job. This is neither!" My mouth was dried out with anger and exasperation, the sour aftertaste of the morning's coffee coating my tongue.

"It was supposed to be easy," Norman said, softer. "Only reason it went wrong is cos of that snake in the grass Swain."

Norman's phone began vibrating on his lap. I glanced over. 'SWAIN' in uppercase letters, all grandiose as if he was a real bigshot. And why just one name? Was he Worcester's disappointing answer to Beyoncé?

Norman's legs shook in sync with the phone's rumbling.

"You gonna answer it?"

"I dunno, boy. You reckon he'll be in good spirits? Cos I got a feeling he ain't gonna be too happy about the piss." He picked up the phone. "You know what, though? I think I will answer it. Let that cocksucker have a piece of my mind." Norman accepted the call and immediately screamed, "CUNT!" My headache wept. "Because you're a bloody Judas, that's why. ... Bollocks! You said July eighth. ... What? No, no, that's American style, you plonker. ... Oh, it isn't? That's ... Ah, shit. Then sorry about the piss, you prick. ... Well, cos you *are* a prick. ... Hey, I don't suppose on August seventh, we'll be able to ... No, fair enough. FUCK! Okay then, mate. Well, you look after yourself, yeah? ... Just board it up until you have the money. It ain't hard. ... Afraid not, mate. But we'll think of something. ... All right then. Bye."

Norman placed the phone back in his lap, then bent forward, resting his head in his hands. He sat quietly,

twitching, snorting like a pig with a blocked-up snout, and …
Wait, was he crying?

"You still want me to head to the station?" I asked.

He looked up, eyes red and sore. "Yeah, yeah. To the
station, boy." He exhaled air. "Had a bit of a mix-up with
Swain, didn't I? Got our wires crossed about dates and that."
He reached into his pocket, pulled out his packet of cigarettes,
then sparked up. "Well, what can you do, eh? Could have
happened to anyone. Drop me off at Shrub Hill station. I'll
take the train back to Kiddy, and you get rid of the car, yeah?"

"Get rid of the car *how*?"

"Oh, easy enough. What do you think the lighter fluid's
for? Bit of fluid and a match and you're golden. Or at least the
car will be cos it'll be covered in more flames than a noughties
goth's shirt, know what I mean?" He laughed hard and
unnaturally, a horse choking on a carrot.

"I don't exactly feel comfortable torching a … I mean, you
seriously want me to burn the car?"

"You don't want this coming back on us, do you?"

"Of course not, but then I didn't want us to steal a fucking
car in the first place," I said. "And what about my million?
You get me burning a car, I'd like to see the money."

"And you will, it's just … Listen, you got a phone?"

"Of course."

"Pass it here then." He held his hand out and I reluctantly
handed him my mobile.

He entered his digits, drop called his number, then
returned the phone.

"Call me when you're done. I've got a bit of business to
sort out in Kiddy."

"I don't get it. I thought we were getting as far away from
Kidderminster as possible because of what went down at the
Tudor House. Speaking of which, what did go down?"

Norman sighed. "We live in a fast-moving world. What
can I say? Things have changed."

"So we're no longer in danger if we return to Kidderminster?"

Norman laughed. "Kidderminster's bleeding. We're always in danger in Kiddy. But we've got to go back there. No other choice with what's come up. Anyway, we're getting ahead of ourselves. First step, you burn the car. Second step, you contact me. You've got to trust me on this one."

Trust him? I had more faith in a politician keeping a promise.

"Look, why don't we burn the car together?" I said. "I don't get why—"

"Cos wherever you burn it, it's gonna be a hell of a walk back and my leg is giving me a lot of gyp. ... Plus, I can't get caught burning a car again."

3

It wasn't easy finding a place to set the car on fire, but when I pulled into the much-neglected nature reserve car park with its overgrown greenery and neither cars nor humans in sight, I knew I'd found my spot. I doused the piece-of-shit motor in lighter fluid, keeping my eyes and ears out for signs of life. Though what I'd say if I was caught mid-act, I didn't know. It wasn't as if hiding the can of lighter fluid would do much good —its off-whiskey odour thickly permeated the afternoon air.

And then it happened. A crisp crunch of sticks snapped behind me.

I shot to attention, stopping mid-pour yet keeping the can in position as if watering flowers—trying to look inconspicuous but, in reality, drawing further attention to what I was doing.

I turned to see a man with a skinhead and handlebar moustache. He wore a leather jacket and beat-up jeans. An eyepatch covered his left eye. He walked towards me with a slumberous gait—half-pirate, half *Sons of Anarchy* cast member.

"You looking to set that car on fire?" he said.

Given the literal lighter fluid, it seemed dumb denying it. I stood there, silent and stupid. For a moment, I wished Norman was with me but then imagined he'd either try to fight the geezer or get his penis out. Both were unlikely to help the situation.

"How about I set you on fire?" the guy with the eyepatch said.

"Please don't."

"Give me one good reason why I shouldn't."

"Cos setting people on fire isn't cool."

"Sure it is. You never watch the WWF in the nineties? Them inferno matches were bostin." He moved closer. "Or if Kane's not for you, then how about that monk who set himself on fire in Vietnam? Sitting down, all covered in flames. That was so hardcore Rage Against the Machine slapped him on the front cover of their first album."

"It was a protest," I said.

He grinned but kept staring as if waiting for some punchline. He scratched the back of his left ear. "Tell you what, I won't set you on fire and I won't say shit about what you're doing out here."

"Thanks."

"Hold your horses," he said, curbing my relief. "There's a condition to it."

"Well, what is it?"

"You've got to suck my dick."

Acid rose from my stomach into my mouth. Eyepatch didn't appear quick on his feet but he had some heft to him and stood between me and the exit out of there. My eyes darted around for a rock or makeshift weapon to protect myself with if he stepped nearer, but supposing I did attack, then what? I wasn't going to kill the guy, but if I left him and the car, then he was going to the police or worse. I had to negotiate with him. To appeal to reason somehow.

"Yeah, you heard," he said. "I want you to get down on your knees and service me."

He wasn't grinning anymore. The geezer looked deadly serious and not the negotiating type. Perhaps I should throw the lighter fluid at him and let the flames engulf him with the car. Recreate some of that WWF inferno match magic he got off on. Plus, if he got caught in the fire, it wasn't quite murder, just a freakish accident.

The car park and surrounding nature reserve seemed empty with no other people in sight. Then again, I'd thought that seconds previous, before Eyepatch had shown up and … *Wait!* I wasn't *actually* considering killing him, was I?

Eyepatch moved his hands towards his flies.

Panic washed over me, freezing me more immobile than Jack Torrance at the end of *The Shining*. He shuffled closer. I tried to move, to scream, to articulate words that might reason with him, but my mind and body were incompatible. Then, just as I thought I was done for, he roared pork-thick belly laughter.

"Your fucking face," he said, voice and laughter wheezing into one. "Course I'm not gonna make you suck my dick."

I gasped but no relief came, and he continued to chuckle—nightmarish joy, delighting at his own sick joke. I felt tears forming but held them back.

His stale laughter gusted into my face and I tried forcing a grin to protect myself from further damage, but my stomach was in knots and if I didn't hold it together, if I strained much more, my bowels would loosen.

This wasn't supposed to be happening. I was supposed to be home, poorer and more in debt—crying over bad life choices, chain-drinking coffee and chain-eating pot brownies, googling new and inventive suicide methods, dropping the odd text message to Amanda—but at least with enough money in my bank account to pay my landlord and solicitor.

"I'm not gonna make you suck my dick," the geezer said

again, but this time there was an edge of doubt in his tone. "I mean, you can if you like."

"No!"

He frowned. "My dick not good enough for you to suck?"

I took a step backwards. "That's not what I meant."

"Good cos I've got a beautiful dick. You want to see it?"

How to even answer that with a guy like him? I wanted to run far away and escape my troubles, but it doesn't matter how far you run, you can't escape yourself.

"Well?" he said. "You want to see it or not? It's up to you."

"Not especially," I mumbled, hoping it didn't trigger further anger.

"Fair enough," he said, then shrugged. "But you're missing out. Anyway, I'm Wild Bo." He held out a mud-covered hand, dark dirt caked underneath his nails like a poor paint job.

Apprehensively, I shook his hand.

"I got you so good with that joke, huh?" he said. "But seriously, I'm what you might think of as an unofficial sheriff around these parts. So if you want to burn that car over there and keep me quiet, there's gonna be a price to pay."

"What's the price?"

"Well, what are you offering?"

"I don't know ... What do people usually offer to buy your silence when burning cars?"

"This isn't a usual occurrence." He chewed down on his lower lip. "What is it you usually pay someone to keep them quiet about you torching an old piece-of-shit car?"

"This isn't a usual occurrence either."

"Hmm ... then we find ourselves in an interesting situation then, don't we? What you might call a bit of a quandy."

"A quandary."

He grinned. "You really don't burn cars often?"

"No."

"Shit. You really do look like a car burner to me."

"What's a car burner look like?"

"Like you."

"Is it the haircut?"

"It's not the haircut." He paused, considering my slicked back hair and the not-quite undercut. "But it doesn't help. Not with this situation. Not with anything. No offence, but it makes people want to slap you." He pulled on the bottom of my shirt. "It's not the clothes, though they feel kind of funny —cardboard stiff. It's probably the way you hold yourself."

"My posture?"

"You're shifty. And you don't give much eye contact, which is creepy. Like a car burner."

"No eye contact doesn't mean I'm a car burner," I said, forcing more eye contact.

"It could mean you're a terrorist … Or a pickpocket. But I caught you burning a car, so it was easy figuring out which of the three you were."

"Well, anyway …" I took another step back and towards the car, lighter fluid at the ready. "I've got to take care of this car, so …"

"Not until you pay me. What did I say already? There's a price, so cough up. What you got?"

"I dunno. Um, fifty quid?"

"I want more than fifty quid! I let the right people know about this and you could be facing prison time."

"For burning a car?"

"For *the reason* you're burning the car. The thing you did in the first place to get to this point. Hell, maybe you *are* a terrorist after all."

"And a pickpocket?"

"Oi. Less of the lip. I'm the sheriff around here, not you. And besides, it's only two out of three maximum. You can't be a car burner, terrorist, and pickpocket. Think about it." He paused, giving me a moment to consider his nonsense. "Now,

I don't know what you did, and I'm not asking you about it. That's your business. But I do know your freedom is worth more than fifty quid. So how about five thousand?"

"Excuse me?"

"5K. It's not a lot in the grand scheme of things, but it beats going to prison, am I right?"

"I don't have five thousand pounds on me. I barely have five hundred."

His eyes lit up. "You have five hundred quid on you right now?"

He got so close to me our heads were almost touching. Deer battling for dominance. Wild Bo was considerably taller than me, with fists like two large shit-covered rocks and the smell to match. Was he about to deck me for my money?

"Well? You have five hundred quid on you or not?" he said.

"I mean, yeah …"

He reached out and I flinched, but instead of a punch, I was met with a hearty slap on the back. "Well, that'll do it, mate. That'll bloody do it. Come on then, pay up."

"I don't want to pay you five hundred pounds."

"That about figures. I don't suppose I'd want to hand over five hundred quid either if I was in your situation. But you want to go to prison even less. So you'll pay up and everything will work out just fine."

I took the money from my wallet and held it out to him, gripping the notes a little tighter when he reached for them, eventually letting the money go and cursing my luck.

"No prison for you then," Wild Bo said. "Smart. Wasn't so hard after all, was it? Now, just so you know, I'll help you out of any situation if you pay me the right price. You best get my number. You strike me as the kind of person who's gonna need it."

———

Black smoke billowed high above the tall trees. I walked the long road back from the nature reserve and towards my apartment. My wallet lighter. My nerves more intact. Wild Bo had overseen the fire and even offered to dispose of the car skeleton somewhere discrete.

Car skeleton.

The way he'd put it and his confidence suggested this wasn't his first time disposing of something … or someone. Perhaps that had been the best five hundred quid I'd spent. A literal lifesaver.

Jace Everett's 'Bad Things' screamed out of my smartphone, an incoming call from Big Load Brian.

Who in the …

Oh, of course. That idiot Norman had used one of his monikers when inputting his number.

I answered the call. "Norman?"

"All right, boy. I've got another job for you."

"You still haven't paid me for the first."

"Patience, patience. It's all in hand."

"And besides, I thought you said it was a one-time thing."

"It was supposed to be. But things went wrong, and now we've got to course-correct. But, if you think about it, that just makes this part of the same job. Now, where are you?"

"A few minutes from my apartment."

"I don't know where that is."

"Near Catchems End."

"Best chippy in town if you ask me. Anyway, can you get another car?"

"What the fuck? I literally just burnt the first—"

"Yeah, yeah. And that was wise. Never use the same car twice, even if you're just going to Sainsbury's—but I need you to pick me up from mine, up on Bark Hill. And pack an overnight bag. We're going on a little trip."

"Where?"

"I'm not saying over the phone. What if it's tapped?"

"Who's gonna monitor our calls?"

"I'm not saying that either. Don't want them to know we're onto them. You've got to use your head, boy. So, get your arse over here."

"And then I'll get my money?"

"Yeah, yeah. We'll talk about it."

"Talk! Will I get my money or not?"

"Relax. Everything's gonna be okay. Now get over here. We need to get going ASAP."

"I don't see why I have to steal a car. It would be much quicker if I just drove over in my own motor."

"I thought you didn't have a car."

"I didn't have my car with me in town, but I have a car."

"Who the hell has a car but doesn't drive into town? That's dumb."

"I needed the exercise and fancied the walk."

"The hell's wrong with you? Exercise! That's the weirdest thing I've heard all week and I know some right wrong'uns down the local." His disgust was so loud my ear popped. I moved the handset away from my head and put him on speaker. "Well, whatever, bring your own car if it makes you happy. Just don't blame me if you get arrested."

"Arrested for what?"

"Vehicle theft … arson … the list goes on. Anyway, I'll text you the address. See you soon."

4

Back at my apartment, I took a quick shower and changed into a fresh outfit, purging myself of the post-fire smells that lingered worse than my early morning regret after a night out in Redwoods.

A text message with Norman's address stared up from my phone. I didn't have to see him. I could ignore it: kick back, listen to some music, and forget about Norman and his antics.

Though that wouldn't resolve my financial situation.

So then, I'd head back into Kidderminster and get that bank loan. After which I could pay the landlord, the solicitor, and even give Norman his £600 back if he kicked up a fuss. He didn't deserve it but it was worth it if he promised to piss off permanently.

My phone lit up: a new message from Harry, the landlord. My heart rate quickened. Any message from him sent me into a low-level anxiety spin because most of the time it meant a demand for money or time or some obscure complaint from an anonymous resident, which meant Mrs. Garton. I opened the message, hands notably clammier:

Hi Wentworth... hope you're okay... I'm trying to figure out whose car this is. Do you know? How long has it been there?

A photo of a black Mercedes parked at the far end of the car park followed.

I hadn't a clue whose car it was. I tried to keep my head low and stay out of other's business. The only cars I could identify were mine and Mrs. Garton's old Ford Escort.

A peculiar text message, but not out of character. Either it meant I was in Harry's good graces or he was building up to a more serious question. You know, like: *where the fuck is this month's rent?*

Whatever. I wasn't answering him now. He needed to respect my time and know I wasn't on standby to answer his dumbass questions 24/7.

Then again, I had just stolen and disposed of a car ... texting Harry might go some way towards an alibi should anything come back on me. It wasn't watertight, but a car burner—as Wild Bo had put it—was hardly likely to casually text his landlord on the job. I wrote a quick message:

Hey Harry. All good this end thanks. Hope you and the family are well. I've not seen the car before but I don't pay much attention to the car park so couldn't really say if it's been there a while or not. I'll keep an eye out over the next few days and let you know if I see anything or if it moves. Sorry I can't be more help. Wentworth

Perhaps a bit too much information, but a quick 'no' is exactly what a car burner would write. Unless the text message's length made it obvious I was overcompensating for what I'd done. Ah, fuck, I really was overthinking this as per everything in my life. I pressed send. Then reread the text message.

Let you know if I see anything or if it moves.

If it *moves!* Bloody hell. I sounded insane. As if I thought the car might be alive. As if Stephen King's *Christine* was nonfiction.

My phone chimed back almost instantly. But this time, it wasn't Harry. It was Norman.

You gonna cum or not?

Presumably 'cum' was just Norman's shorthand for come and not a query as to whether I was on the brink of ejaculation. Either way, I was *not* gonna cum or come. I was staying put.

My phone sounded again. Harry: *Thanks. I'll be in the area this afternoon. About for a chat?*

Another text followed. Norman: *I've got ya money.*

I doubted it but was too poor to call his bluff. Plus, it would get me out of the apartment and away from Harry, who absolutely *would* demand his money if I saw him face-to-face. I could return to the apartment in the evening, when Harry was long gone, after confirming Norman was full of shit.

I shoved some clothes and toiletries into an old sports bag, so I was covered in the unlikely event I really was doing an overnight trip with Norman, then pulled on my boots and headed for the door.

5

My Toyota's engine was still running when Norman rushed out of his council house wearing a Guinness top hat. An old blanket was bundled underneath his left arm and he held a Lidl plastic carrier bag in his right hand.

"Go! Go! Go!" he said, jumping in the car with rushed gusto as if he was a white Jackie Chan in a budget action flick.

I expected someone else to burst out of his house, possibly with a samurai sword, but nothing happened.

"You being chased or something?" I said.

"Yes and no."

I scanned the estate. Eerily quiet, save for a couple of teenagers painting dicks on the side of a house which may or may not have been theirs—the house not the dicks, though I supposed it was possible they were also drawing true-to-life drawings of their penises and if so, congrats, lads, you're really packing some length.

"Looks like no," I said, then eased on the accelerator, heading out of the estate.

One of the teenagers turned at the sound of the car engine, registered me, and made the wanker sign with his hand.

"He's a goodun," Norman said. "Martin McDonald's boy. Started smoking at nine. Fucking legend."

"So, what's the job?" I asked.

"The job is getting us the fuck out of here and down to Mona-on-Sea."

"That's three hours away. I'm not driving there."

"Unless you want to die, you don't have much of a choice. We've got to lay low for a bit. Get us to the motorway and I'll explain the rest later." Norman arched forward, gripping the edge of his seat. "I need to stay alert whilst we're still in the local area. Now put your foot down. You're driving like an old man in a hat behind the wheel of a Honda Jazz."

"Why Mona? Why not Bridgenorth?"

"For one, it ain't exactly far away. For two, I ain't got a place in Bridgenorth."

"You have a second home?"

"A lovely little cottage near the sea. Now keep quiet, drive fast, and all will be revealed in good time."

———

By the time we hit the motorway, Norman had loosened up. He reclined back in his chair, rummaging through the supermarket carrier bag on his lap.

"I brought a few tinnies for the road if you want one. I've got some Kestrel, Tennent's Super, and even a few cans of Carling if that's your thing."

"I told you before, I don't drink. And even if I did, I'm not drinking and driving."

"Carling doesn't count. It's basically piss water."

"No, thank you."

Norman huffed. "Fuck me, if I knew you were gonna be like this, I'd have picked up some Skol or own brand stuff. It's only three percent."

"It's still alcohol."

"Oh yeah? If you got three percent in a science test, you wouldn't think you'd done so well. This is the same thing." He grinned like he'd made a smart point.

"If I'd got 45%, I wouldn't have felt too good either," I said, "but if I go around drinking 45% alcohol, I'll soon feel the effects. Now stop with your bullshit and tell me what's going on here, old man."

He straightened in his seat. "Looks like your testicles have returned. Good for you … So, the people we pissed off aren't exactly the kind of folk you mess around with."

"What's with the *we* talk? I didn't do anything."

"You drove the car, my boy. And that's reason enough to punish you, too." There was a hiss to my left as Norman popped open a can of Kestrel. "That nice place on New Wood Lane I busted into belongs to Tricky Ricky. He's about the worst person you can mess with in the entire Wyre Forest. The bloke's smart as well as dangerous, which makes him one up on the other four who are just dangerous." He knocked back some lager, grimacing. "Then there's the Knox Brothers, Pat and Gary. Pat's head's as bald as a rock with the brainpower to match and Gary's got this weird bleach blonde mullet that's part Jimmy Saville and part 118 Guy, but they'll still fuck you up due to their size alone." He scratched his head. "Pat's kind of the second in command when it comes to Tricky Ricky's lot. The first obviously being Tricky Ricky himself. Gary's got a bit of resentment in him about that, but he won't say shit to Pat. Keeps the peace and that, the fucking square. Anyway, the Knox's will just throw their weight around and crush you. Which is at least a problem you won't have with Pat Knox's boy, Colin." Norman screeched wolf-howling laughter. "*Colin!* Even saying his name is funny. Who calls their son Colin?"

"Pat Knox."

"Exactly. What a loser. Name a strong Colin and I'll write you a cheque for ten thousand pounds right now."

"Colin Farrell was pretty ripped in the *Total Recall* remake."

"CGI, boy. That's all that was."

"There was a feature in one of those men's magazines about how to get into shape like him."

"C.G.I. End of."

This guy was ridiculous. As if he believed Colin Farrell's *Total Recall* physique was a result of CGI. I scoured my memory for strong Colins, then it hit me. "Colin Kaepernick! The American football player."

"Don't know him, so doesn't count."

"You'd know him if you Googled him."

"But I'm not Googling, so I don't know him. And besides, American football's not even a real sport. Just some weird footie-rugby-hybrid with helmets. The yanks invented it because they weren't as good as us Brits at either. Ingerlaaaaand!" Norman raised his hands in the air, three-lions-on-a-shirt victorious.

We rode in silence for a moment.

"Wesker's sister," Norman said. "She's the final member of that merry bunch of pricks we pissed off. The crazy slag with the samurai sword."

"What's her name?"

"Wesker's sister."

"Her name is Wesker's Sister? Like legally, that's what her parents named her?"

"Listen, boy, I don't know her family history or blood type or any shit like that, but her name is Wesker's Sister."

"Is Wesker part of the gang, too? Someone we should look out for?"

Norman wheezed—smoker's laughter squealing throughout the car. "Not after what happened to him. Only gang he's part of is a gang bang, know what I mean? That twat's as dangerous as a piece of piss."

"Is that dangerous?"

"Ask Swain. It damaged his window, didn't it? Got him good with that piece of piss."

"Piss is liquid. You can't have a piece of it."

"Course you can."

I switched the radio on. A string quartet from the 19th century filled the car.

Norman frowned at the music. "This a joke? Or ironic? I know you hipsters love irony."

"I'm not a hipster."

"No? Then what's your favourite coffee shop?"

"Well, there's a good independent that does single origin stuff in—"

"Ha! Hipster answer already. I fucking knew it. So the music's the same, right?"

"It calms me and helps me concentrate. Plus, my chiropractor's branching into neuroscience. He says I'm left brain dominant and need to listen to classical music to help activate the right brain."

Norman squawked. "Chiropractor? More like chiro-quack-tor. You are such a mug. How much you paying this charlatan?"

"Fifty quid an hour."

"Jesus Christ!"

"Speaking of money, when am I seeing my million?"

"Soon, boy. Soon."

"In your text, you said you had the money *now*."

"I do, but … Well, why'd you need it so urgently anyway?"

"To pay my landlord and solicitor. You *know* this. I'm in a custody battle."

"You have a kid?" Norman looked taken aback.

"Not a kid, but a cat."

Norman frowned, then laughed. "The Christ are you talking about, custody battle for a cat?"

"I'm serious. I fucking love that cat. His name's Rory."

Norman rolled his eyes. "Bloody hell ... You are something else."

"Just forget it and tell me why these people are after us? All you've done is reel off a list of names, but none of this makes sense."

"You really wanna know, huh?" Norman took a deep breath. "It was supposed to be an easy job. You see, Tricky Ricky makes a lot of money 'off the record', so has to get creative with how and where he stores it. It just so happens Swain has done dealings with Tricky Ricky and has a little inside intel. Swain and Ricky, they used to be as tight as a pair of leggings on a hippo, but after what happened with Ricky's daughter, things went a bit sour. They were still in business together when it suited them, but the friendship just weren't the same."

"What happened with his daughter?"

Norman waved his hand. "Sorry, I'm rambling. Got a habit of doing that when I'm nervous like. The daughter isn't the point. The point is old Swain found out about the vault in the Tudor House. Swain being Swain, he has a way of charming people, getting on their good side, and finding out all sorts of things."

"Is this the same Swain who chased after us in an open dressing gown? Dick and balls bouncing in the wind."

"There's no one else called Swain on the planet."

I rolled my eyes. Norman seemed to have a disorder that meant every other sentence was bullshit.

"Swain happened to find out the one day the property was gonna be unoccupied," Norman said. "So, he wrote it down for me. Complete with the home security code. All I had to do was stroll in and take the money. If things had gone right, we'd already be rich. So would Swain, given he was getting a cut." Norman sighed. "Problem is, I read the date wrong. Thought Swain had written July 8th, but it was August 7th. So there's another way the yanks stitched us up. If they hadn't pissed about switching the day and month order, we'd be rolling in it. But, as it happens, I busted into the house on the wrong day and came to face-to-face with the whole merry gang of cunts. You saw how it played out from there. And now Swain says they're after us."

"He actually said that?"

"I'll read you the message if you like." Norman fiddled with his phone, then cleared his throat. "'Tricky Ricky and his lot are after you after what you gone and done. You two are fucking dead. FUCKING DEAD. You screwed up big time and went too far. Better get the fuck out of town, knob-end.'"

"What a hypocrite," I said. "Given he's the one who gave you the address and stood to benefit, he should be on the run, too. He's the one who betrayed them for Christ's sake."

"Yeah, well, they don't know that."

"I still think it's harsh they're after me, too. I didn't know anything about—"

"Life ain't always fair, boy. And you're in deeper than a colonoscopy. Which is why we're gonna lay low for a bit."

"Just so we're clear, am I right in thinking you didn't get *any* of the money from the Tudor House?"

"I'm afraid not."

"So how do you have my money?"

He tapped his nose, and I wanted to throw my fist into it and bust him open.

An intense piece by Wagner blared through the car's speakers, matching my annoyance.

I should pull the car over. Strangle the bastard to Wagner. Go full Patrick Bateman on this sorry waste of human flesh.

"You got ZERO pounds from the Tudor House?" I said once more in a maddening attempt to revise reality, like if I asked again, I'd realise this had all been a misunderstanding. That we were golden, literally and figuratively.

"You're a little slow in the head, ain't ya? Yes. That's what I'm saying. I got zero. Zilch. Sweet fuck all."

"This is what I don't get. You got no money. They chased you out of the house. And yet you and Swain are still adamant they're coming after you. After *US*."

"They're a bunch of big shots, mate," he said and started snacking on a burrito—and where the fuck had he pulled that from anyway? In which orifice had it been hiding? "Some of them are the real deal. Some are just acting all billy big bollocks for show, know what I mean? Either way, they don't take too kindly to people trying to rob them. And now they have to make an example out of us, so others don't disrespect them in the future, like."

"If they're that big a deal, they've got more important things to do than pursue a few little fish. We're not even petty criminals. We're failed criminals. We failed so badly we didn't even commit a crime. We did about as much damage as a Jehovah's Witness and wasted less of their time."

"Ouch. Don't talk like that. You might hurt my feelings. Plus, once they find out about the …"

I glanced over at him. He gripped the can of Kestrel tightly. Fingers white at the edges.

"Find out about the what? Jesus, Norman, what did you do?"

"The thing is … It's nothing really but might be it's ruffled a few feathers cos …"

"Out with it."

"OKAY. FINE! I shit a brick on this expensive looking rug in their dining room."

"What?! Why would you …?"

"Cos I'm Shit-a-Brick Rick, okay?"

"What do you mean you're Shit-a-Brick Rick?"

"It's who I'm known as. And I've got a reputation to live up to."

"Who you're known as? You said you were Ninja Fingers and Big Load Brian."

"Yeah, yeah. Them as well. I have lots of names. But to most people, I'm Shit-a-Brick Rick. It's that simple."

"Not Norman?"

"Not really. I'm Shit-a-Brick Rick. Listen, boy, it's my thing. A little trademark I have. If I do someone over, I leave a big old brick somewhere obvious."

"And by a brick you mean—"

"A poo. I do a poo, okay? But not pellets. Not little rabbit droppings. And not any of that liquid diarrhoea stuff. I squeeze out a nice hearty shit. Something strong and leathery. I tailor my diet accordingly so I can lay a brick at any moment. A lot of complex carbs and fibre. Sometimes a little corn if I'm feeling fancy—leave some yellow gemstones in my chocolate delight."

"That's fucking disgusting."

"It's a talent, is what it is. People see that brick and they know exactly who's responsible. Me. Shit-a-Brick Rick."

"But I thought you were trying to be subtle. Wasn't the whole point to get in Tricky Ricky's gaff ASAP, take the money, and get out? Leave them none the wiser as to who'd robbed them. But if you left your … your trademark, as you put it … they'd know it was you."

"Good point."

"Good point?! You really didn't think any of this through, did you?"

"That's my one weakness: I don't think. As you get to know me, you'll find that out."

"What makes you think I'm gonna get to know you?"

"With them lot after us, we're stuck together for a while now."

I shook my head. "Oh no. Absolutely not. I've got work at the Co-op on Monday."

He shook his head. "And now you don't."

6

NORMAN'S COTTAGE was located a few miles east of the coast. The salt-licked breeze stroked my nostrils as soon as I stepped out of the car. I slung my bag over my shoulder and drank in a long, delicious breath of air, appraising my surroundings. Aside from the adjacent cottage, situated so close the two houses were practically touching with a shared driveway to boot, Norman's place was the only building in sight. From the outside, it appeared modestly sized and homely with white paint on the exterior and a window built into the tiled roof. A large back garden, comprised of different shades of green, led onto a stretch of woods big enough for Hansel and Gretel to get lost in.

"She a beauty, huh?" Norman stared up at his home.

I looked at his place, then the neighbouring cottage. There was something off about the way they sat so closely together, almost connected and positioned diagonally, affording a view through each other's window if you got the angle right. Hell, you could draw a straight line between them and you'd make a triangle. I thought of Pythagoras and death cults and wondered if the two cottages were somehow linked, which seemed ridiculous at the time, but now, in retrospect, there's a poetry to it.

The door to the adjacent cottage opened, and a tortoiseshell cat rushed out. A woman wearing oversized sunglasses and a floral summer dress, all peaches and cream, followed.

I eyed the cat's gold and black fur, memories of my dear Rory stabbing at the forefront of my mind—his gorgeous eyes staring lovingly up at me. "So beautiful," I said.

When I looked up from the cat, the woman was beaming at me. I soon realised my faux pas.

"The cat," I said. "I meant the …"

But the woman and cat were out of earshot, already heading towards the forest together.

My stomach rolled around queasily as I tried to erase Rory from my mind—a defence mechanism that had helped me cope with his absence. It felt like a kind of betrayal, removing the cat bowl from the kitchen, putting away the litter tray, taking the toys from the living room—especially his beloved scratching post—and locking his photographs in a hidden folder on my phone I never dared access. But I'd still fought for him, through solicitors and search parties, until I'd run out of money and options. I'd almost sold my computer and Xbox, just to get another week of legal work, but Amanda had discouraged me. Said enough was enough. And for once, I'd listened.

Norman patted me on the back. "Your dicking game needs a bit of work. Need to be a bit smoother if you're looking to wet your whistle."

I returned to reality, Rory fading. "Isn't wetting your whistle having a drink?"

"Not where I'm from. Wetting your whistle is getting your dick deep in the vag canal. I'll tell you some of my strategies if you like?" Norman shook his head. "Christ, boy. Look at the state of you. Stuttering all over the shop cos there's a beautiful woman nearby. I bet you had a stiffy, didn't you?"

"No."

"I bet you still have one."

"I don't."

"Then prove it. Show me. Whip your whistle out."

"Stop calling it a fucking whistle."

"Okay then. Whip your ding-a-long out. Show me your elongated sherbet fountain."

"My what?"

"Your plum tree shaker. Your jingling Johnny. Your shaft of delight. Give us a peek at Jeremy Corbyn's magic wand. Your knick-knack paddywhack. Flop out the silent flute."

"I'M NOT GETTING MY PENIS OUT, NORMAN."

We appraised each other and for a moment I thought he was going to lunge at me, but instead he went, "Coward. You've seen mine. In the car when I was—"

"Yes, I remember."

"So then, fair's fair. I showed you mine, you show me yours."

"I didn't ask to see yours."

"That's part of the fun. I don't wait to be asked. I get it out on my own terms. It shows confidence and manliness. So stop moaning and show me your cheese doodle."

"Absolutely not. Fuck off."

"Then you have a stiffy."

"I don't."

He shrugged. "Well, I think you do."

"I couldn't give a fuck what you think."

"Then why've you just spent the last few minutes arguing with me about it?"

"I'm warning you. Keep this shit up and I'll smack you one."

"Ha! Not likely. Anyway, the neighbour's out of bounds. You can take anyone else to bone-town, but she's off-limits.

We stay out of their business and they stay out of ours. That's the way it's always been. Understood?"

"I wasn't planning on trying anything anyway. I just thought she had a nice cat."

"Is that what the kids call a cunt these days?"

He grinned.

I didn't.

"Well, whatever," Norman said, "let's get inside. There's something important I need to tell you."

———

A dining room table in the centre of the kitchen was already set for two. There were placemats and cutlery, archaic candles straight out of a period piece, and fake flowers in a glass vase in the middle. Somewhat unsettling given this was supposed to be an unplanned visit. It was almost as if Norman had been expecting me.

He caught me looking. "Just in case I have guests. And what do you know, now I do. Welcome home." Norman uncapped a supermarket own-brand bottle of vodka. "Want some Vegas water?"

"I've told you twice already, I don't drink."

"I thought you were joking."

"It's no joke." I rolled up my sleeves and showed him the red lacerations and scars running from my wrists to halfway up my arms. "I tried to kill myself. Okay?"

Norman reached out, tracing his finger along a thick, prominent scar. He pulled away, then shook his head. "Nah. Those are just vanity marks."

"What the fuck? I open up to you, I show you my scars, and you come out with that shit?" I loosened my scarf, exposing my rope-burned neck to him. "And I suppose this is a vanity mark, too?"

"I dunno about your neck but, as sure as I'm alive, them

things on your arms are vanity marks. Something for show. A cry for help maybe, but not a serious suicide attempt."

"You're a fucking arsehole. There isn't an hour goes by when I don't contemplate ending it all. Doesn't matter if I'm smiling or joking, I'm bleeding inside. Sometimes I'm so fucking tired, it's like I'm already dead. Why do you think I haven't punched you yet? It's not because I don't want to. And it isn't because you don't deserve it. I'm using all my strength just to exist."

"Hey. It's okay, boy. I guess you have some pain. I can respect that."

"Respect it? Go fuck yourself."

"But you can't bullshit a master bullshitter. Everyone knows if you want to finish yourself, you cut your wrists vertically not horizontally." Norman took a cloudy water-spotted glass from the cupboard and poured a measure of vodka into it. "Sever the major vein. Bleed quicker. Die faster. Easy enough."

"I didn't know," I said.

"Then it's a good job we met each other. Now if you get the urge to kill yourself again, you can do a proper job of it." He sipped his vodka. "Just not over the carpets, okay? Now, how about that vodka?"

There were no knives in sight. Must have been he stored them in a cupboard or drawer rather than out on the counter. Just as well, because the way he was going on, it was fifty-fifty whether I'd rather take one to his wrist or mine.

Norman groaned, then drank more vodka. "Ah, Christ, I'll even make you a coffee if you want? I mean, it's kind of a pain but if it will stop you moping."

"That would be nice. Thanks. I guess."

He stretched his arms as if about to exercise. "Oh boy, here we go. Let's see, I'll have to turn the tap on, then take the lid off the top of the kettle, fill the kettle with water, put the lid back on, press the boil button, wait two, three, maybe even four minutes for it to reach boiling point etc. etc. And that's not including selecting a cup, putting the coffee granules in and all of that. All told, a total pain in the arse and a time suck but—"

"Jesus Christ, I'll just make my own coffee. It isn't a big deal."

"Oh, isn't it? Well, then I'd have to show you where the kettle is. Another pain in the—"

"It's right there." I nodded to the white kettle to the right of the cooker that looked fresh out of the eighties, much like everything else in this place.

"Okay, Mr. Smart Arse, but I'd still have to show you where the tap is."

I nodded to the tap next to the big window overlooking the back garden.

"Looks like you've got everything figured out, huh? Suppose you're going to tell me where my will is next."

"Thought you said you didn't have one, unless you grabbed a template from Google and drafted one up whilst I was burning that motor."

Norman rolled his eyes.

I took the electric kettle from its base and filled it with tap water.

Norman and I stared at each other awkwardly as we waited for the water to boil. Eventually, Norman took a jar of Nescafé from the cupboard.

"I see the way you're eyeing it, boy. Sorry I don't have the fancy stuff. But that's the best I can do. Now, come look at this whilst the kettle's doing its thing."

I followed Norman into the hallway. Up the stairs and above the main entrance, there were various photographs of an elderly but well-dressed woman with permed hair and silver-framed glasses. A much younger Norman featured in some of the photos. From their proximity to one another, I figured the woman to be a family member. Perhaps his mother or grandmother.

Norman fixed his attention on a dusty, full-length mirror with a gaudy faux-gold frame. He straightened his posture then grinned widely at the relic as if he expected it to snap his photograph.

"What do you think?" Norman put his arm around my shoulder and pulled me close towards him. He smelt of cigarettes and booze and stale pheromones. "You like it?"

"The mirror?"

"Look *in* the mirror. How's that working for you?"

"It's a bit dirty."

"Piss off, is it! It's in good nick."

"There are smudges and fingerprints up and down it."

"You see yourself, don't you?"

"Yeah."

"That's all that matters. You only clean a mirror when it gets blurry and pixelated like an N64 game. It's the same with driving glasses. I only clean mine when everything's fuzzy."

"Sounds dangerous."

"Just you keep looking in that mirror. Now, tell me, what do you see?"

"I see me."

"And?"

"Um, you …"

"Right. You see us. Look at us."

"I am. That's *literally* what I'm doing."

"Properly. Take a good long serious look." Norman breathed out. "We look good together. A right team. Practically identical."

If Norman truly thought we were identical, he needed both the mirror cleaned and his eyes tested. Norman looked like a member of a 70s prog band with his long grey hair and my hair was fresh out of a barber's shop that offered complimentary cups of drip coffee and craft ales.

"I can't believe you haven't cottoned on to what's going on here," Norman said.

"You're definitely going to have to clue me in …"

"APRIL FOOLS'!"

"It's July."

He started laughing. "I know that but … APRIL FOOLS'! This has all been an April Fools'."

"I don't get it."

Norman pulled me in closer, wrapping his arms around me in a suffocating hug. "Look closer, boy. Look closer and understand."

"Just tell me what on earth is going on here."

"Jesus, boy, isn't it *obvious*? I'm your DAD. *That's* what I'm talking about."

"Shut up. That's not funny. I haven't seen my dad in years." I wrestled free from Norman, pushing him away.

"Exactly! That's why I set this up. This has all been one big April Fools'. I GOT YOU."

"I'm sorry, Norman. I really don't understand what the fuck you're saying or doing or …"

I backed away, seriously considering whether to run out of the house before the mad twat murdered me.

"I guess it's a lot to take in," Norman said. "Anyway, the kettle should have boiled by now. Grab your brew from the kitchen and we'll talk about all this in the living room. I'll fill in the blanks and that."

"It's *all* blank. There are literally no parts of what you said that make any sense."

"No? Well then, better grab a big mug. This is gonna take some time. Don't worry. Daddy's got you."

7

THE COFFEE TASTED ROUGHER than a 3am lock-in at an unlicensed bar in the scuzziest part of Coventry, though paradoxically it brought back fuzzy memories of childhood. Saturday mornings, mum and I would play with Duplo blocks and she'd give me rancid hungover kisses that tasted of off-brand Nescafé with a sour vodka under-taste.

The living room walls were plastered with photographs and posters from *Naked Attraction*, including various stills of contestants mid-show. In the centre of the room was a print of the *Naked Attraction* television presenter, Anna Richardson. She was topless and posing as Eve from the Bible—an apple in one hand, a python draped across her shoulders, long brown hair covering her breasts.

Norman entered the room, carrying a stack of photograph albums. He caught me staring at Anna Richardson.

"Isn't she something?" Norman said, seeming genuinely awe-struck. "About as near to godliness as we're going to get on this planet. That was taken in the actual Garden of Eden, you know."

The print was obviously photoshopped.

"It's my life's dream to appear on *Naked Attraction*," he said.

I regarded his 'I was on *Naked Attraction*' t-shirt.

Norman picked up on my confusion. "Visualisation. Put it out into the world and it'll come true. Manifesting and that. I'm not sure I exactly believe in it, but it's worth a shot, right?"

Norman dumped the albums on the coffee table before plonking himself down on the sofa next to me. He retrieved a tattered ripped-at-the-corners maroon album from the pile. The first photograph was of him sitting in a high-backed chair in a hospital. He stared proudly at the camera, love and emotion filled his tired eyes. In his arms, wrapped in a cream blanket decorated with green and orange branches, was a tiny baby. His right hand supported the baby's body, his left the neck. The baby's eyes were scrunched shut, a white newborn baby's hospital hat on its head.

"That's the first time I ever held you," he said, tears forming in his eyes. "I was rocking you from side-to-side because I wanted you to feel safe. You do a bit of rocking and it's supposed to simulate the way it feels in the womb. I was so scared, boy, because I didn't know what I was doing. All I knew was I had to keep you safe. Had to be a good dad, like." His voice cracked.

Norman looked to the next photograph. Another from the hospital—a white curtain in the background affording some privacy. This time the baby wasn't wearing the hat and Norman was kissing its sweat-soaked forehead, right hand supporting the body, left supporting the head. He turned the page to a photograph in a dining room. The baby slept on Norman's shoulder—it was dressed in a white romper suit decorated with animals and flowers. Norman looked at the camera—an innocence and contentment in his face that was missing from the Norman of today.

A single tear rolled down his cheek. More tears followed.

"Keep you safe," Norman said again, his voice strained with emotion. "Well, I fucked that one up, didn't I?" He stood up. "Sorry, this is harder than I thought it would be." He took his vodka glass from the table, downing the remaining liquor in one, then settling in the chair opposite me. "I can't look at them, boy. It's too much. Even now. But have a bit of a rummage for yourself and you'll see all I've said is true."

I recognised the framed art in the background of the photograph in the dining room. It was the same art that had been displayed in my childhood home growing up—a garden of flowers painted by my grandmother: an original, one of a kind. Did this mean there was some truth in what Norman was saying or was this simply another layer to his so-called April Fools'?

I flicked through the album, landing on a page in which Norman and the baby were sitting on a sofa, laughing at the camera—a selfie before selfies really existed. Norman briefly peered over from his chair, but soon his head was in his hands and he was sobbing uncontrollably. I closed the album. Whatever this was, it was clearly affecting Norman, and despite him causing me nothing but hassle since we'd met, I took no pleasure in his pain. Perhaps I could sneak another look at the albums when he wasn't about. To see if his claims stacked up.

"Open the green one," Norman said between sniffles. "It's got a lot of fun outings in it. Places we went together. It's green because of the outdoors and that. The maroon one is off-red cos of blood and creation." He tapped his head. "You see, your old man isn't as dumb as you think."

"I never said I thought you were—"

"Please. Everyone does. And how can I blame them with all the jokes I make? I do it for a reason, you know? It masks the pain and regret. Stops me from taking a fucking blade vertically down my wrists. You see? Me and you. We ain't so different, huh?" He grinned, but it was obviously forced. "Now, the green book. Have a butcher's."

I did as he suggested, turning to a page at random. A sunlit European street—palm trees and cool waters. Norman held onto a leash attached to reins. A child, no more than two years old, ran ahead, turquoise shorts and a pale vest top, flip-flops on their feet.

"Looks like Spain. Or perhaps Portugal?

"You've got a good eye, boy. It's Spain. Not so far from Malaga, but more family friendly."

My mother had told me about a trip to Spain when I was an infant, but my dad was out of the picture. He wasn't supposed to be there, unless … Fuck! Could it be Norman was telling the truth? But if Norman was telling the truth, then mum had been …

I stared at Norman's cigarette-aged face. "Are you really my father?"

He nodded, fresh tears in his eyes. "Yeah." The words rasped out softly, energy diminished.

I stared at the photograph again, then back to Norman. "I don't get it. My father isn't supposed to be there." I turned the page to a photograph in which a toddler sat on Norman's lap, cuddling in a busy café. "How can this be? This doesn't make any fucking sense."

"You starting to remember things, boy?"

"Not remember, but these photos, I've seen similar ones— even down to me wearing the same fucking outfits. The man in the photograph, he sure looks like you, and the kid sure looks like me as a child but …" I felt sick. Necked some of the coffee. My heart hammering, my vision receding. *Concentrate on your breaths. Don't embarrass yourself.* "I need some water."

Norman's blurred form bolted up, then he rushed out of the room.

I took a long, deep breath, inhaling and exhaling, snail-slow. Repeated the breaths a second, then a third time.

The album returned from shades of misty grey to full colour as my vision eased back into full focus, and I found myself compelled to turn to another page. Me and Norman, sitting by a Christmas tree in a living room I recognised from other photographs with my mother. I couldn't have been much more than six months old. I wore a red reindeer jumper: my wide innocent eyes gazing up at the camera, a look of absolute contentment on Norman's face as he held me on his lap. Arms safely wrapped around me.

Norman re-entered the living room and passed me a tall glass of water. I guzzled it all, then closed the album.

"Maybe you'll remember this," Norman said before bursting into a children's song. "Busy … busy … busy little bee."

There was something in his delivery that was almost soothing. My stomach rumbled and there was a feeling in it, something stirring, but it wasn't necessarily good or bad, just … *confusing*. An inner movement filling an emptiness I hadn't known was there. Fragments becoming whole and because of what? An aging rocker in a *Naked Attraction* t-shirt?

Maybe. Maybe not.

Norman had frequently proven, in the few hours I'd known him, just what a conman and bullshitter he was. What was to say this wasn't another elaborate joke? The sickest and cruellest of all.

"You say you're my dad …" I began.

"Boy, I *know* I'm your dad."

"Yeah? Well, maybe I don't. So help me out. How can *I* know you're my dad?"

"Beyond the photos and the busy bee song?" He brushed a hand through his hair. "That's a tricky one to answer, Wentworth."

"You know my name."

He laughed. "Of course I know your name. I'm the one who named you, you know?"

"I didn't know. I *don't* know. Matter of fact, I know sweet FA about you, other than you had a drunken night with my mum over three decades ago and … well, here I am."

Norman laughed, but it was joyless—his eyes glassy and pained. "A drunken night? That's what she told you, huh? Try fifteen years."

"Fifteen years? Nah, that's bollocks. You weren't about when I was in first school, let alone a teenager."

"True enough, but your mother and I were together for over a decade before we even started trying for a baby."

"No … I don't understand. Why would Mum lie?"

"That isn't for me to say. Though she was troubled, to say the least."

Troubled? Who the fuck did he think he was to show up in my life and start talking shit like that?

"Ah heck," he said. "I probably shouldn't have said that. I've got to watch this tongue of mine." He stuck his tongue out of his mouth and stared at it until he went cross-eyed.

Calling Mum troubled … In truth, I couldn't argue, but hearing it made me uneasy, especially from a stranger. It didn't matter what Norman had been in the past, or what he claimed to be now, the guy in front of me was a stranger.

"I've got some photos of the two of us together," he said. "Me and your mother. They're up in the loft, but I could show you if you want."

"That'd be good, but you don't have to get them now. It's okay." I paused, taking a moment to study him and his reaction before saying, "I believe you … I guess."

A few seconds felt like hours as we both processed what I'd said.

Finally, Norman spoke again, "I only put the albums together after the breakup. See, your mum was going around talking shi—" He stopped himself. "This isn't easy. I want to be honest with you, boy, but I also don't want to disrespect your mum. Not that she had any problem disrespecting me to anyone who would listen, but it doesn't feel right. Especially not with you."

"If you've got something I need to hear, you should probably …"

He slapped his knee, halfway between motivating and punishing himself. "Yeah. Will do. Though I suppose we don't need to rush anything." He stared into space for a moment. "Those albums of your mother and me, I created them so I could remember the good times were real. As soon as we were through, she started creating this alternative reality and, at the worst of times, I was questioning myself. Almost buying into her bullshit. But the photos, they tell the truth." Norman looked down at his lap. Was he about to cry? Something had got him choked, words tangling in his throat. "I confided in a few people, but mostly I wanted to run away from that old life."

"That why you ran away from me?"

"I never ran from you. NEVER." He clenched and unclenched his fists. "Sorry. I shouldn't have … But, no, I never ran away from you, Wentworth. Never stopped loving you. Ever."

I heard what he was saying, but *love*, it's a complicated and weird thing. Could he really continue to love someone he no longer knew, or did he just love a past version of me? An idea of me?

"Some people told me that what your mum had done to me was gaslighting, but I don't know about all that," he said. "I mean, for one, I don't like to say anyone does anything to anyone. Things happen. It's easy for us to pass blame and say someone *did* something to us, but maybe we played a role in whatever happened?"

I raised an eyebrow. "That sounds almost like victim blaming."

"Nah, that's not it. Or if it's how it came out, it's not how I meant it. I'm just saying all of us—the heroes, the villains, the in-betweens—we have more control than we think we do. In-betweens … that's all any of us are, you know? Heroes and villains are imaginary. In real-life, the lot of us are just different shades in the middle."

Where was this coming from? The Norman talking to me was wholly different from the Norman who'd thrown a bottle of piss through his mate's window.

He took his vodka glass from the table. "Now my glass is empty, and it looks like yours is, too. So how about I fix us another?"

He scooped up my glass.

"Water not vodka," I said.

"Yeah, yeah. I get it. You have a drinking problem. One glass of Mona's finest tap water coming up."

When Norman left for the kitchen, I returned my attention to the photograph albums sprawled out on the coffee table. One stood out amongst the clutter, a black cover and two red crosses taped over the front—definitely a DIY job rather than part of the original design. I picked up the sinister-looking album and turned to page one. Scrawled in my mum's handwriting, white pen on a black background: *Wentworth Cooper, Year One*. I turned to the first photograph. Norman pulled a dumb face next to my mum as she breastfed me in the hospital. Over much of Mum's face were two large Xs that obscured her eyes. The edit made it look as if she was the victim of some grisly murder. A caption underneath read, *'Our first family photo together'*.

Family … Holy fuck, was there seriously a point she thought of the three of us as a family? Assuming this was real —and it was unmistakably my mum's handwriting—then Norman really hadn't been a one-night thing.

Jesus, that hurt.

I'd longed for a family for much of my childhood. In many ways, it was what I was still searching for. The nearest I'd got had been with Amy and Rory. A season of my life that had abruptly ended when one day I went to work and returned to an empty apartment that was never to be filled with laughter again. For a while I'd hated Amy for that, but with time and reflection, I'd come to hate myself.

"Sorry about what I did to your mother."

I jumped at Norman's voice. The silent drink maker put fresh glasses of vodka and water on the table, followed by the three-quarters full bottle of vodka.

"It was too painful to keep looking at her after everything she'd done." Norman eyed the Xs on my mum's eyes. "Sorry, after everything that *happened*. There I go again, talking about things she *did* when it isn't that simple. I don't mean to be so negative, you know?"

"Guess you didn't mean to be negative when you threw that bottle of piss through Swain's window either."

He laughed. "That's just mates, innit? The kind of shit lads do."

"How about when you shit a brick on—"

"Oh, here we go again …"

"You broke into his place, too."

"*Actually*, the door was unlocked, so I—"

"You were going to steal millions from him."

He shrugged. "That's less about hating him and more about benefiting myself. Big difference. Anyway, how's your mum doing these days?"

I paused, caught off guard. Norman was erratic—there was no telling how he'd react if I gave it to him straight.

"She's, um … well, the thing is, she's …" Feverish sweat built on my forehead. "My mum, she is … She *was* …"

"Ah, shit, boy. I'm sorry. I didn't …"

We stared at each other. Was there some understanding? Had I managed to tell Norman without being explicit? And if so, was he okay? My mum had been a much bigger part of his life than I'd known and here I was, a son he'd only just met, effectively telling him his former partner—the mother of his child—was no more.

"How did she ..." Norman shook his head, stopping himself. "No. I shouldn't pry. It's none of my business."

I shuffled in my seat and he shuffled back—a weird dance of badly choreographed awkwardness as we both scrambled for ways to move the conversation away from my dead mum.

"Here's the thing I don't get," I said.

"Go on." Norman leaned forward in his chair.

"You turned up at the bank today ... But how'd you know I'd be there? And how'd you even know what I look like? You hadn't seen me for thirty years, so ..."

"I hadn't *met* you in thirty years. That doesn't mean I hadn't seen you. I watched you grow up, you know."

"Wait. You've been stalking me?"

"Bloody hell, son. Easy on the *stalking* talk. Absolutely not. Besides, it isn't stalking if it's your own kid."

"I think it might be. Especially if you're going around and—"

"It wasn't always me. Sometimes I'd get others to watch. Take some photos, a couple of videos etc. etc. Report back 'n' all that."

"I mean, that sounds even worse. *Fuck!* The more you say, the worse it gets."

"You're my boy. I had to keep an eye out for you. What kind of a fucking father would I have been if I hadn't?"

"*An eye out for me?* You were creepily watching from the side-lines. That's what weird uncles do, not dads. Dads are supposed to help."

"I did help. Sometimes." He sipped some vodka. "You remember in year six when you were getting bullied by that fat lad, Mickey Poole?"

I hadn't thought of Mickey Poole in decades. Had almost forgotten the way he'd corner and lay into me. Calling me a fucking gaylord and threatening to bum me if I didn't use my lunch money to buy him iced buns and chocolate cookies from the school cafeteria at break time. The irony of his insults and threats were lost on him, but that was the middle school nineties logic.

"You do remember him." Norman grinned. "He stopped bothering you one day, huh?"

Norman was right. It had been sudden. I'd assumed he'd had a change of heart. Had found Jesus or something. But from the way Norman looked at me, it wasn't Jesus he'd found—or should that be, it wasn't Jesus who had found him. He'd moved schools soon after.

"Christ, Norman, what did you do?"

"I looked out for you, is what I did. Same when you were at PC World and that weasel dick, Toby, used to push you around."

I shuddered. "I never asked you to—"

"A boy shouldn't have to ask his old man. A good dad will take care of business. No questions asked."

How much chaos had Norman caused in my name? Had he threatened people? Hurt people? Had he worse than hurt people?

"Maybe I should get going …"

"You'll do no such thing," Norman said. "We've got to stay here at least until things calm down back home. And besides, we're having sausages tonight." He said this last part with genuine pride, as if sausages were enough to make anyone stay—a real game changer.

If Norman went around beating people up in my name, what lengths had he gone to guarantee meeting me? Pins and needles shot through my hands. My head growing lighter.

"Was all that Tricky Ricky stuff real? Or did you do it to meet me?"

"You think I'd stage a heist just to meet you?" Norman said. "Awfully elaborate, don't you think? And besides, that business with Tricky Ricky happened *after* meeting you. We met outside the bank, remember?"

"I'd prefer it if you just answered the question."

"And I'd have preferred it if I'd got to raise my son properly, but here we are." He folded his arms.

"I can't lose my job over this."

"There's worse things to lose. I'm telling you, Tricky Ricky and his lot are after us."

"So it *is* real?"

He nodded, but I wasn't fully convinced.

"Here, take a look at this vid of Colin," Norman loaded a TikTok video on his smartphone and angled it towards me.

An out-of-focus shot of a council estate. A skinny, acne-riddled kid who couldn't have been much older than seventeen stood in front of a heavily graffitied fence. He wore a basketball shirt and shorts that rose too high above the knees.

"What the fuck?" I said, staring down at the very definition of a weak Colin.

"Just watch. He's about to do his thing."

Reluctantly, I continued looking at the phone screen, hoping to hell *his thing* wasn't anything like Shit-a-Brick Rick's thing. Then Colin did some sort of attempt at a gangster gesture that would have embarrassed Ali G and bust into a half-arsed attempt at a rap in a *so-high-my-balls-have-yet-to-drop* West Midlands accent.

"You done messed up when you fucked with us.
Now I'm gonna turn you into a puddle of mush.
Like peas! And I got my White Lightning.
You'm gonna run away cos it's getting frightening.
Frankenstein at the Safari Park.
Got a dog with a limp, and a terrible bark.
When you shit on the floor, you made it personal.
Cos I couldn't get it out with a bottle of Persil.
Better run away, cos we're coming for you.

We're talking Pat and Gary and the rest of the crew..."

Norman stopped the video. "You get the idea ..."

"That was ... *painful* to watch. But if some scrawny-arse teenage boy wearing shorts that rise higher than a cheerleader's skirt is our biggest threat, I think we'll be okay."

Norman shook his head. "Colin ain't a threat, but the rest of them are and, as you heard, they're coming after us."

"Whatever that was, it wasn't necessarily directed towards us."

"He mentioned the poo. It's definitely directed towards us."

"Nonetheless, I can't stay here for long."

"Listen, Swain's monitoring the situation. He'll keep me posted on Tricky Ricky's mood and the lads' movements. We'll go back as soon as we can."

"I don't think you understand the financial predicament I'm in. If I lose my job, I'll—"

"Your job at the Co-op?" he said, and there was obvious judgement in his voice.

"As well as the bar work at the Academy in Birmingham."

"Bloody hell, son. You shouldn't be trekking all that way for a part-time job."

"Some of us don't have the luxury of finding a job that pays enough close to home."

He looked to his feet—his big toe close to poking through a hole in his sock. "I guess not."

"And besides, it's not so bad. By the time I'm finished, it's not long until the first train of the day ... As long as it's a weekday and there isn't a rail strike. Anyway, it pays the rent."

"Pays the rent! You could have fooled me when you went to the bank, bitching and moaning about how your landlord was on your case. Doesn't sound as if it pays the rent."

"I'm doing my best, okay? What the hell do you do for money anyway?"

Norman gestured around the room. "Enough to get a place like this."

"Good for you. Well done, I guess. Though I still don't get what you're doing living up on Bark Hill estate when you have a cottage by the coast. Why not stay here forever?"

"It's a fair question. I suppose mostly cos *you* don't live in Mona. But if you did … well then, I could sell the place on Bark Hill and we could stay here forever."

"That what this is all about?"

"It's a possibility. That's all."

"This has all been a ruse, hasn't it? You thought you could show up and play happy families and I'd stay with you indefinitely. You're deluded, old man."

"Hey! Watch it now, no need to—"

"No! *You* watch it. You lied to me about money, tricked me into committing serious crimes, lured me here under false pretences, and then just thought this was gonna end with a happily ever after. You're out of your fucking mind."

I rose from the sofa—legs shaking with adrenaline.

Norman stood to meet me.

"Wentworth Cooper, you are staying here and that's final."

"Fuck off. You're not my dad. You don't get to talk to me like that."

"I am your dad. What more do I have to show you for you to believe me?"

"You've shown me stuff that suggests you might be my biological father. Not my dad. There's one hell of a difference."

That zapped some of his spirit. He backed away, a burst balloon.

"I suppose you're right," he said, voice frayed. "But I wasn't bullshitting you about the danger we're in. Please don't go. Not yet. At least stay a night or two whilst I find out what's happening with Swain."

Outside, the skies were growing grey. I could stay a little longer if only to avoid a rough trek home, but I needed to get out of the house and away from Norman to straighten my head and process everything before I did or said something I'd regret.

I headed outdoors—body still shaking—wagering that whatever lay outside the house would be less threatening than what lay inside. But my success and wagers were less Blaise Pascal's philosophical pragmatism and more Gary Graham's dole money after-hours on a random horse at the bookies in Stourport.

8

I SKULKED around the nearby forest—the aroma of damp leaves and recently rain-kissed bark permeating my nostrils. The walk would have been almost pleasant if not for my state of mind because how *fucking dare* Norman spy on me for three fucking decades. I had let it slide at the cottage and mostly kept my cool, but the more I considered it, the more absurd everything was. Norman's actions and decisions were a total violation of my privacy. I was tempted to call the police out of principle and have him arrested, but given all the things we'd done together, all the shit that could and *would* come back on me, I held off.

What if Norman had gone further than spying? What if he'd tracked me? Put a device on my car? Broken into my apartment and set up cameras? Considering his obsession, it was a given he'd scoured all my social media and my internet presence. The creep probably had a Google Alert on my name. It was a good job I kept things low-key and didn't document my life on the internet unlike millions of others. But how far did Norman's stalking go? Did he watch my home at night? Observing everything that went on? Did he follow me on nights out? There were things I'd done in my life I wasn't exactly proud of. Reasons I kept trying to tap out, blade-first.

What did this motherfucker have on me?!

The audacity of the man … Trying to use love and fatherhood to justify his interference. Norman was a loud joke that needed silencing.

I picked up the remains of a fallen branch and smashed it repeatedly against a thick oak tree, exorcising my anger and frustration.

"Stupid … stalking … motherfucker. You'll never get on *Naked Attraction*. Never ever. You dumb cunt!"

A soft throat clearing from behind startled me. I peered around to see the woman from next door with the oversized sunglasses staring straight at me. She wore a long red coat over her summer dress and held a dog lead tightly in her right hand. Only there was no dog at the end but the very tortoiseshell cat I'd seen her with before.

"Were you talking to the branch or the tree?" she asked. "Either way, you're right. I've never once seen a branch or a tree on *Naked Attraction*, though I've seen contestants with less intelligence than a bit of wood, so you never know." She giggled at her own joke and the sound was delightful. An ice-cold glass of water on a hot summer's day. "Then again, I don't tend to watch much *Naked Attraction* so there could have been a tree as a contestant. I'm more of a *Naked Lunch* or *Fatal Attraction* woman myself."

"Those are two very different films."

"Well, one's a book."

"But a movie, too."

"Thanks for helping me out with that one. A poor woman like me wouldn't have known without your valid input."

I went to apologise but stopped myself. I was leaving Mona soon. It didn't matter if she got the wrong idea.

Unfortunately, I was incapable of standing the silence for long and said, "I don't like *Naked Attraction*."

"Then that's two things we have in common," she said, brushing a strand of hair behind her ear, which was when I noticed the thin cut on the back of her neck.

"What happened there?"

She frowned and Norman's words returned: *We stay out of their business, they stay out of ours. That's the way it's always been.*

Her cat meowed as if picking up on my faux pas.

"I should probably get going," she said. "There's a storm coming soon. And, trust me, you don't want to get caught in it."

That was probably true, but there was a storm at Norman's, too. Its name was Norman.

We stayed staring at each other briefly, then she spoke again, "You should seriously get going. And maybe just stay out of the woods in general, yeah?"

"Why?"

She tipped her hat at me, offering the crease of a smile, before briskly walking away from the woods and towards the cottages, her cat by her side.

I picked up the remains of the branch I'd beaten before, stood within striking distance of the tree, and gave it a final whack. But I felt nothing. The anger had subsided. It was time to head back.

9

THE THICK SCENT of sausages and cloud of vegetable oil fogging through the cottage was almost suffocating. I broke into a coughing fit when I was halfway in the gaff. Once I'd composed myself, I followed the television sounds to the living room.

Norman sat on the sofa, hand on the television remote control as if he were its guardian. He looked up at me.

"Good to see you, boy."

He spoke cheerily as if there'd been no tension the last time we'd seen each other, as if I hadn't huffed out of the cottage. In that respect, Norman was good at being a dad—not addressing conflict and making as if everything was okay with blind ignorance. That's how my mum's on-off partner, Braydon, had been.

"Norman, I need to ask you about—"

"Shh!" He gestured towards the TV. "Looks like they've found another."

On the television, a Mona-on-Sea news broadcast played. Police officers in high-vis jackets patrolled the forest. Shots of cordoned-off areas, blue plastic tents, and forensic officers in protective face masks. The news reporter announced this was the third body they'd discovered this year. The victim was currently unidentified.

Norman muted the broadcast and turned his attention towards me. "Bloody grim stuff. And right on our doorstep. Those woods are literally a stone's throw from the cottage."

"What the fuck is going on? You got me to drive us here, even though you knew about this?"

"What are you talking about 'knew about this'? This is the first I'm learning of it, too."

"Third body this year!"

"Yeah and? Last one was six months ago. The other a month before that. I thought it had died down."

"You shouldn't have taken me to a town where people are murdered for fuck's sake."

"We just left Kidderminster. You have any idea about the kind of shit that goes on in the Horse Fair every day? How about the number of people killed in Birmingham each week? Don't act like Mona is the only place people are getting offed."

"People don't get murdered often in the Horse Fair."

"Correction, my boy. You don't *hear* about people getting murdered much in the Horse Fair. Don't mean it doesn't happen. There's a big difference between what goes on in the world and what gets reported. You'll figure that out someday." He pointed towards the local news broadcast, which had seamlessly segued from dead bodies in the woods to a local fisherman-turned-author reading a story at a primary school. "Trust me, Mona's a bloody paradise compared to where we've come from."

"I just think it would have been a good idea to mention your place was next to Murder Forest before getting me to drive here."

"Murder forest? You are such a sensationalist! And don't act like you didn't hear about the murders here at the start of the year. For a few weeks, it was all over the national news."

"I didn't see anything about it on Twitter."

"You need to get your news from somewhere other than Twitter," Norman said, then waved a hand dismissively. "Ah, relax. The victims are all women. The two of us will be all right."

"Don't be such an arsehole! Somebody's being carried away in a white body bag and you're acting all bloody chipper because it's women, so who cares, right?"

Norman sucked in a gust of air, evidently irritated. "That's not what I meant, and you know it."

"I don't *know it*. I hardly know anything about you."

"Yeah? Then what do you want to know?"

The past twenty-four hours coalesced with the past thirty years—everything and nothing whizzing past so fast I couldn't keep up. Couldn't speak. Could barely function.

"The sausages will be ready soon, so we can have a proper chinwag over some grub, yeah?" Norman said. "And these sausages are the good stuff. Tesco's Finest."

This prick had violated my privacy in so many ways and now he was acting all jovial about sausages. I gritted my teeth. I needed to keep calm and together, neither of which came naturally.

"Earlier, you said you'd been watching me," I said.

"Watching over you. Watching out for you. Protective and that."

"Cut the crap. You've been watching me for decades. Finding out about me. What exactly have you seen? You got something on me? You gonna blackmail me? Is that what's going on here?"

Norman's breathing quickened. He reached into his pocket, pulling out a packet of Marlboros. "I think I'm gonna need a fag. Can I tempt you with one?"

I knocked the cigarettes from his hand. They tumbled to the floor, scattering like matchsticks.

He scowled, scurrying silently to pick them up, then put

one in his mouth, before wandering towards the front door and holding it open for me.

I stayed in the living room. He remained at the door. Both of us unblinking—deadlocked in awkwardness.

Reluctantly, I followed him into the front entrance because what else were we going to do? Perpetually stay in place until one of us passed out from exhaustion or had to rush to the toilet when bodily needs took over? Then again, given Norman's antics, I wouldn't have put it past him pissing his pants before moving—maintaining intense eye contact and a flicker of a smile as his denim darkened and urine trickled down his leg.

The skies were blackening outside. The threat of rain edging closer.

Norman stepped out of the house, but I remained inside. Less than a foot between us.

"I want to know what you saw," I repeated.

"I've been doing this since you were a kid. You're gonna have to be more specific." He sparked up his cigarette.

This was a game of chicken. I could hardly divulge all the times I'd screwed up over the years. The things I might have been implicated in. And yet, if he was holding something over me, if blackmail or bribery was imminent, I needed to know. I'd been fucked about enough, but not this time. Not by him.

"Norman, if you've got something you want to say to me, you best say it now."

"You smoke something fruity out in those woods, boy?" He furrowed his eyebrows as if genuinely perplexed. "Something happened out there, didn't it? Something got to you."

Everything had got to me. Where to start? What to say? Decision paralysis temporarily sank in, rendering me speechless.

"I'm your dad," he said. "You can tell me anything."

I laughed at that, but it could have easily been tears.

"Whatever's on your mind," he said. "Just say it. No judgement."

I'd known magistrates who'd made fewer judgements than Norman.

"You really want to know what's on my mind, huh? Well, all right. I'm wondering how an obvious waster like you happens to have a beachside house in a desirable place like this? You inherit it? You screw someone out of some money? You break into the place and kill the owners?"

He sniggered. "Don't say such ridic—"

"What really happened with you and mum? Because what you say and what she said are polar opposites. They don't add the fuck up."

"Your mum had a lot of—"

"Stop with the bullshit. The money you promised me … It's gone, right? The chances of getting it are zero. There is no backup plan. You failed. Plain and simple."

"We ran into some trouble but—"

"Was there ever any money? Is Swain even real? The woman with the samurai sword … is she part of the show, too? Is this all a performative and desperate attempt to rekindle our broken—correction—*non-existent* relationship?"

"You think I'm crazy enough to—"

"I don't fucking know. That's the problem. That's what I keep saying. I. DON'T. KNOW. YOU. But what I do know is you're a man of very questionable judgement, lacking in real aspirations. Your biggest dream is to be on *Naked Attraction* for fuck's sake."

Limp cigarette drooping out the front of his mouth, Norman rolled his hands into fists. His face flushed red. "You take that back! You take it back now! No need to make this personal, you little—"

"And why do we have to stay away from the neighbours? I saw the woman in the woods and, to be honest, she seemed all right. A bit eccentric, but aren't we fucking all?"

I backed away, receding further into the hallway and towards the living room.

Norman walked towards me, still smoking, but stumbled, grabbing hold of a standing light at the edge of the living room for balance. The day-drinking taking effect. His raw anger at the *Naked Attraction* jibe transforming into something else.

"What do you mean, you *saw* her?" There was a quiver in his voice.

"She was walking her cat when I was out there. Which, by the way, is a bit fucking odd, but who am I to judge?"

"You speak to her?"

"A little."

"What did you say?"

"Not a lot. To tell you the truth, it was embarrassing. She caught me beating the shit out of a tree branch."

"Why would you do that?"

"I dunno, Norman. Probably because it was better to beat the branch than your fucking face."

He tapped cigarette ash from the end of his fag onto the living room floor, a hand still wrapped around the standing light. "What exactly did she say to you?"

"Nothing important or memorable."

"Try to remember."

"What's going on here? What aren't you telling me? This is part of the problem. This is what I'm talking about. You're always being sneaky. Holding things back. Something has got you ruffled and I've a right to know what."

He finally let go of the standing light, taking a laboured step towards me. Then, as he was taking a second step, his legs gave out. It was as if someone had kicked the back of his knees from behind. He fell to the floor, clipping his head against the sharp edge of the coffee table in the process.

"Norman!"

I raced over to him. His face had drained of colour—so pale he was practically anaemic.

"Norman! Norman, get the fuck up already, you arsehole."

He stayed stone still on his back, eyes glazed over and unmoving. I knelt over him. Checked his breathing, then his pulse, but both came up empty.

"Shit. Shit. Shit."

I dialled the ambulance on speaker phone and tried administering CPR. Clumsily pushing my sweat-nervous hands rhythmically down on Norman's chest with bugger all effect. I started humming AC/DC's 'Back in Black' cos I had this vague recollection that it was the perfect beat for CPR. But no matter how much I pushed, or how hard I hummed, it wasn't working.

Because Norman was dead.

And I'd been the one to cause it.

10

After just over four minutes of 'Back in Black' CPR, I gave up. It was obvious Norman wasn't coming back, and I'd pushed through the entire duration of the song, so there was nothing left to sing.

I sat cross-legged on the living room floor, sipping water and staring at Norman's inanimate body, waiting for the ambulance to come. The whole world stood silent aside from my restless mind.

So it starts, so it ends.

The day had begun with no parents, I'd briefly gained an unreliable father, and as the day grew to a close, it would end with no parents.

"I'm an orphan," I said aloud to the unfeeling room.

A few seconds later I received an answer: a sharp blaring alarm from the adjacent room.

There was so much smoke in the kitchen, my eyes stung. I opened the oven and black mist flew towards me. We'd forgotten about the sausages and set the smoke detector off.

After turning the oven off, I opened all the windows wide and wafted a tea towel underneath the smoke alarm hoping to halt its screams, but like a stubborn toddler its cries refused to cease.

Just as I was about to take a rolling pin to the alarm and silence it permanently, I realised it had stopped and the whine I was now hearing came from an approaching ambulance. I ran to the front door, rolling pin still in hand, where I saw the paramedics marching up the drive: two men and one woman, each in official forest green uniforms.

"It's my dad. He's in the living room. I think he's dead," I mumbled in hurried panic.

They stepped inside the cottage and I moved out the way for them to enter the living room.

"What's the problem?" one of the guys said, confirming my incoherence.

Though shouldn't it have been obvious? There was a dead man lying down in the middle of the living room. What would you think the problem was? A sore throat? Lost too much blood after a paper cut? Vicarious embarrassment after watching a *Naked Attraction* contestant drop a sloppy jalopy on national television?

I limped into the living room after them, my right leg deciding now was the opportune time to play dead like my dad, which was when I saw Norman, sitting straight up on the floor and smiling at the ambulance crew.

I felt the floor falling beneath me and, just as my vision was receding, the woman shouted, "We've got a level five zonker!"

11

So MAYBE THE woman hadn't said *zonker*, but she'd definitely shouted something as my consciousness and unconsciousness switched place.

When shapes and colours came back into view, the paramedics were standing over me, my shirt fully unbuttoned. The beardiest of the paramedics was enthusiastically rubbing gel into my chest hair. Before I knew what was happening, he sheared a square into my fuzz with a BIC razor.

"Stop shaving me and tell me what's going on. He was dead!" I screamed, pointing at Norman like he was the OG living dead man, Lazarus.

But the paramedics remained stoic. Looking straight through me as if I hadn't said a word. If it hadn't been for the cold-arse electrodes they started taping to my body—as if I was cosplaying Pinhead on a budget—I might have thought *I* was the one who was dead.

After running a bunch of tests on me, they turned their attention to Norman and finally the truth came out. Not that it made much sense. See, it turned out Norman had a rare condition in which he passed out when under intense stress and panic. What made Norman's medical malady distinct from others was he'd been clinically dead eleven times in his life thus far.

As Norman later told it, he was being all chirpy and chatty with the paramedics as soon as they saw him. Then seconds later, I fainted, and all attention turned to me. I was only out for under a minute, but they wound up running more tests on me than they did him.

In the end, both of us were given the all clear and told to contact our GPs for a referral to a stress-management and anxiety specialist. Not the most satisfying conclusion to a '999' call. Then again, the NHS is overstretched these days, so perhaps it's the new norm. The woman further advised we reduce stress and triggers where possible. As if 1) it wasn't bloody obvious and 2) it wasn't bloody difficult. You try spending a day with Norman and see how easy it is for you to remain zen. Before the paramedics departed, old beardy told us we didn't live in the easiest of locations to drive to and we might want to think twice about calling an ambulance in a non-emergency situation. As if thinking somebody had died was not an emergency.

———

Norman and I slumped on the sofa, trays on our laps, and plates overflowing with a combination of reasonably cooked fresh sausages and cancer-black lumps of misshapen meat that tasted more like charcoal than the spiced pork originally promised. A pre-recorded episode of *Naked Attraction* played on the TV in front of us.

"Well, that was quite the eventful evening, huh?" Norman's grin was too wide for someone dead an hour previous.

Norman bit into a charred sausage, the crunch so vicious I wouldn't have been surprised if he'd chipped his tooth in the process. He washed the meat down with a splash of vodka.

"Should you be drinking after what just happened?" I asked.

"Definitely. Shit, boy, if you came back from the dead, you'd celebrate with a tipple, too."

"I mean, if I drank, then I guess … But maybe it's the excessive drinking that caused it in the first place?"

"Absolutely not." His teeth ground against the sausage so hard my own enamel weakened witnessing it. "You made a right fucking spectacle of things, boy. Calling an ambulance like that. The paramedics were right. You really should only call 999 in an emergency."

"You're taking the piss, right?"

"There's a non-emergency number. If you dial 111, then someone from the NHS will—"

"I thought you were dead! You can't put a dab of Savlon and a plaster on a corpse, you daft twat!"

He forked up another burnt sausage, solemnly shoving it in his mouth, and avoiding eye contact. When he was done chewing, he looked up. "There's no need to be like that. I was just trying to help. I didn't know about 111 until a few months ago myself."

———

As the evening progressed, we wound up watching taped episodes of *Match of the Day* hosted by Des Lynam. Norman said he was only interested in matches from the 1992-93 and 1995-96 season because they were the glory years of Aston Villa and Des Lynam was a lot less politically charged than that crisp wanker, Gary Lineker.

"I mean, Des Lynam did vote for UKIP, so he's not exactly politically impartial," I told him.

"Very few of us are politically impartial, but we don't

make the whole bloody programme about it," Norman said. "I'd vote for Des Lynam if he ran for Prime Minister. Imagine him and Ron Atkinson as co-leaders. Dream ticket right there!"

"Politics aside, they're both in their eighties. This is England, not America."

"For now," he said. "But the way they're privatising everything, it soon could be, know what I mean?"

"Lynam-Atkinson sounds like something you'd need to see a doctor about."

Norman groaned as if he'd heard that one before, then proceeded to spend much of the Villa-United game with his arms folded and face lemon-sour like Big Ron himself. Whether it was Norman's strong focus as he prayed the Villains would hold on to their lead—perhaps suffering from some bizarre amnesia in which all past games and results were forgotten—or if he was still annoyed about my dismissing his Lynam-Atkinson dream ticket, I'd never know.

When the final whistle blew, Norman sighed deep relief and picked up his vodka glass once more. "If the weather's nice, I can show you around Mona tomorrow. Give you a proper tour of the town."

"Thanks, but I'll need to get going."

"I get that. Which is why Swain's working fast to give us an update. But I figure we'll be here at least a day or two longer, so why not make the most of it?"

"I told you already, I'm not losing my job over this."

"Better than losing your life," Norman said, then snatched a glance at my scarred wrists. "I mean for most. Shit. Sorry. I …"

"It's fine."

He snapped his fingers together with merry gusto. "I've got it. You can work the docks out here."

"Work the docks? What does that even involve?"

He shrugged. "To tell you the truth, I'm not sure myself,

but it's something I hear people say down the local all the time. *My boy works the docks.* That's what they say. Sounds impressive actually."

"You're full of shit."

"That's not a kind thing to say to your dad. Just work the docks and make some bank. Inhale the fresh sea air. It'll do you good to have a job."

"I have two jobs already. Jesus, you never listen to me."

"Well, there's another reason to work the docks! You work the docks, and it'll pay enough, you'll only need one job."

"I thought you said you didn't know anything about working the docks."

"I know it pays good." He scratched his nose. "Don't mean I know the practicalities. Same with being a surgeon. I can tell you it's a nice little earner, but it don't mean I can you tell how to do it, know what I mean?"

The television was paused on a shot of Des Lynam presenting in his shoulder-padded work-appropriate nineties suit. His iconic Einstein-esque moustache watching over us, judging us, as if sentient. The silence between Norman and I lingered, and it occurred to me we were both staring at Lynam as if waiting for his guidance on the matter.

Should I stay or should I go?

That's how The Clash had put it. Though rather than the dichotomy of divorce, my dilemma was different: stay with my estranged drunkard father in a seaside cottage or go back to my grey hometown where I was saddled with debt, decay, and now, thanks to Norman, a bunch of bastards baying for my blood.

Des Lynam's moustache seemed to twitch. An omen of sorts. I made my decision.

"I'm going home in the morning," I said. "It's not just the job. There's Amanda, too."

Norman stretched his arms above his head. "I knew it!

There's always a bloody girl. Thinking with your dick, aren't you, boy? Christ, what are you like?"

"You've got it wrong. Amanda's—"

"You'd sell out your own father for a slice of snatch. Go gallivanting back to Kiddy for a taste of the fairer sex and leave me here to die."

"Die? Hold up! You said this was a safe place. Somewhere they couldn't find us."

He shrugged. "It's what I hope. But if they do find us and there's two of us, we can defend ourselves better and all that."

I looked to Lynam. He nodded. Gave me strength. As if to say: *Go on, son. It's okay. Say your piece.*

"I don't think there's anyone coming for us," I said. "It's a hell of a trek. And even though they're angry about the whole shit thing—"

"It was a big one, boy. An absolute whopper lumped dead centre on the fanciest rug I've ever seen." He beamed like a proud parent at his kid's first football game—though ironically, the cunt had missed mine!

"Yeah, whatever. Despite all that, if these guys are as important and as big as you say they are, they've got better things to do."

Another silence stretched out, then, "Nah. Even if they don't want to do this, they have to. Out of principle. They'll be searching for us for a long time. You go back and they'll soon find you, which will put me in danger." He chewed down on his lip. "Maybe you'll keep quiet at first, stay loyal to your old man and that. But there are limits. And once the waterboarding starts, you'll be spilling my whereabouts faster than Dwight Yorke scored that header against Coventry at Highfield Road."

"You can't be serious!"

"I am! Look it up. End of September 1995. It's still the fastest header scored in the Premier League to this—"

"Not about the fucking goal, you idiot. About the waterboarding. You're telling me these Kiddy thugs go around waterboarding people? Please."

"You need to stop underestimating them. They are not just Kiddy thugs. They're some of the most dangerous people you'll ever meet."

"Nonetheless, I told Amanda I'd—"

"You can't have even been with her that long. Didn't you say you recently split up with some chick over a cat?"

"We didn't split up over a cat and that was more than a year ago."

"You've been involved in a custody battle for a cat for over a year?"

"Yeah. Kind of. I mean, I'm not now. I lost. But I've still got bills to pay."

"Absolute mug!"

"Piss off."

"You know, I get where you're coming from. Not about the cat, that's bloody bonkers. But about the girl. See, I was the same as you back in the day, boy. Waded through so much pussy I had to wear wellies."

"Norman, I don't need to—"

"I'm serious. I'm great at oral, too. Want some tips? I'll tell you about the pancake."

"Please don't."

"Or the white-water rapids. That's a good one … Bet you've never heard of the angry Jeremy Corbyn, have you, boy? If you'd have given your ex the angry Jeremy Corbyn, I guarantee you she wouldn't have left you."

"I didn't say she left me."

"Pretty obvious. She took the cat. She could hardly take the cat if you'd left her."

"Maybe I split up with her and she took the cat later."

"That how it happened?"

I lowered my head. "No."

"Ah well. Cheer up, boy. Do the angry Jeremy Corbyn with Amanda and she'll never leave you."

"She's my boss!"

Norman's smile was wider than the Mailbox Bridge. "That's my boy! Fucking the boss. Absolute power move."

"You've got this all wrong. That isn't what I said. It isn't like that. I'm not just fucking her. It's more than that."

"Oh, Jesus, don't tell me it's love. Is that what it is?"

"What it *is* is none of your business. Amanda's a good person and I won't bail on her like that. Not at such short notice. Which is why I'm going home in the morning."

"You could die."

"We're all gonna die eventually."

"Yeah? Well make sure each moment counts before that time. Don't make the mistakes I did. You were obviously in a cunt of a relationship, and it's left you wounded, but you can't let that stop you from living now."

I nodded. "You're right about that, at least. Though whether I was in a cunt of a relationship or the cunt in a relationship, I don't know anymore."

"Yeah." Norman stood up from his chair, a new sombreness to his face. "I get that, boy. I honestly do. Well, anyway, if you really do have to go, you have a safe trip back, yeah? And stay in touch. I don't want to lose you again."

Norman was heading towards the kitchen when a banshee-high scream boomed through the walls. Hefty rhythmic thuds followed—boots on a floor or somewhere worse. Then the deep guttural voice of a man who ate cigarettes for breakfast. An immediate desperate protest from the woman, an angry murmur from the man, and then, so clear she could have been in the room, the woman said, "Help me! For the love of god, help me!"

12

FUCK! This was surely the woman with the oversized glasses —all peaches and cream, and summer dress, and cat on a lead. She'd been good to me in the woods. Had given me a warning of sorts about the forest and the murders, which was more than Norman had done. And now I had to do something for her.

Awash with clarity, I stood up. Norman held both hands out in a lazy combat stance as if drunkenly preparing to fight me off. Come to think of it, he might well have been.

"Easy now, boy. You just sit yourself back down. We stay out of their business and they stay out of ours. Remember?"

I didn't advance forward, but I didn't back down either.

"Anything else is too dangerous for all concerned," Norman said.

A series of thumps and groans in quick succession. Though who was thumping what or who, and who was protesting, it was impossible to tell. And how was it so clear anyway? This was a detached cottage Norman was living in. True, there was little space between the buildings, but the sound was as crisp as if we were in the same room. Sound sure did travel differently around here.

The woman yelped as if a dog kicked in the stomach.

"What if something happens to her?" I said.

"It won't."

The thumps continued, but the protests diminished. I pictured a military boot stomping on a face until it transformed into a puddle of human mulch.

"What if she dies?" I said.

"She won't."

"You don't know that. You *can't* know that."

"It's a regular occurrence. Has been going on for months now."

I wanted to shove past Norman but couldn't let this turn into a fight. I had to keep my wits about me, and if we were squabbling, I wouldn't be able to hear what was going on next door, which would mean if anyone was in danger, I wouldn't be able to help.

"Going on for months," I repeated. "Why?"

"Refer back to the whole *we stay out of each other's business* thing," he said. "But seems to me they have a very European relationship. It's intense, fiery, passionate. *Fight hard, fuck hard.* Anyway, how about an old episode of *Naked Attraction* to take your mind off things?"

"We should check on them. We *need* to check on them."

"Boy, you're not listening to me. It's fine. Seriously. They've got their energy out of their system and now they're getting on with their evening, just as we should. Christ, if you hear them fucking, are you gonna ask if we should go on over and join in?" He paused. "Actually, that's not a bad—"

"Don't be such a prick."

I tried squeezing past Norman, but he moved in step with me as if performing some bastardised salsa dance.

"Norman, get out of the way. I just need to see if they're—"

"What do I keep saying? We don't ask questions. We don't

involve ourselves. And in return, they don't ask us questions either. We're off the grid. That's the arrangement we have."

I tried to walk around Norman, but once again he blocked me. Was the only way forward through? Did I have to take a shot at the old bastard?

"I won't be long. Now please move."

"THAT'S the arrangement we have," he repeated, firmer and louder.

"There is no *we*. That's an arrangement *you* have with them. I get to make my own decisions thank you very much."

"Don't be so cheeky. Just give over and watch *Naked Attraction*."

"You can't talk to me like that. I'm thirty years old. I don't have to take this shit. I came here cos you practically forced me to. But stop acting like … I dunno, like you're my dad."

He glared—a snake ready to strike. But then he backed down. Injured. As if he were the one who'd been bitten. He gave up, folded like a bad hand of poker, and stepped aside. I finally exited the room.

"Go on then," he called after me. "Do what you want. Just don't get me caught up in your bullshit."

I turned back to Norman, wondering if he was aware of the irony. After everything he'd put me through, he wanted to ask *me* not to get *him* caught up in *my* bullshit. I went to say as much but thought better of it. I laced up my boots and rushed out of the cottage.

13

THE NEIGHBOUR'S cottage was eerier in the dark. Trees cast long shadows over the driveway with jagged edges and barbed contours threatening to cut those who trespassed. It was almost enough to send me back to Norman's.

Almost.

I tip-toed towards the front door—a socially awkward hipster Elmer Fudd out hunting, though instead of a rifle, I packed anxiety and a moral compass that had been dropped so many times it was as reliable as a rice paper umbrella. I'd have been better armed with Fudd's rifle. As I was about to step up to the porch, a bright light illuminated me and it may as well have been accompanied by the *Metal Gear Solid* "gotcha" sound because I threw my hands up in the air lightning-quick in a "don't shoot officer, stance."

Of course nobody shot because I hadn't been caught and it was just an automatic lighting system.

Once my heart rate returned to near normal, I moved forward until I was staring at the neighbours' off-white front door with its frosted glass and time-weathered paint. I pressed my ear against the door, listening for signs of life and struggle. I couldn't hear a thing, so pushed closer, inadvertently bearing too much of my weight against the frame and squeaking the evidently ajar door open. I threw out a hand to prevent myself from falling face first into the hallway, then scrambled to stop the door from smacking against the inside wall.

I was about to close the door and be on my way when I heard grunting and heaving as if two people were struggling to carry a large sofa up a narrow flight of stairs—only the sound wasn't coming from upstairs but from the adjacent room. Soon there was wheezing like an asthma attack on a treadmill. When the screaming started, I realised it wasn't struggle or pain, but pleasure and ecstasy. Whether they had or hadn't been fighting earlier, Norman's neighbours had made up for the time-being.

Fight hard, fuck hard.

Norman's words had not been hyperbolic but a statement of fact.

And what else had he said?

Christ, if you hear them fucking, are you gonna ask if we should go on over and join in?

I was not gonna do that. I would never do that. Though apparently I was already the aural alternative to a peeping tom because I'd been standing there a good thirty seconds.

I clambered hastily to close the door, then bolted out of there faster than a hairpiece in a hurricane.

14

THERE WAS STILL tension between Norman and me as we slurped up 7 a.m. cornflakes that had lost their crunch from a packet so worn it could have been excavated from a burial ground.

I packed my bag and left the house whilst Norman was in the shower, hoping to hit the road early and begin my journey home without confrontation.

As I was leaving the cottage, so, too, was the woman from next door. She wore an oversized hat with a wide brim and the long red coat I'd seen her in the previous day. No cat in sight.

"Morning!" I called out.

She jumped, more startled than a cockroach on an electric fence, and scrambled to retrieve her sunglasses from her coat pocket, which she hastily donned despite the newspaper grey clouds in the sky. She was quick but not so quick I didn't see the purple punctuating her eye.

"Lovely day," the woman said, though her tone and the weather suggested otherwise.

"Right … Hey, last night, what were you—"

"I've got to go." She clicked a button, unlocking a convertible the same red as her coat.

She was in the car before I could say as much as "see you around" or "have a good day" or "did your fella do a number on your eye before or after the sex and was it malicious or some kind of consensual kink?"

She jetted off into the distance, sharp pangs of guilt and regret stabbing at my stomach for my inaction. No wonder she'd had no qualms about being out in the woods when the more immediate danger resided in her own home. I sighed, short and sharp, and it felt good until a bear paw slapped my shoulder from behind.

Norman grinned at me. His hair straggly and wet. He smelt of cheap shampoo—floral, sickly, and artificial.

"I told you not to involve yourself with the neighbours, boy."

"I was just being friendly."

"Don't." He gestured to the bag in my hand. "You're really leaving then?"

The knots and needles in my stomach intensified and, for a moment, I thought I was going to pass out *again*. But instead of my vision receding, my stomach rumbled violently. Seconds later, the fiery vibrations progressed lower.

I dropped my bag, racing past Norman and bolting for the bathroom to evacuate my bowels.

15

SITTING ON THE JOHN, a layer of sludge that didn't quite make it into the toilet bowel slopping in the bottom of my pants, I called Amanda.

"Finally," Amanda said upon answering. "I was beginning to wonder what had happened. You all right?"

"I won't be able to make it to work this afternoon."

There was silence on the other end of the line, but the connection was crystal, which meant Amanda was upset. Likely furious.

I braced myself for the onslaught. Waiting for the phone equivalent of a violent beat-down, but instead she said, "Something did happen, didn't it? Shit ..."

I wanted to tell her about the way the woman had screamed as if her life depended on it, the dog-like yelps, and her masquerading silent smile conveying more truth and wounds than words would have. Moreover, I had to tell her about what was going on in Mona. The news reports and grisly findings in the forest.

Yet I couldn't. I froze up.

Amanda spoke again, her tone softer still, "You go quiet on me for the best part of a day and then ring me last-minute to cancel your afternoon shift without so much as an explanation. You need to tell me what's going on. I deserve better than this, Wentworth."

Christ, when she put it like that, I hardly had much choice.

"You know anything about the murder forest in Mona?" I asked.

"Huh?" Confusion clouded her voice. "You talking about a film or something?"

"There've been a number of murders in Mona-on-Sea this year and several more disappearances. Coverage has been limited, but it's picked up recently. They found another body this week. Anyway, it's obvious they're all connected. The media's being coy about the details but, from what I gather, the victims are always mutilated. It's as if the victims have been attacked by some kind of wild animal."

"Maybe they have. They've recently reintroduced wild boars to the UK."

"This isn't the work of a pack of lunatic wild boars. It's a human. The police know that at least. Besides, wild boars tend not to meticulously remove the teeth and fingernails of their victims." I paused. "You honestly hadn't heard about any of this until now?"

"I don't really watch the news. If there's something worth hearing about, I'll find out eventually."

"Exactly!" I shouted, remembering the way Norman had mocked me. Claiming it had been all over the nationals—it hadn't. It had taken an awful lot of digging via local news websites and Reddit threads to find out as much as I had.

"Um, okay," Amanda said, obviously unaware of Norman's mockery and presumably thinking I'd further lost touch with reality. "But why are you taking such an interest in something happening in Mona? I asked you what was going on with *you*, but instead of answering me, you've jumped into one of your bizarre circuitous stories. It's a bit ... *random*."

"It isn't random. It's connected!"

"How? Start making sense, Wentworth."

"Because …" I began, and this was the point of no return. Either close off the conversation or transform what Amanda and I had forever. Lay out everything about Norman, his neighbours, and the true extent of my financial woes. It'd either scare her off for good or bring us closer than ever.

Talking was a risk, but so was saying nothing.

I spilled my truth and bled for Amanda.

————

The phone line lay in awkward silence after I'd finished and, for a moment, I thought the connection had been cut for real this time, but then she spoke. "I don't understand why I'm only hearing about all of this now. You've made some bizarre and frankly bloody stupid decisions in the past 24-hours. The least you could have done was send a text message."

"Yeah," I conceded. "I thought about it but—"

"But what?"

"I didn't want to worry you."

"Well, I wish you had. The sooner you'd spoken to me, the sooner I could have talked you out of getting deeper into this mess. I can't believe you followed this idiot in the first place."

"He's my dad," I said, though the word tasted funny in my mouth.

"Yeah. Apparently. But you didn't know that at first. Look, I can get your shift covered today, give you some time to straighten your shit out and clear your head, but you should come home. You *need* to come home. Okay?"

"I will. Soon. Though I have to stay with Norman a little longer."

"But he's not a good person."

"Are any of us? What is a good person anyway?"

"For fuck's sake, Wentworth!"

"You said I should clear my head. But I can't do that if I leave Mona. The sea air is—"

"Bollocks! You know there are other ways to clear your head that don't involve staying with someone who forces you into committing numerous crimes."

"I guess. But things are so unresolved here."

"The way you're talking, this obviously isn't just about clearing your head. I can't believe you're still holding back. Give it to me straight!"

"Truth is, I don't want you involved."

"After all we've discussed, I'm already involved. It's about the murders, isn't it?"

Shots of blue plastic tents and white body bags filled my mind. Waves of sickness gurgled from within. At least if I lost control of my bodily functions, I was still sitting on the toilet.

"And there's something about that neighbour," Amanda said.

My heart rate quickened.

"Do you like her?" Amanda asked.

"I barely know her."

"But you're worried about her."

"I'm worried about people doing harm to others."

"You're thinking about her a lot. Obsessing, even. It's in your nature. It's who you are. She's the real reason you don't want to leave."

"Nah, it's—"

"I know you, Wentworth. And you know I know you. Please don't deny it."

"Amanda, if you'd seen the state of her eye and heard the way she begged for help last night, you'd feel the same. Norman wouldn't go round or call the police if he heard a chainsaw rev up and witnessed some halfwit spinning Leatherface-happy around the garden. He'd just sit in front of the telly, repeating their deal like a fucking mantra: *we stay out of their business and they stay out of ours.*"

"Don't be daft. There are obviously limits and—"

"We heard a man beat the shit out of his wife and all Norman could do is tell me to stay out of their way, so they stayed out of his. And that kind of insanity got me thinking, what is it that Norman's hiding?"

"And what are the neighbours hiding?" Amanda said.

"So now you understand why I have to stay."

"To save the woman."

"Perhaps."

"That's your problem," she said. "You always want to save people. But you never stop to consider what it is *they* want or need. You're playing with fire. And you know what they say about people who play with fire."

"They get burnt?"

"They're bloody stupid."

"I'll come home soon. I promise. I just need a few more days. To get a sense of what's really happening. And leave things better with Norman. Right now, they're tense and—"

"You want to get your million off him, yeah?"

"We both know there's no million."

"Yeah," Amanda said. "Difference is, you took the bait in the first place. How could you be so stupid?"

"It was desperation, not stupidity."

"If you say so … Either way, from now on, you keep in close contact with me. You text or call every day and let me know what's going on. Starting tonight. And if you need help with anything at all, don't hesitate to get in touch."

"Right you are."

"I mean it, Wentworth. You like to play the hero, and you hate asking for help, but this isn't a situation to fuck around with. You keep in touch, and you get out of there as soon as you can. And if you need to call the police, you do exactly that. Fuck Norman's 'we stay out of their business' bollocks. You do the right thing," she said. "And no more going along with any more of Norman's insane plans either. If he tells you to steal a car, to break into a house, to burn the evidence or god knows what else, you DO NOT DO IT. That isn't who you are, and it isn't who you're going to become."

16

After I'd cleaned my disgraced underpants and taken a damn good shower, I headed out the back for some air. Basking in the fresh sea-licked breeze was soon interrupted by a hell of a clattering and commotion. I made my way to the front to investigate the noise. The sun was out and so were Norman's legs as he paraded around the garden in light blue jorts and a faded ZZ Top t-shirt that was crop-top short. He muttered to himself as he hammered nails—assembling some kind of structure. Big blocks of wood, around waist height, surrounded the house's entrance. A shabbily put together faux fortress. Norman locked eyes with me before darting behind one of the blocks.

"Stay back, you trespassing cunt!" He crouched down, soon popping back up with a bow and arrow. He pointed the arrow right at me, firm against the taut drawstring, ready to release.

"Norman, what the Christ are you doing? It's me. Wentworth."

He stayed in position at first, but then recognition flickered across his face and he lowered the weapon, standing fully. "I thought you'd gone back to Kiddy."

"My car is literally on the drive and my bag of belongings is next to it."

"Yeah? Well, given the hurry you were in, I assumed you'd decided to lose the car and leg it home instead. Not a bad idea, all told. If you don't burn a car you've used in a job, you should at least abandon the fucking thing."

"That makes no sense on any level. Are you mentally … You know what, never mind."

Norman shrugged, then emerged from behind the wooden block, leaving the bow and arrow on the floor. He patted the block merrily as if praising a workhorse or kid done good.

"Self-defence," he said as if it was obvious. "Hide behind one of these bad boys, then when an intruder approaches, you can go *Call of Duty* on their arse."

"Go *Call of Duty*?"

He bent behind another of the blocks of wood and retrieved what looked like a medieval helmet. He'd affixed a miniature England flag to it. It looked out of place and flimsy —would have been better suited to a desk, affixed to the lapel of a jacket, or atop a particularly patriotic birthday cake.

"What do you reckon?" He tapped the top of the helmet. "Good bit of protection, no?"

"A bullet will go straight through it."

His smile faded, and he looked sullen. "Yeah? Well, this is England, pal. Nobody's gonna shoot me. It's all about knives. And this thing will murder a knife."

When I didn't respond, Norman threw the helmet to the ground in irritation. It conked so hard he probably damaged the thing. It was less King Arthur and more the Tin Man from *The Wizard of Oz*.

He stepped out from behind the badly constructed self-defence unit and opened his arms wide. "Well, come here then. Give your old man a hug. I knew you'd come back."

"I didn't go anywhere! I was upstairs on the shitter."

"I *knew* you'd come back," he said, sounding more convinced the second time around. "You're a good lad. A real daddy's boy. Now come here."

His hands beckoned me, arms still outstretched, ready to embrace.

Jesus, the guy looked so pathetic. I shuffled forward, giving him a hug more half-hearted than Theresa May's attempt at a Brexit deal. Norman overcompensated, pulling me in hard, and hitting me with so much force it was as if I'd got something stuck down my windpipe.

He released his grip, and I gasped for breath. Then he wrapped an arm around my shoulder, and we lumbered towards the house side-by-side. When we got to the front door, he held it for me.

"In you go, boy," he said, and I did just that, scraping my boots against the welcome mat.

I was about to step further inside the house when he screamed, "Mind the shit!"

Norman's eyes were more distressed than a punk's jeans in the 1970s.

I almost stood in it. A great big curler of a turd, just past the welcome mat, in the centre of the linoleum floor. Judging by its size, it must have been laid by some beast of a dog. I stumbled over the turd and to the other side of the hallway as one of the photographs of the well-dressed woman with the permed hair seemed to follow me—her eyes locked onto me as if trick art.

"You let some dog shit on your floor and didn't clean up?!"

"That ain't from a dog," he said, grinning. "That's daddy's finest. I laid a brick, son."

A second of confusion, followed by a second of realisation, followed by anger and disgust.

"Why the hell would you—"

"I'm marking my territory."

"But it's your house, you bloody idiot!"

"That's the point! And if somebody breaks in, they're gonna find out. This is *my* yard. They'll be walking around smelling of my pheromones."

"You're not right in the head."

Norman stepped over the poop, walked through to the kitchen, and started opening cupboards. He began taking cans of food from one of the higher shelves.

"Are you seriously not gonna clean that up?" I looked back at the dump in the middle of floor. "I can't believe you did that and didn't even warn me …"

"You weren't exactly about. Like I said, I thought you were halfway to Kiddy. Though, turns out, you were just upstairs planting a brawny brown of your own. You see? We ain't so different. Like father, like son."

He pulled a couple of tins of vegetable soup from the cupboard and shrugged, reaching for the canned peas. "Give us a hand going through this, would you? I'm making an inventory of all the food we've got and sell-by dates in case we need to get more supplies. I need to know how long we can survive here. Given everything kicking off with Tricky Ricky and his merry bunch of pricks, there could be a situation where we're unable to leave the house for a bit … The fuckers might surround the gaff. Have us cornered and that."

"A standoff?"

"Could be." Norman scratched his head, putting three cans of peaches in a corner and stacking corned beef a little to the left of them.

Was Norman a prepper? This seemed as if it was about more than Tricky Ricky. Perhaps later he would deliver his conspiracy theorist manifesto about an impending apocalypse.

"You got any money, boy?" Norman asked, skittish and hopeful.

"Not really."

"What about that loan you went to the bank for? Has it come through yet?"

I glared. "I didn't apply. You stopped me. Promised me a million pounds!"

He laughed as if that was too funny. "That I did. Well, anyway, we could do with more money."

Scalding anger sizzled inside me. Norman seemed to sense it cos he went, "Not to worry, boy. We'll figure something out."

He continued sorting and stacking cans. I started taking stock of packets of breakfast cereal, giving my shaking hands something to do other than punch Norman. I kept my lips pursed and tried willing my heart rate to slow.

Norman continued talking, but his words were white noise and aural dirt. A distant whirring at a frequency I couldn't understand. Norman had lured me into this situation under false pretences, promised me riches he didn't have, and rather than acknowledge his behaviour or apologise, he just went about things untroubled, expecting me to comply, shrug, and join in with his inanity. This less-than-a-man had no personal accountability or sense of morality.

"Right, that's it," I said, angry but unable to look at Norman. "For once in your life, I want you to be honest. There's no way I'm ever seeing that million pounds, is there?" My fingers wobbled under a packet of Crunchy Nut Corn Flakes.

"I mean, *ever* is a long time. We had a bit of a setback, but Swain has a few other schemes that could get us close, so—"

"No more bullshit. Be real with me, Norman. Be a dad."

He stopped stacking cans.

"I'm sorry, son." There was a sadness in his voice he

hadn't exhibited before and I wanted to look at him—to see if he was for real—but I couldn't.

"I really did think I could give you a million," he said. "All that I told you about Tricky Ricky's and the money was true, but the moment I turned up on the wrong date was the moment that opportunity went away."

"So why didn't you tell me that at the time?"

"Cos I was embarrassed. And selfish. Could hardly push you away minutes after reconnecting. Plus, I thought there was a chance I could turn things around and get the million after all. Though I guess *thought* isn't right, more like hoped, wished … Truth is, I'm just a fuckup. A deadbeat dad. It's probably a good thing I wasn't around for your childhood."

Silence hung more awkwardly than the letters on the *Fawlty Towers* hotel sign.

"I'd just waited so long to be back in your life …" he said.

"We live in the same town. Have done for many years of my life," I said. "By your own admission, you've been watching me. You know where I live. So you could have just knocked on my door. Introduced yourself that way. But instead, your idea of the *right opportunity* was to implicate me in a burglary. A damn-near heist. That was your way of getting me on side and back in your life."

"I knew you needed some money," he said softly. "If I'd had someone hand me a million pounds in my youth, I'd have lived a much better life. That person would have been a hero to me."

I looked at his sorry-arse-face. Dejected and useless. If stupidity was a sport, he'd be representing England at the Olympics.

Norman clicked his fingers and grinned as if he'd landed upon a good idea. "You remember when I hot-wired that car? I was thinking you could hot-wire a load of motors in town. See what we can sell. A lot of fancy cars around these parts.

Many people only live here half the year. Holiday homes and that. And those that holiday here are pretty minted, too."

"I'm not doing that."

"It's as easy as taking a piss. If you don't remember how I did it, then just Google it."

"I'm not saying I *can't* do it. I'm saying I *won't* do it."

"Fair enough. I suppose it's not for everyone," he said. "Another option is a bit of low-level burglary. You don't take anything that might be sentimental, and you treat the house with care. A respectful burglary."

"Burglary is disrespectful by definition. A total invasion and violation of somebody's sacred space. A respectful burglary is an oxymoron."

"I'm no moron," Norman said, proving the opposite. "You just search the place for hidden money. Under beds, in drawers, in a jar in the toilet's water tank, bookshelves, pantries, suitcases, etc. A lot of old fucks start taking their money away from the banks and storing it in the house. A good way to minimise inheritance tax and that. Though, if you think about it, it's a kind of fraud. We're just helping restore the balance and taking the tax those fuckers are avoiding paying."

"You steal candy from babies, too? Or do you just go up to prams and punch the kids dead in the face?"

"Don't be so hysterical. Them old fucks will be dead in a few years. And it's not as if they can take the money with them. I'm basically Robin Hood. Taking the money from the rich and giving it to the poor."

"Hardly. The only person who benefits is you."

"You benefit, too. No more shit from landlords or legal bills to worry about. You could even restart the legal case to win your cat back or take your girl on holiday. Somewhere nice like Malaga."

"I'm not doing it, and I don't want any part of it. Not only is it illegal, but it's immoral. It's obvious you couldn't care less about breaking the law or hurting others, but that isn't me ... Ugh, you really are beyond contempt."

He shrugged. "Well, there's obviously something you like about me, otherwise you wouldn't have decided to stay."

"I didn't stay because of you, Norman."

"No? Then why'd you stay?"

17

Norman was in sombre spirits when he realised I really hadn't stayed because of him. He started medicating the only way he knew how, pouring himself a large measure of vodka, before sitting down at the kitchen table.

"Well, I'm glad you stayed, at any rate. If you'd have gone to Kiddy, the bastards might have got you."

"You're just being paranoid."

"I don't think so. You see Colin's TikTok?"

"What? No. Why would I ..."

"Because, Swain aside, it's the best way to understand what they're thinking. Here, check this out."

Colin stood in front of the same graffitied fence he had in the first video and wore the same basketball shirt and shorts. He began rapping if you could call it that.

"Got my dick in my hand.
Got my dick in my shorts.
Got my dick in your arse.
Got my dick on the door.
Got my dick over there.
Got my dick on my stick.
That's my hockey stick.

But you can just call it my hockey dick.
WOW!
I'm a crazy guy.
Fucking Bramley apple, I'm American Pie.
Shoot Clapton from a rocket, that's Eric in sky.
Write Greek poems, shoot yourself. Homeric 'n' die.
A businessman is mad at you. Hysteric in tie."

"Um … what? I don't get it," I said. "What's this got to do with us?"

Norman peered over at the phone. "Ah, shit. Wrong one."

He flicked to the next video.

Colin was once again in front of the same fence, wearing the same clothes. He obviously took the Steve Jobs 'wear the same every day' approach to fashion.

"This one goes out to the cunts who stitched us up the other day.

You bitches gonna get what you deserve.

Turn it up, turn it up, Ian. Here we go …

Norman Cooper's a filthy cunt.

And his piss-eyed son is a little runt.

Here's what we're gonna do to you.

So, listen up, son, and pay attention.

Wesker's Sister's furious.

Cos she's …"

Colin scratched his head and said, "I dunno how to say it in a rap."

"Then just say it normally," a voice off-screen that sounded just as young and pathetic as Colin said.

"But rapping's my thing."

"Why'd you tell me to press record if you didn't have your rap ready, you bellend?"

"I dunno. I thought it would come to me, like, but it didn't."

"So, say it. I'm still recording."

"Shit." Colin started pacing. "I really do think it should be a rap. I kind of *have to* rap. It's what I'm known for." The camera lingered on a progressively more frustrated Colin. "You *still* recording?"

"Yeah."

"Fuck, man. This video's gonna be shit."

"So edit it down."

"I don't do edits. I believe in giving people reality. That's why my rhymes are so powerful."

"Just tell them."

"Fine." Colin took a deep breath. "Norman, you and that inbred son of yours are dead. Wesker's Sister's gonna show you why they call her the Slicer. Pat is gonna batter you like a piece of cod from … well, any fucking chippy—Merchants, Catchems End, that one on the Bewdley Road, though I always forget the name."

"Bewdley Road Fish Bar."

"That's the one! And as for Gary, he will … will … well, he'll probably give you a good kicking, too. And if Tricky Ricky turns up. Well, better hope he doesn't, know what I mean?"

The video ended.

Norman rested his elbows on the table and waited for my response.

"I'm not sure if I feel threatened or relieved. That was all very confusing," I said. "One thing's for sure, though, these guys are amateurs."

Norman knocked back some vodka. "No, mate. That's where you're wrong."

"You're telling me that video was—"

"That video is just Pat's boy screwing around, but the operation Tricky Ricky heads up is serious. They *are* a threat. If I told you *the real* reason they called that sword-waving loon 'Wesker's Sister', you'd get it. But I hold some things back to protect you, you know?"

"I *don't* know. That doesn't make any sense," I said. "Plus, every time you hold something back, it just results in a bigger headache for me in the long run. You've got to start being more transparent."

Norman groaned. "Put it like this, Tricky Ricky's her father, but he won't even call her by her real name. There was an accident, years back now, after old Ricky had had too many bevvies, and let's just say, the wrong kid got incapacitated."

"Incapacitated?"

"Wesker's a bloody potato, mate! And Tricky Ricky had him lined up to be the heir to everything, so he keeps his name alive via Wesker's Sister. She's so bloody psycho because she's trying to prove herself to daddy, but he couldn't give a shit about her. It's sad really. A tale as old as time itself." Norman stopped talking, clearly thinking about something. "There are rumours Tricky Ricky ... Well, shit, it's all hearsay, but let's say the way he treats her, or at least *treated her* when she was younger, is a lot bloody darker than not calling her by her birth name. I'll leave it at that for the time being." Norman stood up, eyeing the tinned food that remained. "Anyway, I've got work to do, boy. Thanks for the chinwag."

I left Norman to return to his food inventory and headed outside to mow the parts of his front lawn that weren't littered with junk or newly erected wooden defence blocks. I fed into Norman's paranoia and told him I'd do it to help raise the property valuation in case he needed to make a quick sale due to the impending threat from Tricky Ricky. Though, in reality, I wanted to be close to the neighbours for when the woman with the oversized sunglasses inevitably showed up. Her convertible wasn't on the drive, and I couldn't see or hear anything from within the cottage, so it was a safe bet she was still out.

When the lawn was cut, I started weeding the garden and pruning the limited beds of flowers Norman had accidentally cultivated, doing anything I could to keep myself occupied and out at the front of the house.

I worked until the skies darkened and rain began to drizzle down, at which point Norman emerged to announce, "I'm cooking sausages for tea, frozen, from Morrison's. They're cheap as a cup of cum, but if you drench them in barbecue sauce, they'll taste as good as the scran you'd get at a five-star restaurant."

I stayed outside a little longer, but as the rain intensified, I relented and headed back inside, disappointed not to have seen the woman.

18

NORMAN HAD GONE ALL OUT with the food, preparing some oven chips and almost in-date onion rings to complement the sausages. The food and bottles of sauce lay on the kitchen countertop, ready for us to devour.

"I thought about warming a can of baked beans on the hob but can't deliver Michelin quality nosh too early. Got to save something good for next time, know what I mean?" Norman said. "Now, you want to have trays on our laps and watch *Corrie* or sit at the table like a couple of benders?"

"The table's fine," I said, shifting uncomfortably.

"You think you're better than *Corrie*?"

I ignored the question and took the plate to the dining table in the centre of the wide kitchen.

Norman followed, his fists clenched.

The first bite of sausage tasted more like old carboard than meat. Norman silently slid a bottle of barbecue sauce towards me. I squeezed sauce onto the plate.

"You really should respect *Corrie*," Norman said, clearly not done with his *Coronation Street* spiel. "You're British, aren't you?"

"You should know, seeing as you're my dad."

"Just checking you're not a bender."

I put the fork down. "Do you even know what bender means?"

"It's just something you say to get a rise out of people. We all used to say it back in the day at school. Nothing bad about it. Just having a laugh. Why've you got to be so sensitive like that?"

I tried one of the onion rings. It was almost as bad as the sausage.

"Do you think less of men who are attracted to other men?" I asked.

Norman fidgeted awkwardly in his chair. "I don't see what that's got to do with anything."

"Would you think less of me if I was attracted to other men?"

"Are you?"

"What does it matter?"

"It doesn't." Norman pushed his shoulders back, straightening. "You attracted to me then? I used to be good looking in my youth. I've got some topless snaps if you're interested. In '88, I was the talk of Bodmin Beach."

Norman's awkwardness was interrupted by the loud rumbling of a nearby car engine. I shot up from my seat, much to Norman's chagrin. "The hell are you doing? We don't leave the meal table until we're done eating!"

But it was too late, I was already dashing to the living room, narrowly avoiding Norman's still present pile of poop in the adjoining hallway.

Through the living room window, I watched as the woman from next door got out of her sports car carrying several large shopping bags, a triangular logo emblazoned on the most prominent, bringing to mind the Pythagorean death cults I'd considered earlier. It was now dark outside, but the woman was still wearing her oversized sunglasses. Had she been driving in them? Was it even possible to see through the windscreen in shades? She was struggling to walk with the weight of the bags in each hand, her feet dragging rather than stepping forward as she advanced towards the front of the cottage.

A light came on inside and the door opened, but I couldn't see anyone there to greet her. So, the bloke she lived with—presumably her husband, partner, lover—couldn't be arsed to give her a hand with the bags or even say hello. What was she even doing with him?

The woman glanced over her shoulder and looked towards me as if hearing my thoughts. I wanted to duck down, to walk away, to make as if I wasn't watching her, but we soon locked eyes and the light behind me made my presence in the window apparent. I raised a single hand in recognition. She nodded back before retreating into the illuminated darkness of her house and slamming the door.

19

NORMAN'S EVENING entertainment was the same as always. A can of lager in hand and an old episode of *Naked Attraction* on the box.

On the telly, a group of lads baring all, stood in a horizontal line. Norman scrutinised their tackles. "Bigger dick than him, bigger dick than him, bigger dick than him, bigger dick than—ah, wait, that lad's got a right flesh hanger, could be a grower *and* a shower—bigger dick than him, bigger dick than him, bigger dick than him."

"Do we have to watch this?" We were only three minutes in and I already regretted my decision to hang out with Norman.

"It's an important part of television history. Plus, it's fun. Look closely and you might see someone you've boned before."

"Do you often see people you've boned on *Naked Attraction*?"

"I once saw this trans woman I noshed off behind Merchants Fish Bar. I mean, she noshed me off, too, so it was fair game." Norman smiled at the memory. "She wasn't a contestant but part of the studio audience, though it still counts. And believe you me, if she'd been part of the game, she'd have won. Nobody was gonna turn her down."

I sipped my glass of tap water. I'd hoped in spending time with Norman, I could get him on side and find out what was going on with the neighbours. Given the agreement he had with them, it might be he knew more than he was letting on. It was proving useless thus far, but I was learning things about my supposed dad, so there was that. Though, admittedly, I was learning things no one ever needed to know about their parent.

Norman pointed towards the telly. "I know it's just a clothed woman checking out some blokes at the moment, but she'll take her kit off soon. Later on, there'll be a bloke checking out a bunch of birds. That's when it gets *really* interesting."

"I know how the show works, Norman. It's a dating show in which one person chooses which of the six naked contestants they fancy having a date with."

"I mean, it's a bit more complicated than that. You don't see the full body for a while, parts are revealed bit-by-bit. Suspense and that. And there are all sorts of questions, too. Still, I'm glad you get the gist of it. I'm proud of you, boy."

Norman sat on the edge of his seat, absorbing every detail of the show.

"If there's someone I like the look of," Norman said, "I start bashing one out. Unless I'm eating my tea, mind. Don't want to get any pubes in my baked beans."

"Ugh, gross." I felt congealed sausages stirring in my stomach, threatening to re-emerge.

"*What?* I said I *don't* bash one out if I'm eating. But if there's no food in sight, I give my man-wood a right good sanding if you know what I mean? It's completely natural. And healthy, might I add. Those who shake hands with the milkman have lower rates of prostate and testicular cancer. That's a fact."

"I really don't want you to start rubbing one out when I'm here."

"Don't be weird, boy."

"Sorry. It's just from the way you were talking, I thought you might."

"No, I mean, don't be weird *about* it. You think you're the result of an immaculate conception? Where'd you think you come from? How'd you think it happened? I'll tell you the where *and* the when. Back of Halford's car park, summer of '91."

Norman stared at me, waiting for a reaction I wasn't giving, then went. "You can bash one out, too, if you want. Over the men or the women or the legends in-between." He cleared his throat. "Just don't get any jizz on the carpet, curtains, or cushions, okay? Them's the holy three Cs."

A bump from next door jolted with such violence and noise, I thought something was about to explode out of the neighbour's place, burst through Norman's shabby walls, and join us in the living room.

Norman and I exchanged a look.

"Ignore it," Norman said. "That isn't for us. But she …" He gestured to the blonde tattooed woman, completely starkers on-screen. "She certainly is."

20

THERE'D BEEN no follow-up or further sounds from next door, so, much to my discomfort, we'd continued watching *Naked Attraction*. I tried asking Norman questions about the neighbours, but he refused to discuss anything not directly related to the show whilst it was playing, claiming it was disrespectful to *Naked Attraction* and one of the seven tenets he lived by.

Beer-glazed, Norman got sleepy halfway through the second episode and we made our way to our respective bedrooms. The room Norman had offered me was painted in varying shades of green and barely bigger than a shoe cupboard with a cheesy odour to match. It looked like the kind of guest room even an elderly hoarder would be embarrassed by. I cracked a window open, but it did little to improve the smell. I lay on the bed for a moment, hoping I wouldn't contract something.

When I wagered Norman was conked out, I crept downstairs to the living room, where I perched on the window ledge, looking out at the neighbour's cottage. Rain beat down hard, making it difficult to hear anything else outside, but there were no thuds or screams from within. I couldn't settle on whether that was reassuring or disturbing. Silent screams are reserved for the pain that hurts the most.

My phone buzzed in my pocket. A text message from Amanda: *How's everything going with your dad?*

Ah, shit. I'd forgotten to check in with her.

It hadn't helped that Norman had gone all medieval on me with the wooden blocks. Then there'd been the whole shit-a-brick debacle, the sausages, *Naked Attraction*, and the mental drain of any and every interaction with Norman. I'd had limited room to whip out my phone, more concerned with preventing Norman from whipping out his pink gherkin.

I began drafting a quick text: *Things are weird but as expected. Not had a chance to talk with the woman next door but ...*

I backtracked. Deleted the last sentence. Didn't need to mention the woman again until there was something worth mentioning.

I went over the message once more, and was considering deleting the whole thing, when my phone started vibrating in my hands.

An incoming call from Amanda.

I picked up. "Hey, you."

"Saw you were typing, so thought I'd save you the trouble. Now a good time?"

And this was one of the many things I hated about modern technology. The invasiveness of the "is typing" message. Only second in my list of things that should well and truly get in the sea to the so-called read receipt.

"It's late," I said. "Got to keep quiet so I don't wake Norman. But I can chat for a few."

"You made any progress?"

"Not really. Unless you include answers to questions I never asked. I found out I was conceived in Halford's car park."

"Your life story just gets sadder by the minute."

"Thanks for the support. All this time with Norman and I was beginning to feel depressed, but you've got a knack for making me feel better about everything."

She laughed. "I see he hasn't drained you of your sarcasm. So, how about the woman? You speak to her?"

"Speak, no, but I saw her. Carrying a bunch of shopping bags into the house. Nothing special." No need to mention I'd practically camped out in the garden all day looking for her or that she'd caught me looking from the window.

"I read up on the murders," Amanda said. "You weren't kidding. It *is* grim. It's the little details that get me. The torn and bloodied child's vest jacket with the rabbit ears. The Mickey Mouse handkerchief that was more red than white after what happened to the poor lass."

"Hold up, what are you talking about, child's jacket? The victims were all adult women. Twenty- and thirty-somethings. There've been no children I've seen."

"Well, be grateful you haven't. I can't get the images out of my mind. The dark web is an evil place for breaking a story and leaking photographs: the *Paw Patrol* backpack, empty save for a half-full bottle of kids' orange juice, the broken necklace with an emergency contact number for the child's mother, also murdered at the scene. It's so fucking sad."

"There were no children! You've got your wires crossed. You're looking at the wrong thing."

"Today," she said. "A few hours ago. They found another body. The daughter of the woman they located two days ago."

"You can't be serious? This can't be happening!"

"Is it not being covered on the locals?"

"I haven't seen much."

"They're not reporting on it?!"

"I don't know. I've barely seen anything other than *Naked Attraction* and old episodes of *Match of the Day*."

"What the fuck?"

"It's Norman's telly, so he controls what we watch."

"I thought you cared about the murders. Isn't that part of why you're still there?"

"Jesus Christ, *of course* I care, but it isn't that simple. You don't know what Norman's like. I'll keep track of things more, I promise. I'm doing my best … or at least I'm *trying* to."

There was silence and, for a moment, I thought the call had been disconnected.

Amanda breathed deep, then said, "There was *so much* blood. Did you know the necklace the little girl had been wearing was—"

But my imagination was too visual. I was going to puke, pass out, or both if Amanda didn't slow down.

"Just stop it! For fuck's sake, Amanda. We should stay informed, yes. But we shouldn't be reading up on the murders in that kind of detail. No good will come of consuming grief porn."

Amanda cleared her throat but didn't speak straight away. Without video on, I couldn't be certain how she was reacting.

Raised voices quarrelled in the distance. I strained to listen but, before I could make anything out, Amanda was talking again.

"It isn't grief porn. There's a purpose to it. A responsibility to keep on reading. We might find something that will save your life or someone else's."

The sounds were getting louder. The argument next door escalating. The cat began mewling—a cry for help or a plea to stay away?

"It isn't porn," Amanda said again. "There's no pleasure from it. It isn't gratuitous. Far from it."

"Yeah," I said, removing the phone a little from my ear, pressing closer to the cracked-open window as if I could channel next door's sounds towards me.

I recalled the horror scene Amanda had laid out. That fucking necklace and the writing, *"Please call my mummy if found."*

I wanted to run away from the world and hide until it became kind. Or better still, just regress to a time in my childhood when I'd been protected from the cruelty of man, even if it had been short-lived, for fewer years than a childhood rightly should be.

"So then, you agree?" Amanda said. Had she been talking the entire time? "We are obligated to keep reading. For the sake of the victims, past and present."

There was another noise from next door, not a voice, but movement, and if we were helping would-be victims, I should get off the phone and follow the sounds. I should *investigate*.

"If you text me the address, then I can come to you," she said. "I'll get a few days off work and see what I can—"

"Slow down. I'm not sure Norman will agree to that and—"

"This isn't *about* Norman!" There was a loud bang, but this time it was from Amanda's end. She breathed deeply before speaking in a softer voice. "Maybe the woman will respond better to another woman."

"I know you're doing your best here, but we have to tread carefully. A to B, not A to C, and certainly not A to Z. It's easy to let our minds race ahead with everything going on, but we can only respond to what we see and hear."

"I know, I know, but …"

"GET YOUR FUCKING HANDS OFF OF ME!" The sound of a woman, part-terror, part-warning.

The cat's grating siren silenced.

There was a light on in the large front window next door. It had to be the woman, and I had to do something, for the price of inaction is often far greater than the price of making a mistake.

"Amanda, I've got to go."

I hung up the phone and raced out of the house and towards the neighbour's cottage.

21

I CLOSED in on the neighbour's place. The enraged couple threw words and objects back-and-forth. A television remote control crashed through the window and into a bed of flowers.

I stepped off the lawn and onto the pathway leading to the neighbour's front door. A kaleidoscope of light and movement glinted from the front window. Then something caught my shirt collar, wrenching me from behind and pulling me down onto the ground. My skull thunked back onto the lawn. Acute pain invading my head. A pressure pushed into my shoulders, pinning me in place on the grass. I looked up to see Norman. A cigarette dangling out of his mouth, maroon dressing gown half open, revealing chest hair and paunch. His face couldn't have been more puzzled if it was a Rubik's Cube.

"What are you doing, boy?"

"Get the fuck off of me," I said, spit flying from my mouth to his face.

He tightened his grip, puffing cigarette smoke towards me. "Son, you've got to get back in the house."

"I haven't got to do shit. And besides which, I can't go anywhere unless you let go of me."

"Tell me what you were doing out here."

"Same as you," I lied. "Going for a smoke."

"You keep your cigarettes in the neighbour's place or something?" He looked over his shoulder towards their cottage.

"Of course not. My fags are in my pocket."

Norman's eyes lit up. "So, you really are a smoker then? Daddy's proud." He relaxed some of the pressure on my shoulders and I kipped up, pushing him off me. "What the hell are you doing, you little bastard?"

Norman grabbed the bottom of my jeans as I struggled to my feet. I kicked him away, driving the heel of my boot into his forehead. He groaned, then launched a fist towards my face, which I dodged before backing away from him and edging closer towards the neighbour's. Norman threw another punch but failed to connect. He looked like a blind man fighting a wasp's nest, the cigarette still in his mouth as if permanently glued there as he whipped his fists around haphazardly.

"Get the fuck away from me," I said.

"No, *you* get the fuck away from that cottage."

"They need my help!"

"Bollocks! They don't need a bloody thing from you."

I took another step backwards, closer to the house.

"Go back inside, Norman. Let me handle this."

He charged forward, spearing me to the floor.

When my head hit the ground, there was no grass for protection, just gravel and concrete.

Norman threw a fist at my head and this time it connected, thwacking my forehead square in the centre.

"What the fuck are you doing, you animal?"

"You started it," he said, touching the broken skin on his

own forehead. "So you got one back. It's what's known as a receipt. Fair's fair."

I punched the arsehole in the lip, busting him open, and slapping the sound right out of his chops. He fell off me—the cancer stick finally dropping from his mouth. I clambered to my feet once again, staggering towards the neighbour's gaff.

"You stay down," I called as Norman looked up at me, shuffling on the grass to retrieve his now soiled cigarette, damp and limp like overcooked spaghetti. "Don't you even think about starting shit unless you want another fist to the face?"

He grinned, blood leaking from his mouth. "You think you're a hard man, do you, boy?" He spat blood and saliva onto the ground. "You've got another receipt coming for that, you little prick."

"No. That was *my* receipt for you conking my head on the floor, you dozy dick."

He hawked more blood to the grass, then threw the bent and damaged cigarette on top of it, staring at it mournfully for a second, then went, "Nah, boy, you drew blood. That means I get to draw blood later. Might not be now, but it's coming for you."

"Get fucked!" I screamed, turning for the neighbour's place, which was when I thudded into a big bloke who wore a dirty apron and smelt like a butcher's shop had taken a bath in cheap aftershave.

He towered over me like a teacher in first school, with well-muscled arms, a lumberjack beard, and coarse hair that was so dense it wouldn't have surprised me if a bird's nest was buried within.

"What's all this racket?" His voice was diesel fuel and elk meat.

I backed up. I didn't fancy my chances in a one-on-one fist fight with this giant. His once white apron held an assortment of time-worn stains from oil grease to sawdust to blotches of paint and off-red marks that looked fresher than the rest of the blemishes.

"Well?" he said. "You have any idea how late it is?"

Norman was on his feet and walking towards this mountain of a man.

Norman's hands pressed together in a prayer. "I'm terribly sorry about this. It's just me and my boy had a few too many tinnies. We were having a celebration of sorts and … Well, things got out of control, as you can see." Norman wrapped his arm around my shoulder and pulled me close like we were best buds.

Man Mountain eyed the two of us. My heart hammered and my knees shook under the adrenaline and pressure of it all, but thankfully it didn't appear to be visible through my jeans.

"Just keep it down, yeah?" Man Mountain said, then turned away from us, heaving back up the driveway.

The woman in the sunglasses stood in the front window of the neighbour's cottage. She sipped something from a wine glass, watching us intently.

"I'm really sorry about all of this, Richard," Norman called after the big man.

What the fuck? Norman was actually grovelling. The man was as thick as a tank and as tall as a truck, but from the concern etched across Norman's face, I reckoned this was about more than physical intimidation.

The woman continued observing us as we watched Richard, though when I stopped glancing at her in my periphery and turned to her directly, she quickly shut the curtains. There was no embarrassment to it—she was just decisive in keeping us locked out and her locked in. I couldn't help but recall Amanda's sentiments about some people not wanting to be saved.

Richard entered the house, closing the door with an authoritative slam.

Norman dropped his arm from around me and slapped me on the back. "Come on, boy. Best get going. We've caused enough trouble for one night."

22

THE FOLLOWING MORNING, I found Norman in the living room, pacing frantically and stuffing handfuls of supermarket brand knock-off Monster Munch into his mouth.

"They found a kid," he said between crisp crunching. "This has gone too fucking far."

He dropped to his knees, weeping, and there was nothing false or exaggerated about it. Norman was hurting.

On the television, there was a photograph of the newest victims, Elizabeth Raleigh, twenty-six years old, and her daughter Liliana, just four years old.

I put an arm around Norman, patting his shoulder awkwardly, attempting to comfort him. Being a son to Norman came unnaturally. This was a dance we were both figuring out, with neither instructions nor rules.

He stood up suddenly, decisiveness in his eyes. "We've got to fix this," he said. "To take care of business and bring the sorry fucker to justice."

Norman switched the TV off, and I heard a man (Richard?) from next door shout, "You're behaving like a cunt, Alex. A selfish cunt-bitch."

A glass smashed, and Norman closed the window, muffling the commotion.

"We can't be concerned about that right now," he said, his eyes bloodshot and face feverish. "They've been at it for the last hour. And Alex, she gives as good as she gets … Now, tell me, boy, do you know how to shoot?"

"Norman, I'm not playing this game. You tell me about the neighbours, and you tell me what the hell happened with Richard last night? Why were you so afraid of him?"

"I'm not afraid," Norman shouted. "Jesus, you're not gonna drop this neighbour nonsense, are you?"

"You've got to give me something."

The boiler whirred to life in the adjacent room.

"Okay, fine," Norman said. "Richard and I, we have a thing going. A secret. He knows something about me, and I know something about him."

"What?"

"Well, if I told you, it wouldn't be much of a secret, would it? Plus, it's a burden."

"Your secret or his?"

"Both. Trust me, my silence is doing you a favour. It wouldn't be good for you. It's not good for anyone."

"You sure about that? If this has anything to do with the murders, then I have a right to—"

"It has shit all to do with the murders!" Norman said, agitated. "Now, do you or don't you know how to shoot?"

"I can handle myself if necessary."

Norman blinked. "How the hell do you—"

"I don't want to get into it. And it's none of your business anyway."

Norman frowned. "No? Well, it might become my business if we're in a life and death situation, so less of the lip. Besides, I need to see it for myself, which is why we're gonna practise shooting today."

"I don't have to prove myself to you. And anyway, I thought I'd just—"

"Just *what*? Sit on your arse and read a book? Eat Weetabix all day long? Go down to the beach and surf with some of the locals? This isn't a bloody holiday camp, boy. I need to make sure you're in fighting shape. And for more than one reason. Firstly, I want us to start patrolling the woods for that killer. Murdering women is one thing, but when you start fucking with Mona's children, that's another matter entirely. If the police won't stop it, then *we* will."

"I don't think the police are deliberately *not* catching the killer. It's all over the local and even the national news now. The case is picking up steam."

"As it bloody well should, but it's not quick enough." Norman folded his arms.

"So, what's the other reason?"

"That should be obvious. Tricky Ricky's gang of merry bastards could show up here any day now. And when they do, we need to give them hell and run them all the way back to Kiddy."

"As I keep telling you, I don't think they'll go to such extremes."

"With respect, you don't know a damn thing about them, so how can you *think* anything?"

"Listen, Norman, you didn't make off with any of their money. You're just being paranoid."

"Swain sees things differently. Says they're looking for me and you. Like *really* looking. More than just words on TikTok. Matter of fact, Colin's been snooping around your gaff."

"Colin?"

"Pat Knox's lad. You got dementia or something? The shit rapper. You've seen his videos. And sure, he's as stringy as a runner bean with the intimidation factor to match. But trust me, if Colin's there, the rest will follow. Now please tell me there isn't anything lying around at yours that will lead them here. You didn't write my address down, did you? Or leave a Post-it note on the fridge saying you'd gone to Mona or any shit like that?"

"Slow down. How could they be at my place? Even *you* don't know my address. This doesn't make any sense."

Norman thrust his phone in my face. "Perhaps this will help you make sense of it. I got this from Swain."

An on-screen photograph showed Colin standing in the middle of my apartment's car park. He wore his trademark basketball shirt and shorts cut so high if he took another inch off, his ballbags would bounce out the bottom. He limply clutched a baseball bat with as much confidence as a virgin at an orgy.

"What the hell is this?"

"Don't worry," Norman said, scrolling through his photographs. "Your photo looks better."

The next photo showed me in the bathroom, topless, and washing blood off my hands.

"What the fuck? That's a violation of my privacy, you piece of shit."

"A funny way of saying thank you," Norman said. "Look at your shoulder definition. That's some seriously good lighting. It don't pop like that in real-life and yet here we are. You look like a piece of prime beef."

"You are unbelievable!"

"Unbelievably sound at taking pics. A good job we had that scrap on the lawn, huh?" He touched his mouth, slightly swollen at the lips. "I have to say, I wasn't too happy with the way you busted me open, but it worked like a charm for the shot. Blood on your hands, top off, shit hair ruffled so much it almost looks manly. If I didn't know you, I might think you could handle yourself in a fight."

"I handled you last night, didn't I?"

"I went easy on you, boy. But, anyway, we're getting away from the point. I sent that snap to Swain. Told him to tell Pat Knox you could deck his lad as easily as taking a piss."

"Why the fuck would you do that?"

"Because Pat was talking shit. Saying his boy could batter you. I ain't no bitch and neither are you. They can't cuss us out like that."

"This isn't middle school. If someone says they can beat me up, I don't need to respond to it. Let them think whatever they want."

Norman groaned. "That's how you become soft, my boy. Never let someone think they can deck you. You show them what's what."

"All this talk reminds me of that old saying, better to remain silent and be thought a fool, than to open your mouth and remove all doubt."

"What the bloody hell are you going on about, you pebble?"

"At least you only sent it to Swain."

Norman looked down at his feet.

"You did only send it to Swain, right?"

"I only sent it to Swain," he said. "But the thing is, well, Swain might have forwarded it to the rest of the lads. I mean, maybe not all of them, but at least Pat and Gary."

"You sure about that?"

Norman navigated to a text on his phone from Pat Knox that read: *You and your boy are dead when we find you. And we WILL find you.*

"Satisfied?" Norman asked.

"What part of any of this makes you think I would be satisfied?"

Norman shrugged. "I must have got proper shit-faced last night. From the looks of my message history, I sent Pat a load of stuff about the lot of them having small dicks. Look here, I photoshopped their faces on some stills from *Naked Attraction* and also sent a mirror selfie pic showing them I was much better hung than the lot of them."

Norman shoved the phone in my face. His hanging Cumberland was the first photograph I saw. I swatted the phone away as if fighting a mosquito, but the damage was done. My dad's dick was now an image that would forever be burnt into my mind.

"Whenever people mess with me, I photoshop them into the least flattering *Naked Attraction* photos I can find."

"You are obsessed with that show."

"Yeah, *and?* Better than being addicted to smack. Now stop with the playground talk and follow me. We've got some shooting to do."

23

NORMAN TOOK me to a secluded spot in the woods where he'd set up his own DIY shooting range. I'd figured it would take less time to follow rather than fight him. Whilst it was by no means a good shooting range, it looked like a pro setup compared to his so-called barracks. There were a bunch of cans with their original labels torn off. Taped in their place were photographs of celebrities Norman had issues with. I didn't recognise everyone, but amongst the famous faces were Tony Blair, Gary Lineker, Helen Mirren, and Tom Jones.

"She's one of the worst," Norman said, pointing to a woman with a thicket of blonde curls. "Lauren Harries, former child prodigy and *Big Brother* contestant who got her lack of knickers in a twist on *Naked Attraction* because someone said she was too old. When she stormed off in a huff, she caused a right atmosphere. Didn't even give the bloke a hug. That's like refusing to stand for the national anthem or not shaking the hand of the interviewer when you go for a job. It was one of the worst nights of my life. I almost couldn't finish my beans on toast."

"It sounds terrible. Much worse than our foiled attempt to become millionaires."

"Boy, I'm not even joking when I say I'm not sure which is worse. I didn't leave the house for about a week after Lauren pulled that disgusting stunt. There are others I hate, too. Dame Sheila Hancock moaned about having to watch *Naked Attraction* for *Gogglebox*. Which is like moaning because McDonald's serve you Wagyu tenderloin. Luckily the producers of *Gogglebox* know what's what and fired her dumb arse. I'll never understand people who think they're better than *Naked Attraction*. NEVER EVER," Norman said. "India Willoughby. Now there's someone with integrity. One of the greatest people to ever exist. She was all set for a celebrity-edition of *Naked Attraction*, but there weren't enough others interested, so it got axed. Google it if you don't believe me."

I reached for my phone to do exactly that, but Norman scowled. "Not now, you clown.

I slipped my phone in my pocket, but not before I caught a glimpse of a text message from Amanda: *Staying at yours for a few days. The neighbours round mine are partying again. Sleep deprivation is making me sick and nauseous. Need some proper sleep.*

"Have a hold of this," Norman said. "Feel its weight." He passed me a charcoal black rifle that looked in good nick. "It's a Ruger. American made. Guns are one of the few things the yanks are actually good at."

I pointed the rifle towards Lineker. "You want me to take a shot and get this over with?"

"Not with that. That one's for me. I just wanted you to experience its power. Something to motivate you." He snatched the rifle back. "I got another gun in mind for you, my boy. Something more *appropriate*, shall we say?"

He gestured to a relic of a gun propped up against a tree. It looked like it belonged in a museum, but not in a good way. It was rusted at the edges and made *Resident Evil's* broken shotgun look state-of-the-art.

"Does it even work?" I said.

"Cheeky bastard. Just aim for Micah Richards and make a man out of yourself."

"He's from the Midlands and played for the Villa for four years! He's one of our own. What the hell have you got against Micah Richards?"

"First of all, the lad grew up in Leeds. Second, I didn't like his tone on *Gogglebox*. He never explicitly said he didn't like *Naked Attraction*, but there was something a bit off in his commentary. As if he didn't recognise the show as a high art form."

"I'm not comfortable with this … I really don't see why I should prove myself to you."

"And I wasn't comfortable with the time my uncle gave me a colonoscopy in a shared bathroom, but I got through that, so you can get through this. Now, get on with it."

I pointed the gun towards the can baring Micah Richards' grinning face. He looked so pure and innocent, like eating candyfloss for the first time.

I glanced at the gun. "There's a layer of dust on it for fuck's sake. The damn thing looks like it might blow up in my face the moment I pull the trigger."

"Only one way to find out."

I rested the gun back against the tree. "Not a chance."

"Just take the shot, you pansy."

"Fuck this, fuck that, and fuck you."

"Less of the lip, you cheeky …"

But I'd heard enough and took off into the woods, leaving Norman and his archaic guns. I wasn't sure where I was going, but anywhere away from Norman was a marked improvement.

A few minutes later, I heard nearby gunfire. The first shot jolted me out of my run. My heart hammering. I spun around, searching for the source. When the second, third, and fourth shot clapped, the answer as to who the gunman was became obvious, though in truth I should have figured it out from the first. It was just Norman, letting off steam, and filling Micah Richards with more holes than a lace knit sweater. I caught my breath before resuming my run. A whining meow soon interrupted it.

Staring straight at me was a tortoiseshell cat, followed by the woman from next door, out of breath and wearing her oversized sunglasses.

"Alex," I said.

She frowned. "I didn't tell you my name."

And she was right. I'd heard it earlier when her husband had called her a cunt. I blushed, realising my error.

"I'm Wentworth," I said, extending a hand as if it made up for my tactlessness.

She took my hand, shaking it firmly as if a CEO asserting her authority. "I know."

Temporary paralysis kicked in. Rock-heavy with the weight of the situation. This woman was the reason I'd stayed in Mona. To look out for her. To *save her*, as Amanda had put it. And to find out exactly what Norman and his neighbours were hiding, and why they were so adamant about staying out of each other's business. Yet the woman had drawn the literal and metaphorical curtains on me, was holding herself as if she'd rather be anywhere but next to me. As if *I* was the threat.

"What are you doing here?" she said.

"Going for a jog."

"In heeled boots and a cravat? What's wrong with you urbanites?"

Urbanite? Kidderminster was hardly a metropolis, though compared to a place like middle-of-nowhere Mona, it could well be seen that way.

"I didn't intend on jogging. It just happened. I was originally going shooting. Or, should I say, Norman wanted me to show him I could … you know what, it doesn't matter."

She shook her head. "I don't think so. You're not a shooter.

And besides, that doesn't make what you're wearing any better. Though it explains the noise. Anyway, I didn't mean what are you doing *right now*. I meant, what are you doing *here*? In these woods. I told you to stay away."

"Why did you tell me to stay out of the woods?"

"Do you not watch the news?"

"Yeah but … Hold up, why are *you* in the woods?"

"Because it's the best place to walk my cat." The cat meowed as if in agreement, then squatted down onto a log, spread its hind legs, lifted its tail, and began to pee.

"Why do you even walk a cat anyway?"

"Because cats need exercise, and I don't want to let little Rufus out of my sight. He's a house cat."

"Rufus … My cat was called Rory."

"So?"

"There must be other places you can walk a cat around here. Especially if these woods are … a danger."

"It's peaceful here." A shot fired in the distance, then another. "*Usually*. These woods are the one place I can really get away from it all. To be alone and think."

"What exactly are you getting away from?"

"We don't ask questions like that around here."

"Norman said much the same."

"And yet here you are. Asking questions."

I kept quiet to see if she'd fill the silence with an answer. When she didn't, I said, "Must be a hell of a thing you're trying to escape if you'd rather spend your time in a place people are getting murdered."

"It doesn't happen often."

"Once is permanent enough."

She stayed silent as if considering it, then shrugged. "So, maybe I want to die."

"Do you?"

"What relationship do you have with Norman anyway? I haven't seen him with anyone up here since …" She stopped herself and was this a test? Was I supposed to ask her to finish the sentence? To go a little crazy about her leaving it incomplete? I tapped my foot against the soil and leaves, gritting my teeth.

"Well," she said, "what's your relation to Norman?"

"I guess he's my dad."

"What do you mean, you *guess*? Either he is or he isn't." The tortoiseshell ran over to Alex, and she petted the cat before it pattered off to play with some nearby leaves, diving into them as if a child in a ball pit.

"He says he's my dad but ..." I thought about the photographs, and it all lined up. "He's my dad."

"Well, I never," she said, shock flattening her voice. "I thought the two of you were friends."

"I look that old to you? Because I know he doesn't look that young."

"Age has nothing to do with it. If you think people should only be friends with those their own age, you've got a lot of growing up to do, kid."

I recoiled at her condescension. Not least when there had to be less than a decade between us.

"It's just Norman never struck me as the fatherly type," she said.

"I didn't know you knew each other well enough to have an opinion on the matter."

"Oh, we know each other. At least we used to." She played with her wedding ring, and it was the first time I'd noticed it—faded gold with a diamond that had lost much of its sparkle. "Norman, a dad. I never would have imagined he'd be any good at that."

"I'm not sure he is. I mean, he hasn't seen me for over two decades, so—"

"He abandoned you then."

"That's not how he tells it."

"Never bloody is. Absent fathers ..." She shook her head

as if it was personal and I wondered how her father had damaged her.

"When I was a child, I used to think I was the normal one and everyone else had problems. When I got older, I realised I was the most fucked-up of all," I said.

She frowned as if I'd spit in her soup. "Did you abandon your kid, too? History has a habit of repeating itself. Your parents fail you, so you do your best to rewrite things, but when it's all said and done, you wind up hurting your kid far more than mummy and daddy ever hurt you."

"You have a kid then?"

"You answer my question first."

I looked at her cat, Rufus, and thought about the way I'd been separated from Rory. It hadn't been my choice, but we were apart nonetheless. How the hell was a cat supposed to know I hadn't intended it? For all Rory knew, I'd left him. He didn't know how much I'd fought to win him back. It was the results, not the effort, that counted.

"I guess in a way, I did," I said.

She glared. "Then what the hell are you doing here with me when there's a child out there that needs you?"

She called her cat, and it raced back to her side. I'd never seen such obedience from a cat before. I could call Rory until my voice was sandpaper raw and it wouldn't make a difference. He'd return in his own time. On his own terms.

"I need to get going," she said.

"Wait. It's not a cat. It's a child," I called after her.

She looked at Rufus, then back to me. "Say what now?"

"Sorry, I meant it's not a child, it's a cat. I'm separated from my cat, Rory. And I did fight for him. I fought until I got in so much debt, I couldn't afford to take out any more loans. So don't tell me I didn't do my best. But solicitors, they're expensive, you know?"

She took a lead from her pocket and attached it to the tortoiseshell before returning her attention to me. "That's a lot to process. But I really should get back to mine, and you should get out of the woods, too. Not that I suppose you'll take my advice this time either."

"So, we'll head back to the cottages together."

"Excuse me?"

She looked nervous and, ah shit, another faux pas. "I didn't mean ... Forget it. I'll take another route."

"It's not a problem for me, but Richard ... I dunno. He's not best pleased with you."

I put my hands up. "Say no more. I don't want to cause you any further trouble ..."

"Oh, sweet innocence. No, no, no. My husband isn't a problem for me. It's you I'm worried about."

And was she not aware how easily the sound travelled from her place to Norman's? Did she not know I'd heard the fights between her and Richard? Both the physical and verbal brawls.

"Stay out of the fucking woods," she said, her voice hot iron and sharp razor. "And stop trying to play the white knight when you're dealing with a king. I've been civil, but now I'm telling you to back off. Don't concern yourself with my life. Concentrate on the person who really needs saving. Yourself."

24

"I FINALLY SPOKE to the woman next door and I'm more confused than ever," I said to Amanda, who was walking back from her shift at the Co-op, traffic rumbling in the background. "I thought if I told her about Rory, it would bring us closer together, but it had the opposite effect. She got pretty ... Well, *cunty*'s a bit harsh but ... Her whole demeanour changed, you know?"

The sound of beeping at the traffic lights rang out on Amanda's end. "Wentworth, I've told you this time and time again, but your situation with Rory ... It's *weird*. And unrelatable. People love their cats, sure, but you don't pay tens of thousands of pounds to a solicitor trying to gain custody of your cat. That's just not reality."

"Don't act like I'm the first person to have a pet custody battle. I did my research before contacting a solicitor. There have been countless cases. Jesus, if you don't believe me, you can Google it." As the words spilled out of my mouth, I realised I sounded like Norman.

"I *have* Googled it. Not long after we met. Or more precisely, you Googled it in front of me when all I honestly wanted to do was watch *Squid Games,* but you were drunk and upset, so I humoured you."

"Stop speaking like you don't take my love for Rory seriously."

"I've comforted you, supported you, been with you throughout *all* of this. But I'm also a realist and you have to stop telling people about it. I can't stand how they laugh and take the piss out of you."

"I guess it's just … It's hard to let go. I don't want to forget Rory."

"And you don't have to. But the reality is, you lost the case. So move forward. Speaking of which, maybe it's time you come home. You felt guilty about leaving the woman without finding out what was going on, but now you've spoken to her, there's nothing more you can do."

"But maybe there is."

"Wentworth, she told you to stay out of her business. She's set a boundary. Don't push it. You're better than that. Come home."

Amanda made a compelling point, and yet returning home meant facing my troubles. The debt, the dead-end job, the imminent eviction notice and potential bankruptcy if I didn't get my shit together fast. Staying in Mona was an escape from reality, but the more I considered it, the more it wasn't real. I was masquerading worry and concern for Alex, when really, I was deflecting from my own problems.

"Perhaps I should come home," I said. "But, honestly, I'm nervous. The gang we pissed off are after us. And coming back to Kiddy seems like the equivalent of walking into a police station, holding my hands up high, and saying, 'I'm the one who done all those murders, officer.'"

"You're exaggerating as usual."

"They keep sending Norman weird videos and messages. And they know what I look like because … well, Norman sent them a photo of me right back."

"Why would he—"

"Because he's a fucking idiot … Maybe this is the universe's way of telling me I should get out of Kiddy. My landlord's on my back, there's a gang after me, and it's not as if I have a great job or family keeping me there. I need a fresh start."

"And what about me?"

"You could come with. You *should* come with."

"I'm not sure I can. Kiddy's all I've known. And shit, Wentworth, I really lucked out with this management job at the Co-op. People like me don't get put in positions like that. I can't go back to the bottom of the ladder."

"You're great. Hard working, dedicated, loyal. You could have any job you want."

"You know that's not reality. Now, *please*, Wentworth, don't make me beg you cos I'm not that kind of girl. Just come home, yeah?"

"I wish I could but … Well, what would I tell Norman? He'd be gutted."

Static sizzled in the background and, for a moment, I thought I'd lost Amanda until: "What do you actually want, Wentworth?"

And it was a big question. An ambiguous question. But before I could formulate so much as a thought, Amanda cut in again. "You need to figure out what you want. And start taking responsibility for your own actions. I like you, Wentworth. A lot. But …"

"Wait! What are we talking about here?"

"Hold on …"

Hold on?

"Shit, I've got to …" And there was something fresh and timid in her voice, starkly removed from ten seconds previous. "Listen, I've got to get going, but it might be best we don't speak to each other unless you've got a handle on things. When you know what you want, we'll talk. But until then …"

"Amanda, wait."

"And don't worry about the gang. I'm looking into them, okay?"

"What do you mean, you're *looking into them*?"

"So they won't be a problem for you."

"They're fucking dangerous, Amanda! One of them has a sword for fuck's sake. She as good as decapitates people."

"I really do have to go."

"Amanda! Wait! Listen."

"I'm sorry, Wentworth."

"For what? We're not done here. Amanda!"

But she'd already hung up.

25

NORMAN WAS up in the master bedroom, frantically stuffing jumpers into a tattered suitcase overflowing worse than the River Severn after a rainstorm.

"It's all bastard fucked," he mumbled. "I try my best. I do my best. But it doesn't matter how hard I try. Or what I do. It's all bastard fucked in the end." Each staccato sentence was separated with an aggressive shoving of a singular jumper onto the woollen pile.

It was then I noticed the entirety of his wardrobe covering the floor: trousers, shirts, jackets, vests, all creased up and crinkled, sprawled out as if patchworked.

"What's going on, Norman?"

"What's going on is what always goes on. I'm being shafted. And why? I pay my bills. I help people in need. I look out for my fellow citizens. But it's all for nothing. I don't know why I bother." He punched a maroon jumper. "I used to be well respected, you know? A big deal around Kiddy. The Boss of Bewdley. People got nervous when I rocked up in Stourport. But now I'm a joke. And why? Because I made some mistakes. Tried to rob the wrong man on the wrong day. It's the hypocrisy that drives me nuts. It's not as if Tricky

Ricky got all that money through honest means. In many ways, I was just restoring the balance. But people don't see it that way. They're all so self-centred. Even you."

"Excuse me?"

"Oh, *please*. I show up as a father. Offering board and support. I give you love. Frozen sausages. Episodes of *Naked Attraction*. The good life. But, in the end, you'll leave me. Just like everyone else."

"You've got a bloody nerve."

"Yeah, yeah, yeah. Less of the lip." He waved his hand as if dismissing a child. "Go sort your suitcase, boy. I'll see you at the car in ten minutes."

"What makes you think I'm going anywhere with you?"

"You don't have a choice. That bunch of bastards will be here soon enough. Ah heck, I had a good run here in Mona, but now it's time to move on. *Permanently*."

"You can't just up and leave your own house."

"Oh, believe me, I *can*, and I *will*."

"Where exactly are you going?"

"How the hell should I know? We get in the car first and decide where we're going later. Like the old days. That's how everyone did it in the eighties."

"Tell me what happened, Norman."

"I've got a sixth sense. And not like the film. Though I do see dead people. Me and you if we're not out of here ASAP."

"What do you *really* know about the people next door?"

"I know we stay out of their business."

"Was it always that way? Or only since the so-called *secret* you and Richard share?"

He stopped heaping up the jumpers in the already impossibly stretched suitcase and closed the gap between us. "What's this all about, boy?"

"You know more about the neighbours than you're letting on."

He grabbed a half-empty can of Skol from the chest of

drawers, slugging back a generous mouthful, then grimacing as if it had been there for some time. "So what if I do?" Norman belched out stale lager. "We stay out of their business and they—"

"Stay out of ours. Yeah, yeah. I know. You keep saying, but it isn't good enough. Alex says she knows you. Or, at least, she used to. The way she tells it, the two of you were close. *Really* close. Is that what the secret is about?"

Norman staggered towards me, an accusatory finger pointed at my face. "Now, listen here, boy, I told you to stay away from her."

"Yeah? Well, I didn't. Now. What. Do. You. Know?"

"You're making a mountain out of a molehill. So pack your things and let's leave it at that."

Norman reached for a sweat-stained t-shirt scrunched up on the floor. I slapped it out of his hand.

"You want us to get close? To have a relationship? Father and son? Well, fathers and sons, they confide in each other. They talk."

He squealed hyena-pitched laughter. "No, they don't. Dads and their kids don't talk about shit. Why do you think so many people are messed up by their dads?"

"Stop stalling. The neighbours, Norman ..."

"I know nothing about them, other than they make too much bloody noise. Fighting and moaning all hours of the day. Then, no sooner have they fallen out and they're making up again. Fucking throughout the cottage. Knocking over framed photographs, vases, glasses. I mean, I don't know that's exactly how it plays out because I've only got my ears to go by and I blew them out years ago listening to too much Fleetwood Mac, but you get the idea. One time they made love in the bath, and she started using the shower attachment like a power-hose on his arse."

"Bullshitter! You couldn't hear that through the—"

"I didn't hear it, boy. I felt it. Rumbling through their

house, across the garden, and right into ours. If you don't know how that works, then you don't get science and you've never been on the power-end of a hard fucking." Norman folded his arms. "Then there was the time he did the literal wheelbarrow with her out there in the front garden. She was collecting leaves as he fucked her. Bagging them up and everything. It was very impressive. In many ways, it brought to mind me and your mother back in our glory years."

"So many bullshit stories and ramblings about nothing. Why do you always do this?"

He looked at the can of Skol, then thought better of it.

I stared him down, waiting for an answer. Norman responded by huffing out more air than a leaf blower, frantically looking in every direction but mine until he eventually screamed, "Men are allowed to have secrets, you know?"

I headed for the door.

"Where are you going?" Norman said.

"To pack a bag."

"That's the spirit. I knew you'd come round."

"I'm going home."

"Not a good idea. Got to go somewhere far away. The Lake District maybe. I've always wanted to go there. Nice and remote. A right bastard of a phone signal 'n' all. Dated a girl who moved there, and the phone signal was so bad it just kept going to voicemail. A few weeks later, it was disconnected."

"Who fucking cares? You're doing it again with your anecdotes! Though, for your information, I don't think that was her phone signal."

Norman looked to the clothes on the floor as if they might provide reassurances or elaboration. "Well, anyway, I'm told it's a lovely area. It's made several 'places to go before you die' lists. So might be apt we go there soon, know what I mean?" He started laughing to himself.

"I'm not going to the fucking Lake District. I'm going home."

He put a hand on my shoulder. "You don't seem to get it."

I slapped his hand away. "ALONE. I've wasted too much time here when I should have been with Amanda. You know, someone who actually fucking cares. Who tries to make life better for me. Who looks out for me. I had a real chance to make it with her, but the moment you showed up, I got obsessed with … well, this and that, and it took my attention away from the one person who truly mattered. It might be too late for us now, but I've got to get back to Kiddy even if it means a run-in with Tricky Ricky. Because I've got to try. For Amanda. I wish I could say it was nice knowing you, Norman, but …"

I left the room.

"Wait," he called as I was halfway down the corridor. "Stop there and I'll be straight with you. About Alex. About Richard. The neighbours. *Everything*. But I don't think you're gonna like it. And I'm *definitely* not gonna like it." He exited the bedroom, catching my arm by the stairs. "Please stay. If only for a few minutes longer. We'll head to the living room. Do this over a bottle of voddy. You might change your mind about the whole not drinking thing by the end. Now, come on."

26

NORMAN SPENT the first minute slouched in an armchair, building up his strength and slugging back vodka as if a chronic asthmatic sucking on an inhaler. Hot summer rain beat down outside, warning us against leaving Mona.

"This little cottage used to belong to my mother, your grandmother. I've lived here for the best part of a decade or so," Norman said.

So she was the matriarch pictured in the photographs lining the entrance. That also explained the odd decorating choices, the antiquated carpets and rugs laid throughout the place, and the strange musty rose odour, particularly popular with old biddies, that permeated the air.

"When I was younger, I used to visit mum once a year, twice tops, but as time went on and her Alzheimer's got worse, I wound up seeing her every week. A hell of a trek when you haven't got a car, the local train network is almost non-existent, and taxis cost an arm and a leg and sometimes a bloody kidney 'n' all. In the end, it was easier to move in with her temporarily." Norman refilled his glass with vodka. The bottle had a fancy logo emblazoned across it. By no means premium stuff, but it was a significant upgrade from the own-brand paint stripper he often drank. "Moving in meant I saw more of the neighbours. It was about that time I got to know a bit about Richard and Alex. Though back in those days, it wasn't just them. There was Kevin, too."

"Who the fuck is Kevin?"

"Their son."

"And where in the hell is he n—"

"Calm down! I'll get to all that. Bloody hell, boy, you've no sense of pacing. Let me tell it my way."

"This isn't about entertaining me with some story. This is about getting to the facts. We don't have time to piss about. You said so yourself—Tricky Ricky's lot could show up at any minute."

"Right you are. So, the thing is, I got close to Alex. Like *really* close."

"I fucking knew it."

"Slow your judgement and let me finish. Honestly, I think Richard had his suspicions, but he didn't say shit to me or to her as far as I understand. Would have made him a bloody hypocrite given how close he was to Alex's bestie, Leah, if you know what I mean."

"So, you were fucking Alex and Richard was fucking Leah?"

Norman grimaced as if swallowing soured milk. "I didn't say that, boy."

"Didn't deny it either."

He put a dismissive hand up and went on. "Things came crashing down around the time my mum died. Matter of fact, she died exactly there. Where you're sitting."

I wriggled on the faded pink armchair, patterned with gaudy flowers and miscellaneous stains, feeling decidedly less comfortable.

"She weren't murdered or anything," Norman said. "And she didn't have a rectal prolapse if that's what you're thinking. So just relax."

It had not been what I was thinking, and his words didn't relax me.

"How'd she go?" I asked.

"I couldn't tell you exactly, but she went peacefully enough. In her sleep or at least in my sleep. See, we were both in front of the telly watching *Animal Hospital*. I drifted off and when I came to, she was out for the count, but like *permanently* out." He swept a hand through his greasy hair. "Such a beautiful way to go really. Post-lasagne, watching a bit of telly. That's magic, that is. It's how I want to go, all-told, but instead of Rolf's animal noncing, I'll be watching *Naked Attraction*."

Norman clicked his fingers as if he'd had a lightbulb moment, which likely meant whatever came out of his mouth would be as useful as a plaster for a brain injury.

"Say, if you're about when I'm on death's door, please make sure *Naked Attraction's* on in the background. Even if you can't find an episode, a quick clip on your phone would be something. Especially if I'm in a coma or paralysed. I need *Naked Attraction* playing at all times. Those are my wishes, boy. Promise me you'll make it happen."

"Um, okay."

"Promise it. Say, 'I promise.'"

"I ... promise."

He let out a sigh of contentment.

"Now, could you get on with what you were saying?" I said. "Your mum, you said you didn't know how she died cos you were asleep, but what did the coroners say?"

"This was a 91-year-old woman with Alzheimer's. There weren't no need for a coroner, boy. Nothing suspicious about it."

"So it was natural? That's what was written on the death certificate?"

Norman sniggered and muttered, "Death certificate," like it was the dumbest possible thing.

"A few days later," Norman said, "I'm doing a bit of gardening out the back. Which was when everything kicked off. There I am, just digging a hole as you do, when I—"

"What do you mean 'digging a hole as you do'? Nobody digs a hole for no purpose."

"Sure they do. You never heard of sandcastles and moats at the beach."

"So you were making mud castles in your back garden? Do you really expect me to believe that?"

He looked to the front window where the driveway and so-called barracks lay.

"What was the hole for, Norman?"

"I was just digging a hole as you do," he shouted. "Bloody hell! Why do you keep getting fixated on insignificant parts of the story?"

"I just don't think you were digging a hole with no purpose."

"Oh, there was a purpose," he said. "Good lord was there a *purpose*. But let me tell it how I want to tell it. So, there I am, minding my own business, digging a hole—"

"As you do … Yeah, yeah. Speed it up …"

"Then there's a hell of a commotion next door. Now, granted, that's no strange occurrence, as you know. And, in fact, it was even more commonplace back then. But then it goes very quiet, very suddenly. We're talking pin-drop quiet. So quiet I can hear the ants running in the soil I'm shovelling."

"Piss off could you hear ants running!"

"Next thing I know, Richard's in the garden, spitting distance from me, digging a hole of his own. We both acknowledged each other and never spoke of it again. I broke things off with Alex the next day." He slugged back some vodka. "Anyway, that's why we don't talk to each other."

27

A HEAVY THUD thundered from next door as if someone had upended a cabinet. Indistinguishable yelling broke out, shattering the silent deadlock as Norman and I appraised each other.

I clasped my hands together, considering everything Norman had said and the implications.

I leant forward in the armchair. "Sorry to be so dense, but I'm not sure I get everything you're saying here. I think I do, but ... well, could you spell it out for me?"

Norman breathed heavily as if he was really put out, then forced a smile as real as the designer watch I'd purchased from a car boot after a drunken night in Moseley.

"Boy, I've just told you things I promised myself I would never tell anyone. Don't make me go further."

"But the story isn't finished. You and Richard were digging holes. You caught each other in the act but ... I mean, why were you digging holes? For what purpose?"

Norman glugged back vodka.

"For *who*?"

Norman's hands were shaking as he poured himself another measure of voddy.

"There's no death certificate because …" I started.

And now it was my turn to take a deep breath. I could have done with some of that voddy myself, but if I went down that path, I'd likely be dead by the morning.

"Because …" I repeated.

And was I really going to go there?

I didn't have much of a choice. Norman sure as shit wasn't going to spell it out. Yet we desperately needed transparency and realness. Something that had been lacking in our conversations thus far. Hell, something that was lacking in most of my interactions. Most of my bloody life. I gathered my courage, sucking in another gust of musty rose and cigarette glazed air.

"*Because* you buried your mother in the back garden."

"Keep your bloody voice down," Norman scolded in a whisper.

"And Richard saw."

Norman kept poker-faced.

"Why'd you do it? To avoid inheritance tax?"

He shook his head. "If only it were that bloody simple. I looked after Mum for the best part of a year, but she went and left everything to my older brother, Timothy. And he did sod all for her. Not so much as a call. But because he went to uni and works in finance, she bloody worshipped him. Put that cunt right up on a pedestal, good and proper. And the joke of it is, not only did he do sweet FA for her, but he was embarrassed by her. Considered her as favourably as he would dog shit on his Tom Ford brogues. There's no way he'd have been seen out in public with her, let alone introduced her to partners or friends."

"But she was still his mother," I said. "And different people have different ways of showing love. Maybe you got him wrong."

"No! Absolutely not."

"So you wanted the house for yourself?"

"Wanted?" Norman said. "Don't make it sound like I was the one in the wrong here. It was about doing the right thing. Timothy was ashamed of her. Didn't you hear me the first time? Plus, he's absolutely loaded. He didn't need the house or any more money. It would just be another hassle for him. A lot of paperwork and that. But for me ... Well, it could make a real difference. It *has* made a real difference."

"Wait a minute, are you telling me your brother doesn't know his own mother is dead?"

He waved a hand. "She's been as good as dead to him for years. It's no big deal."

"No big ... A woman's dead! Does anyone know she's dead?"

Norman sipped vodka.

"Did Richard *see*? Does he know what you did?"

Norman looked away and towards the window.

I leant forward, forcing Norman to acknowledge me. "Wait. If you haven't told anyone, does that mean you're cashing her pension? Her benefits? Other bits of money here and there? Christ, does she still get birthday cards with cheques and cash that you pocket?"

Norman grinned as if I'd told him some smutty joke. "I've said more than enough."

"And what about the other hole? The one Richard was digging ..."

"I told you already, we don't ask questions."

"You said they had a son. Kevin, was it? But he's not around anymore. You also said Richard was fucking Alex's best friend. I don't see her anywhere either. So who was the hole for? Which of them did Richard off? Or was it someone different? You've got to tell me."

Norman folded his arms, his smile a rictus of repulsion. "These questions, these are the things we don't ask."

"So you didn't see? You don't know who he buried cos you weren't looking?"

Norman's mouth twitched.

"You did see, didn't you? *Fuck*. It's all starting to make sense now. That's why Alex told me to stay out of the woods but had no problem walking there herself. Because it's Richard. He's the killer."

"Steady on, Pizzagate! Nobody's said that. Stop jumping to such wild conclusions."

"Nothing wild about it, so don't take me for a fucking idiot. Richard's the killer. Alex knows that. And you know it, too. That's why your nose was so far up his arse it was practically dripping with chocolate. You *know* what happens if you get on the wrong side of him."

Norman swallowed. He glugged back vodka from his glass, then straight from the bottle. "Now, now, boy, slow your roll for a moment. You're adding two and two together and coming up with six. Let me explain."

"Fuck this. I'm out of here. You can explain to the police. I'm done with you. And I'm done with this fucking town."

I charged out of the living room and for the door. But as soon as I opened it, I was greeted by Alex. She stood there with a face full of blood and eyeliner running down both her cheeks.

"I need to stay here for a bit."

28

ALEX CLUTCHED a small red handbag close to her chest. Who was I looking at here?

A victim?

An accomplice?

Someone in between?

The knuckle-thick purple underneath her eye didn't suggest she was an accomplice. Neither did the blood spread down her face, much of which emanated from her nose. But these murders, they'd been going on for over a year now, and if she'd been in on it, then she'd as good as gutted some of the victims herself unless ...

Had she been a prisoner of sorts?

Scared of losing her own life?

What if the death of her son or best friend was an execution she'd witnessed, serving as both a threat and a promise?

"*Please,*" she said, and I realised I hadn't spoken since opening the door. "Look, I know I was off with you earlier ... Okay, I was a dick. A *cunt* even. I shouldn't have said any of those things. You were trying to help, and I was condescending, when, the truth is, I *do* need your help. I just didn't want to admit it." She scratched her head. "I'm not a king. Barely even a bloody pawn right now." She shuffled on the spot. "I'm sorry. Truly. At least let me in, if only to clean up, and then I'll leave."

I glanced behind her.

No sign of Richard.

I hoped if I invited Alex in, I wouldn't open myself up to further trouble. All I wanted was to get home to Amanda and never see Mona, Alex, Norman, or any of this life again. But Alex was in a right state. Bloodier than Carrie White at the prom. I could hardly turn her away.

I moved aside. "Go on."

Then, as she was stepping into the cottage, I noticed Norman's turd, still planted there, and called to Alex as if in some slowed down nightmare, "Look ouuuuut!"

She covered her head as if someone was going to lob a brick at her, then saw the excrement and course-corrected, narrowly avoiding the steaming stool in the middle of the floor.

"He likes to mark his territory," I said as if it was perfectly normal and explained everything.

Instead of disgust or asking for an explanation, she sighed like an overworked nurse and said, "I can't believe he still does that." Then, without missing a beat: "Anyway, could you please show me to the bathroom? And if it's okay with you, I'll keep my shoes on."

I looked down at the floor. I'd seen squat houses that were cleaner.

"Come on," I said, leading her upstairs. Then to Norman, lingering in the living room: "We're not done here. Not by a long way."

I stood outside the bathroom, holding Alex's handbag, as she ran hot water and tended to her wounds.

"Do you need me to get you some clean clothes or anything?"

"Richard and I are going through a rough patch," she said.

"What's he done?"

She frowned. "Why would you assume he's *done* anything?"

Shit. Her guard was up from the off. I had to tread carefully.

"You're covered in blood. And something tells me you didn't do that to yourself." I heard her splashing water. "You don't have to stand for that. You *shouldn't* stand for that. It will be hard at first, most things worth doing are, but it'll get better over time. Taking the first step, that's the most difficult part." The bathroom sink gurgled, draining water. "Whatever he's done, and however long he's been doing it, it isn't too late to go to the police."

She opened the bathroom door. Her face was clean from blood, accentuating the bruise underneath her eye. She took her handbag from me and retrieved a miniature bottle of facial mist which she silently spritzed over her face. When she was done, she squeezed a pea-sized blob of primer onto a makeup sponge, slowly spreading it from the centre of her face towards her cheeks, chin, and forehead.

She kept her gaze towards the mirror. "It isn't what you think."

"What if it is?"

For a moment, she turned towards me, eyes cold.

She hurried the rest of her makeup, losing some of her poise.

"Just tell me what happened," I said.

"Excuse me?"

"Easy now." We both turned to see Norman climbing the stairs. "Leave the woman alone and let her rest. You can lie down in the master bedroom if you want."

Alex appeared uncomfortable, likely remembering how unsanitary Norman's quarters were. The kind of place that might open wounds and give you gangrene just from looking at it.

"I need to walk and think," she said. "Got to clear my head of all the noise. But I'll be back."

"I should come with, just in case—" I said.

"Wentworth!" Norman's voice exhibited an uncharacteristic firmness. "Let her go."

We cast a look at each other before Alex spoke again. "Well, I'll just finish up here and be on my way. It's okay. It will all be okay."

But whether she was saying this for us or herself, I couldn't be sure.

Reluctantly, I headed to the spare bedroom. I didn't want to let Alex go without answers, but if I came on too strong, she might shut down forever.

I dialled Amanda, finally knowing what I wanted. To be away from the chaos and back with her. To travel to a time where angsty landlords and low bank accounts were the worst of my worries. Albeit this time I'd do things without fixating on sweet Rory. He was gone now. But Amanda wasn't. I had to stop the past from poisoning the present.

The phone kept ringing out.

"Pick up, pick up, pick up."

But Amanda didn't pick up.

Not on the first try, or the second, or even the third.

A text message then.

I panic-wrote the following:

I think the murder forest killer lives next door to my dad.

I stared back at the message.

The blinking white cursor jumping and judging me like a salty probation officer.

I reread then deleted the message.

Took another stab at things:

I'm sorry I've been difficult lately. But I know what I want now. You. I'm coming home soon. I promise.

That wasn't quite right either.

What the hell did I think this was?

A romcom?

A happily ever after where all the shit would line up in just the right order?

I deleted the second attempt and paced the bedroom—which, given the size of the glorified shoe cupboard, meant taking three steps forward, turning, and repeating.

Norman knocked at the door.

He stood on the landing, staring at my half-packed luggage. "You going?"

I shrugged.

"Are *we* going?" he asked.

"I guess, now Alex is here, we both have to stay put. I know you don't have the best track record, but I reckon even you draw the line at abandoning beat-up women."

He chewed down on his lip, considering the statement, then went, "I best go put some sausages on the grill then. Looks like we'll be here quite some time."

29

A FEW HOURS LATER, sausages consumed and wreaking havoc on my belly, Alex returned to the cottage, less on edge. There was still no sign of Tricky Ricky or any of the Kiddy lads Norman had claimed were gonna show up, Amanda had yet to return my calls, and Norman himself had been in the bathroom for a good half an hour after announcing, "I don't reckon I cooked them sausages right. Got a bit too excited to eat them like. Anyway, I'm going for a poo and a wank."

Alex and I sat at opposite ends of the sofa, the gap between us as awkward as the words unspoken. I kept looking at my phone, waiting for it to light up—some message or call from Amanda. I longed to call her again but, at the same time, didn't want to run the risk of being overbearing or clingy.

So I gave her space.

Waiting it out.

Exchanging periodic glances with Alex. Neither one of us knew how to pick up from where we'd left off. I mean, how do you sensitively ask someone if their partner is a serial killer? There are some things even Google can't answer. I fucking know cos I tried asking, and all I got was a bunch of

Richard Ramirez fan sites and mockery from a bunch of sweary teenagers on Reddit.

Then Alex began to talk. "I want to talk to you. Really, I do. I've been holding onto something for a long time. Lord knows I want to set it free. Lord knows *I* want to be free. Not least a good person. But the truth is, I'm scared. Scrap that, I'm bloody terrified."

"I get that. I know what it's like to hold a secret and be scared of saying shit. I've been in the same position myself … I mean, not the *exact* same position, but I've held secrets so tightly I thought I'd burst. I'm telling you, the not telling can kill you. It chips away, gnawing through your ear canal, boring a tunnel, infecting your brain."

"Sounds like you're talking about a parasite."

"Secrets *are* parasites. And if you play host for too long, they'll eat you from the inside."

Alex looked down at her lap, straightening her dress's fabric. "The problem is, with some secrets, the telling can kill you, too. It's a lose-lose situation."

Norman burst into the room. The inner door whacking the wall with a heavy jolt.

"Wentworth, we've got an emergency, I need you to …" Norman stopped himself, looked to Alex. "Ah crap, you porking the neighbour now?"

"Obviously not." I gestured towards the literal seat between us.

"No judgement if you are. Or if you want to. I guess things are different now, so I won't get in your way if you want to give her the old *how's your father*."

"I am here, you know," Alex said, standing up. "And, for the record, I have no interest in getting *porked* by either of you."

"What if we were the last people on earth?" Norman said.

"If you were the last people on earth, I'd be dead. But

you'd be free to pork each other. Anyway, I'm off to the bathroom."

"I wouldn't if I were you, love," Norman said.

"Alex, we seriously need to ..." I started.

But she left the room.

Norman stared at the door, gormlessly grinning as he wracked his lack of brain for something witty to say. When he came up empty, he shrugged and said, "Women, eh? Can't live with them, can't live without them."

I didn't bother pointing out he didn't live with any women and, to the best of my knowledge, hadn't lived with a woman besides his mother for a very long time.

"You ruin everything, Norman! She was seconds away from telling me something vitally important, you stupid bastard."

Norman reached into the rear pocket of his jeans, pulling out a pistol. He threw it my way, all blasé, as if flinging a frisbee at the beach.

I barely caught the gun. "The fuck you playing at? Throwing a gun around like that."

He took his phone out and snapped a photo with a click and a flash, and said, "That," before writing and simultaneously reading aloud a text message: "We're packing, you pricks. So stay away and eat my son's little dick."

"Who the fuck are you sending that to?"

"The lads are on their way, and we've got to show them we aren't gonna be scared off by a bunch of knob-cheese gobbling dickwads."

"What does that even mean? What are you doing? Did you really send that message? And *my* fucking photo?"

"Course I bloody did. I'm showing them we're in charge."

"In charge of *what* exactly?"

"Mona, mate. You and me. We're the Mona massif."

"A group of mountains?"

"A squad, boy. Don't act like you don't know what I'm talking about. Now get ready for a fight."

"What happened to getting the hell out of here? I thought you chose flight not fight."

"Yeah? Well, then your new girlfriend showed up, and everything went to shit. It's too late for flight anyway. They'll be here any minute. There's only one way to the cottages. Better to meet them here than on the road where they'll *Destruction Derby* our arses!"

"You said they were on their way before, but they never showed. Maybe they'll bail again."

"Before was an inkling. This time's for real."

I handed the gun back to Norman. "You've caused me enough trouble. I don't want any part of this."

He snatched it out of my hand with contempt.

I wrote Amanda a quick text message: *I hope you're doing okay. Things are crazy here. But I'll be heading back to Kiddy soon. Call me if you get a chance.*

I sent the message. A phone chimed almost instantly, but it was Norman's. He started laughing to himself.

"Don't think they're scared of you, boy."

Norman tilted his phone screen towards me. A photo message showed a toddler in a red t-shirt with yellow trousers, holding a gun in a limp hand and crying. Below the photograph the sender had written: "Looks like your boy."

"This isn't funny," I said. "How *the fuck* is this funny?"

"Take a proper look at his face and the gun. You've got to admit, there's a like—"

"A gang of mad bastards are coming for us. Possibly including that absolute loon with the samurai sword. And all you're doing is laughing over a picture like they're your mates. They're psychopaths, Norman. Get a grip!"

I stomped upstairs, towards the bedroom. It didn't matter that Norman said they were so close I'd see them on the road, I'd take my chances. Norman was the anti-Nostradamus, his predictions as reliable as a watering can with a hole in the bottom.

So what if they passed me on the road?

It was Norman they were really after. As long as I didn't have him with me, they'd let me go.

I was on the landing, almost at the bedroom, when Alex charged out of the bathroom and threw me against the wall, her hands against my collarbone.

"No more bollocks. What did you see?" she whispered.

My heart started hammering faster than a DMX rap. "What the fuck are you talking about?"

"Don't play dumb. You clearly saw something in my house or you wouldn't be talking about secrets so much."

"Wait, you were the one who brought up secrets not—"

"You know something and you're going to spill."

"I don't …"

"You saw something," she said. "Or you heard something. Or somebody told you something. So spare the lies and come out with it. I reckon it was when you were on our lawn. Around the time Richard caught the two of you fighting like a couple of pub drunks."

"Look, I was halfway up your driveway, I admit that. And, for full transparency, there was another time before that when I accidentally kicked your front door open but—"

"You did *what*?"

"I didn't know it was ajar. But, anyway, you and Richard were—"

"So then you did see something. I knew it!"

"Not really."

"Not really isn't not at all."

"Then not at all."

"You see a cage?"

"No."

"You see what was in the cage?"

"What are you talking about? What cage? I didn't see a fucking cage."

"You came into my house," Alex said. "You were snooping. Trespassing. Why would you do that?"

"I didn't come in. I swear to god. Now, what's this about a cage?"

"Why did you come up to the front door in the first place? What were you looking for?"

"For you! To save you! You were screaming."

"How can I trust you? I don't think I can. And if I can't trust you, that means—"

"Oh god! Please don't kill me! I'll do anything. For the love of god, I don't want to die."

"What? I wasn't planning on—"

"I'll be on my way. I just need to grab my things. Then you'll never see me again. I promise."

Alex let go of me and, for a moment, I thought my entire being was going to dissolve into liquid piss.

"Why did you think I was going to kill you?" Her voice was calmer.

"Why did you think I saw a cage?"

My phone chimed in my trouser pocket and we both looked towards it.

"Don't you want to check that?" Alex said.

I took the phone from my pocket as reluctantly as a teen uncovering a porno mag to his parents and held it up like a soiled wank sock.

The text was from Amanda. My whole being flooded with relief. Then, as I read the words, I realised it wasn't actually from Amanda but someone with Amanda, and really it didn't make any fucking sense.

A photograph of Amanda. A black blindfold concealing her eyes, ropes wound around her waist, sitting in the back of some vehicle.

A text message followed:

Don't need 2 cum 2 Kiddy. Kiddy cumming 2 U!

30

AFTER I'D STOPPED HYPERVENTILATING, I ran downstairs, Alex chasing after me. Norman paced the living room, bottle of vodka in hand, news broadcast on the TV discussing mutilated bodies discovered in the forest. But it was all background noise to me. Those fucks had taken Amanda, and the only thing that mattered was getting her back.

"They've got Amanda," I said, pushing the phone in Norman's face.

He took a step back and considered the screen, then gave a lecherous grin. "Quite the looker, ain't she, boy?"

I swung for Norman. He made no attempt to dodge the blow in his inebriated state and got punted square in the jaw. Norman spat blood onto the living room floor and shook his head.

"You're getting stronger by the minute, boy. Keep it up and you might be able to give Tricky Ricky's lads a run for their money after all."

"You're a piece of shit, Norman," Alex said.

"Yeah? Probably about right. But no time to flirt with me, love, we've got to bail."

"Oh, I'm bailing all right," Alex said. "Just as soon as I find out what it is your son knows."

"He don't know nothing about nothing. Just a fanciful imagination is all. Pay him no mind. Been nice knowing you, Alex. We had some fun, didn't we? But now, me and the boy are out of here."

"Out of here?" I screamed in Norman's face. "What the hell are you talking about? Last time I tried to leave, you started banging on about *Destruction Derby* and road blockages. Now you're all for running again."

"The *Destruction Derby* thing was an exaggeration. I thought about everything you said and, you know what, you were right all along. Flight is better than fight."

"Too bastard late. Now Amanda's with them, we stay put."

Norman waved his hand dopily. "You're not thinking straight. You can't put our lives in danger because of some bird. She's yanking your Brian Jizzman."

"Yanking my what?"

"Your Brian Jizzman. Like the author. Jizzman. Jazzman. Asimov. Asman. Aslan the Lion. I don't bloody know. Anyway, he wrote some book about fucking a house. Or something like that. I never read it. But I got it. Liked the title. I can go get it if you like. Read it to you on the motorway or something."

The rumble of an engine from outside interrupted Norman's absurdity.

An old workhorse of a Volvo pulled up, followed by a larger, more expensive looking black car.

Norman looked out the front window. "Ah, shit. They're here."

31

"THE DOORS! Lock the bloody doors, boy," Norman said, closing and double locking the living room windows.

I ran to the hallway at the front of the house, securing the front door and picking up several unopened letters that lay where a welcome mat should have been. I stuffed the overdue bill notices and mostly junk mail into my back pocket and away from Norman's shit-brick.

Alex bolted upstairs.

"Good, lass," Norman said, then scanned the hallway. "Shitting Christ! This wasn't supposed to happen."

My mind was a bonnet of bees and noise—discombobulated waste and rot.

"Maybe we should leg it out the back, then backtrack round and ambush them from behind," I said.

"It's all just forests back there," Norman said. "And walking back round will be more obvious than a streaker at a footie match. There's no element of surprise."

"You got a basement? A loft? Somewhere we can hide whilst we figure out what the hell we're gonna do?"

"I don't know."

"It's your house! I mean, not legally given what you said

about your mum, but you've been here long enough. You should know what's what."

"I don't play hide and seek, so how should I know a good place to hide? I'm an adult man."

"This isn't about hide and seek. This is about —"

"Stop!" Norman started slapping himself in the forehead, skin flapping louder and wetter than a sweat-soaked athlete delivering backshots to his sidepiece on a hot clammy day. "This is all a bit much. I'm going blind with the pressure of it all. Plus, I dunno if you noticed, but I'm kind of drunk."

"You're always drunk!"

"Then you understand. All these questions, they're hard to process."

A hard knock rattled the front door.

We crept away from the front entrance and into the kitchen.

A Midlands voice that was half the worst part of Dudley and half the roughest part of Birmingham with a scuzzy Kidderminster under-taste spoke. "Open up, Norm. We need to have a word with you and your boy."

Norman looked at me. "If he says he just wants a word, maybe I should let him in."

"Well, of course he says that, but it doesn't mean it's reality. You open that door and chances are you get a big boot to the head."

"Good point," Norman said. "You should be the one to open the door."

"Piss off. I'm not taking a boot for you."

"I cooked you sausages!"

"It always comes back to sausages with you. Like it's your crowning achievement. Martin Luther King had his 'I Have a Dream' speech and you have your sausages."

"Why you saying that with such derision? Ain't nothing wrong with daddy's sausages."

"Gross … Anyway, we've got to be careful with how we deal with them. These shit-stains have got Amanda after all."

"Maybe. Maybe not."

"I saw a photo of her for fuck's sake. So did you."

"Exactly. They want you to think they have her, but you've no idea when that photo was taken or what happened to her afterwards. Tricky Ricky's lot don't play fair. Never have, never will. Seeing ain't believing, know what I mean?"

A weak knock at the back patio that sounded like a branch scratching a window grabbed my attention. I turned around to see one of the gang staring straight through. He wore a t-shirt that said, *"Everything woke turns to shit."—Donald J. Trump*. He had the haircut of Tweedledum and Tweedledee from the Disney version of *Alice in Wonderland*, and the body of a bulimic who barfed up celery sticks. The kid couldn't have been more than twenty and by the dozy grin on his face, I'd say if he were ever cast in Disney's animated feature, he'd be Tweedledumber.

I stepped away from the patio and closer to Norman at the far-end of the kitchen.

"What are you doing?" The boy's voice squeaked out higher than Snoop Dog on April 20th. "Come back here. I know you're there. I can still see your reflection, you idiot."

I didn't know what I was reflecting off but, given the amount of outdated metallic kitchen appliances, it made sense.

I edged back into the kitchen. Stared at the kid. He stared back.

"Can he see you, boy?" Norman whispered, remaining at the far-end of the kitchen, closer to the cottage's entrance.

The kid and I kept our eyes locked on one another as if in some 'who will blink soonest competition'.

"Yeah," I said. "I'm pretty sure he can see me."

"Shit," Norman said. "Okay. Let's see now … Maybe if you hide, he'll forget he saw you. It's an old army technique."

"I didn't know you were in the army."

"I wasn't, but it's what I heard."

"Where?"

"Telly."

"*Naked Attraction*?"

"Stop yabbering and hide somewhere. Under the table's a good 'un. The tablecloth is long enough to conceal you. Wait it out and the dumb fucker will soon piss off. Army magic."

I backed away from the window again.

"Oi!" the kid squeaked from outside. "It's not an army technique, you pumpkin."

"How the hell did he hear all that?" Norman said.

"Lipreading or something?"

"Nah. Unless he's got binoculars, he won't be able to see back here."

"Your glass isn't soundproof," the kid said. "I can hear everything."

"The glass is double-glazed, you cheeky sod," Norman shouted back. "Honestly, who is this mug? Thinking I do things on the cheap!"

Another knock from the front door, harsher and harder than the first. Norman tutted as if somebody had cut him off in rush hour traffic.

"What does this squeaky mouse of a man look like anyway?" Norman asked.

I moved closer, taking him in. "Looks like his mum cut his hair with a pudding basin and he's thin as a streak of piss."

"Oi!" the kid squealed as if it was his irritating catchphrase. "I'm bulking up. Got a kilogram of Weight Gainer from Myprotein on its way."

A third knock on the front door, this time with more rhythm and officialdom to it. Less the rozzers trying to storm the place, more a door-to-door salesman making a business call.

"I can hear you talking, so open up," the Dudley-Birmingham mutt said.

"Hang on. Hang on!" Norman put a hand up to the front door as if the bloke on the other side could see it. "I'm talking to the geezer round the back, so you just wait your turn, okay?" With that, Norman bumbled into the kitchen with all the threat and urgency of an arthritic grandad in slippers, emerging for a mid-morning breakfast.

Norman was barely at the dining room table when he began guffawing with laughter.

"Oh, this guy is a right bloody dweeb." Norman hunched over in hysterics, his stomach no doubt hurting given his gurning. "He's not even one of the main gang for Christ's sake. They must have been short on men to take this used tampon along. That or it's some sort of pro bono charity work. A life experience for the little lad."

"I can hear you!" he squawked.

"Even you could take him, boy. Probably with one hand tied behind your back. The good one at that." Norman grinned. "Know what they used to call him at school?"

"Shut up!" the kid yelled.

"They had this nickname for him—"

"Don't say it. Don't you say it!"

Norman scrunched his nose up as if the kid's words were a bad smell.

"They used to call him Cummy Ian cos anytime he saw a girl he liked, he'd cum in his pants."

"That's not true!" Ian shouted. "None of it's true!"

Norman glared over at Ian in annoyance. "How in the hell can he hear all of this? I swear to god these windows are double-glazed. I really don't get it. Boggles the mind."

"I mean, we do hear a lot from the neighbour's place," I said.

"Yeah, that's in the living room. This is the kitchen. Different kettle of piss altogether. Maybe young Cummy Ian has superhero hearing or something. There's cum in his pants but not in his ears, know what I mean?"

"The window's open!" Ian screamed.

I looked towards it. He was right. The window lay half open.

Norman breathed out sweet relief. "Nice one. I was getting worried the lads hadn't done a good enough job with the windows and I was gonna have to get them back at short notice. This kid's not just a pants-cummer after all. You have your uses, don't you, young Cummy?"

"Stop saying that!" Ian said. "It was one time, and it wasn't how they said it was."

Norman lent over the kitchen sink and closed the ajar window. "Piss off, cum-stain!"

Ian continued jabbering, but this time he made as much noise as a ventriloquist dummy without its master.

Norman turned to me. "The cheek of the kid—cums his pants, then tries to claim he's been painted in the wrong light. As if a bit of cum leakage is par for the course, but a pond in the pants is a no-go. I don't care if you only get a drop of cum in your pants every time you see a lass who takes your fancy, I'm still calling you Cummy Ian, know what I mean?"

"We should ask them about Amanda," I said, voice so low it was almost a whisper.

"We've got to tread carefully with that one, my boy. They see you're scared and they'll use her kidnapping to their advantage. Got to act like you don't give a shit."

"But I *do* give a shit."

"I know, I know. But … shit, boy … it's a hard one. I dunno what to tell you. These bastards are sadistic. You open a wound and they'll pour in vinegar, know what I mean? You've got to remember what Tricky Ricky did to his own daughter. He's operating on a different level."

"You never did tell me what he—"

The geezer at the front door doubled down on his

knocking, slamming with such ferocity, he had to have been shoulder barging it or worse. If he kept up like that, it wouldn't be long before the frame started to buckle.

"Bloody hell!" Norman said, marching towards the front of the house. "Take it easy, would you? The door's only a few years old."

The shoulder-barger didn't stop or slow down. The door was taking more of a pounding than a dead pig on a boozy night out with Alexander Cameron.

"I've spent good money doing this place up," Norman said to nobody in particular. "It might not look like it, but there are little details here and there. A lick of paint in the master bedroom, a new door at the front, double glazing in the kitchen and upstairs. And how am I rewarded? A bunch of bastards from Kidderminster surround the place and do their damnedest to undo all my hard work. You can have a problem with me, but don't take it out on the property, you monsters!"

The door took such a blow from the other side, the noise reverberated throughout the entire cottage.

"Stop damaging the bloody door!"

But they didn't stop and on the next shot, the door flew off its hinges and Norman stood face to face with three blokes holding what looked like a police-issued battering ram. They dropped the battering ram and one of the lads—badly dyed blonde hair, salt and pepper scruff on his face, black rugby shirt clinging to his belly like plastic wrap—charged towards Norman but halted, almost as soon as he started, when he stepped in Norman's big fat Cleveland steamer.

"Yes! Yes!" Norman whooped, holding his fist in the air. "That's what you get, Gary. That's what you get for running into Shit-a-Brick Rick's gaff like you own the place, you piece of crap. Ha! Ha!" He turned to me. "You see, my boy, you've got to mark your territory and they'll know exactly who's boss. They'll bloody well know."

Gary lifted his dirty Hi-Tec, examining the sole. Brown excrement clung to the bottom as if chewing gum. "What is it?"

Gary went to sniff the stuck-on excrement and Norman damn-near choked on a laugh.

"I wouldn't if I were you. That's my own organic brick. Years of sausages and voddy, cigarettes and Maccy D's, to cultivate such a piece. If you think about it, it's art. Just like the poo-cake I laid at your boy Tricky Ricky's place. Speaking of which, where is he?" Norman peered behind Gary at the other two, a skinhead in his fifties who'd have fit right into *This Is England*, and a teenager with a wisp of a moustache and more pepperoni on his face than a New York pizza.

Wait just a minute! I recognised the lad from the videos. He was wearing the same basketball shirt and shorts that drew attention to his gangly legs.

"Colin," I whispered.

The kid must have heard me cos he smiled as if finally his TikTok videos had gained him some notoriety.

And if the kid was Colin, then I'd wager the skinhead was his father, Pat Knox, the second in command.

Meanwhile, Gary opted to balance on one leg rather than put his black and yellowed at the edges, once white, Puma-branded sock on the floor for fear of stepping in something worse than Norman's shit. His fears weren't unwarranted. If you rolled around on the hardwood floors long enough, you'd probably catch chlamydia.

"Look at fucking peg-leg over here," Norman said as Gary struggled to hold his weight on one leg. "Captain fucking Pugwash, hobbling around, searching for his very own Seaman Staines."

Gary balanced his Hi-Tec against the wall, then slowly smeared it across the width of the paper, leaving a chunky beige trail over the faded pink roses.

"Oh, no, no, no! Don't do that!" Norman said. "Them's the

wallpapers, you heartless animal. My mother picked out the pattern herself and now she's dead."

Gary grinned, putting his Hi-Tec back on and gingerly stepping over the flattened remains of Norman's log. "Don't you worry about your dead mom, you'll be reunited with her soon enough."

Gary took a combat knife from his back pocket, pushed past Norman, and pointed it straight at me.

"Time to die, arsehole."

32

I BACKED up until I met with the wall, keeping my eyes on the knife's blade as if it was a clock's pendulum and I was about to be hypnotised.

"You the one with the girl?" Gary said.

"What girl?"

"The one we got." He studied my face. "You can keep quiet if you want. Pretend she doesn't exist and you didn't get the photo if that's your thing. But if you act like she doesn't exist, I'll make your fantasy permanent and fucking gut the bitch. You get me?"

"Keep your hands off her!" I screamed.

Norman frowned as if he'd seriously expected me to keep calm when a lunatic was threatening to disembowel my girlfriend. Rich coming from the guy who'd lost his temper over burnt sausages.

"*Please*," I said, and Jesus I sounded pathetic.

"Or what?" Gary waved the knife so close he almost gave me a haircut. "Or fucking *what*?"

"Don't be scared of him, Wentworth," Norman said. "This dweeb brought a knife to a gunfight. Now show him what you're packing!"

Gary stepped back, his confidence faltering, but kept the knife directed towards me.

Pat stepped forward, his boy, Colin, cowering behind him where the door once stood.

"Wentworth. The fuck kind of name is Wentworth?" Pat spat out the word as if he'd found half a maggot in his apple.

Norman started sniggering. "I know, I know. Wentworth! Pretty dumb, right? But, listen, the boy's more than just a name."

"Hang on!" I said. "I thought you were the one who named me."

"I was," Norman said, "but I was so blasted off my mind I thought Andi Peters was Beyoncé. Had a wank over him whilst he was presenting *Live & Kicking*."

"Beyoncé wasn't about back then. And anyway, Wentworth's a strong name."

"It's made up!" Pat shouted.

"It is not," I said. "The main actor in *Prison Break* is called Wentworth."

"The fuck is *Prison Break*?" Pat asked.

"Ah, that's a good drama, that is," Colin said. "Saw it on Now TV. Wrote a rap about it once."

Pat glared at him and, for a moment, I thought he was gonna lamp him. "The fuck you have a Now TV subscription for, you fucking pansy? I thought I raised you better than that."

"Hey, there's some good stuff on Now TV."

Gary shook his head. "The only thing you need is Channel 4, mate. It's got *Hollyoaks*, *The Crystal Maze*, and *Naked Attraction*."

Norman brightened up and immediately raised his hand towards Gary for a high-five as if he wasn't pointing a fucking knife towards me. "*Naked Attraction*! MY MAN!"

Gary looked at Norman with confusion.

Eventually Norman lowered his hand, muttering, "Well,

whatever, I definitely *did* have a wank to Andi Peters and if I didn't think he was Beyoncé, it must have been some other chick. Germaine Greer, perhaps. She was well good in *Jackie Brown*."

I didn't point out Germaine Greer was a poet and he meant Pam Grier because what in the holy Christ was going on anyway? These fucks had abducted Amanda, or worse, and now everyone was talking about their favourite television programmes as if we were having a pint down the local. And the knife—the god damn knife—was still very close to my face.

"The main character in *Prison Break* is called Michael Schofield so I dunno why you're pretending he's Wentworth, you liar," Colin said, apparently gaining some confidence but still so close to the doorframe he was practically holding onto it like a handrail.

"Amanda," I said. "Where is Amanda?"

Nobody responded.

"That's my girl," I said. "Okay? You satisfied? I got the photograph. I'm not pretending she doesn't exist. So just tell me where she is and what I have to do for you to return her."

"Michael Schofield's a fucking nonce," Norman said. "I'm glad ITV fired his arse."

"Norman, what the fuck? I'm trying to get Amanda back and you're still talking about—"

"I just think it's best we address the elephant in the room. What he did with them boys wasn't right. I wouldn't be surprised if Michael ends up doing some jail time, know what I mean?"

Gary nodded as if Norman was making a good point. I didn't want to join in but there was only so much idiocy I could take before biting.

"You're confusing Michael with Phillip, you fucking moron," I said to Norman. "And you're confusing the actor with the character," I said to Colin. "Michael Schofield is the character. Wentworth Miller is the actor. The fuck is hard about that, you dunce?"

Gary piped up, "There's a reason they didn't call him Wentworth, you know? Bent fucking name if you ask me."

"No!" Norman said firmly. "As long as you're under this roof, you can't say bent or bender. It ain't right. My lad taught me that the other day, and I Googled it and he weren't even joking. We'll fight, we'll have a bit of banter, we might even fuck each other, but there's a level of respect that must be maintained, and I won't tolerate that kind of language."

Gary pivoted, pointing the knife towards Norman and finally away from my face. "I said what I said," he spat. "I don't see what your problem is, Norm. Unless you're a bender yourself. Is that it?"

"Gary, that's enough," Pat said. "We're not animals. We can show some respect."

"Fuck off! He didn't show any respect when he laid a brick on Tricky Ricky's carpet, so why should we respect him now?"

Pat and Gary sized each other up. Two lions, deep into a crate of Stella, fighting for supremacy. Gary took his knife off Norman, pocketing it, and put his head so close to Pat's noggin I thought they were going to touch. The bloated Kiddy alternative to a couple of stags butting heads or an especially aggressive UFC weigh-in.

Then there came a London accent fresh out of a Guy Ritchie film from outside. "Because we're better than them."

Pat and Gary backed away from each other and straightened up.

Through where the door once lay was a balding man, advancing up the driveway. He walked with a cane in his right hand and had a head so shiny it could have been varnished. The white hair that remained was tied back in a ponytail. He wore a fancy suit with immaculately shone shoes. He walked away from a black Mercedes Benz with blackout windows and towards the cottage. Each of his fingers had a different gold ring on and he wore a chain to match.

"Evening, squire," he said, looking straight at me. "I don't believe we've formally met, though I've heard about you. The name's Tricky Ricky. And you, my lad, are in a bit of a pickle."

33

"Norman," Tricky Ricky said, his voice worn from years of smoking, yet commanding and sounding of old money. "I see the years have been as kind to you as I expected."

Norman rolled his eyes. "Yeah, yeah. Nice to see you, too, old friend."

Tricky Ricky pointed at the shit in the middle of the hallway, then turned to Gary. "Get rid of it."

"How, boss?"

"It doesn't matter how, only that you do it."

"But I haven't got any gloves."

Tricky Ricky appraised him with a neutral expression, but behind his eyes he was as cold as a fisherman's corpse discovered in Alaska.

"It's shit," Gary said. "Human shit. I don't want to get it on my hands."

Tricky Ricky spoke softly. "Listen here, sunshine, I don't give a good god damn how you get rid of it. You can twist your hands behind your back, dive towards the floor like you're apple bobbing, and gobble it up in your mouth, for all I care. But I'll tell you this, if you don't dispose of it within the next ten seconds, then I will dispose of you. Are we crystal?"

"Yes, boss."

"Then step to it." He held up a liver-spotted hand, dotted with cigarette burns as he began to count. "Ten."

Gary scanned the room frantically, settling on the stair bannister upon which Norman's faded denim jacket was draped. Using the jacket to protect his hands, he scooped up the stool and ran out the front, hands panicked as if juggling a hot potato. Then he lobbed the jacket and the turd as far as he could, which was approximately the length of Norman's property to the road outside. It narrowly missed Tricky Ricky's Mercedes.

Tricky Ricky turned his attention back to Norman. "Well, here we are. The whole gang. Not feeling so tough now, are you, Norman? Do you fancy running your mouth with us standing here in front of you, darling?"

Norman clenched his fists but kept his eyes to the floor.

He looked up sheepishly, then said, "What have you got, Wentworth?"

"I haven't got anything," I said, appalled he was turning to me as if I should start insulting the bloody lot of them. As if Tricky Ricky's question hadn't been rhetorical and I should give it my best shot.

The men started laughing. Even that ropey piss-stain of a rapper Colin, which really hacked me off. Why should I insult them? To what end? Much like Paris Hilton's sex tape and Brexit, I didn't reckon much good would come of it.

"Your boy is such a bitch," Gary said, sneering at Norman as if he hadn't been reduced to picking up shit a few minutes previously.

"Oh yeah? Well, what about yours? He's just standing there like a wet wank blanket." Norman pointed towards Cummy Ian, who remained behind the patio door in the kitchen.

"Cummy ain't my boy," Gary said.

"Not what I heard," Norman said.

"Oh yeah? What you heard?"

"That he *is* your boy."

"He isn't."

"I heard you fucked his mother."

"Everybody's fucked his mother. Even you, Norm!"

Norman nodded. "Fair enough. But the difference is, you fucked her and then nine months later this literal lump of human shaped spunk exploded out of her vag canal. And I absolutely do mean exploded. I heard the kid was a flyer. People say he shot out right-quick like Michael Schofield's boner anytime a teenaged boy interned for *Good Morning Britain*."

Colin started laughing. "It's funny cos it's true."

Gary's face turned postbox red, then his embarrassment transformed to anger, and he directed it all towards Cummy Ian. "Get your arse in here, you fucking gobshite!"

Cummy Ian remained still, staring in at the cottage as if a lost cat.

"The fuck is wrong with him?" Gary muttered to no one in particular.

"He can't hear you," Norman said proudly. "Double glazing, innit? I told you. This shit works!"

Gary pushed past me and Norman, marching into the kitchen and towards the patio door. He grabbed the handle and, to his surprise, the door slid open easily.

"It wasn't even locked, you donkey!" Gary said to his probable son.

"You didn't lock the door?" I said to Norman.

Norman shrugged.

"You dumb cummy bastard, why didn't you try to open the door?" Gary said.

"I assumed it was locked!" Ian said.

"You assume nothing in this game, you fucking oxygen thief. Honestly, I've shot blanks out of my dick with more intelligence than you. Now get inside, you silly cunt."

Gary slapped Ian round the back of the head for effect, then grabbed him by the long locks of his pudding basin haircut, pulling him into the hallway with the rest of us.

"Jeez, dad, that kind of hurts."

Gary hit Ian again, much harder and in the stomach. He folded like a deckchair.

"You never call me that," Gary said. "We've been over this time and time again."

Pat and Norman were grinning. Gary was apoplectic. Ian was on the verge of tears. Colin looked confused and awkward, like a snow leopard in Hawaii without any of the menace. Tricky Ricky silently watched the circus clowns.

"Well, anyway," Pat said, trying to maintain some order, "here we all are. The head honcho himself, Tricky Ricky. Me and my boy," he pulled Colin awkwardly closer. "You and your boy. And, as luck would have it, we've got our Gary here for good measure."

Gary grinned as if he appreciated the nod.

Norman frowned. "What about Cummy Ian? Doesn't he get a mention?"

"Norm, mate, even Cummy's dad won't claim him as his own. The kid's about as useful as a sieve as a water catcher."

"Then why bring him along?"

"Court mandate, innit? Custody and that."

Gary nodded as if to confirm.

"But he's in his twenties," Norman said. "Ah well, my boy had a custody battle for a cat, so these things happen, don't they? Funny what they'll let into court these days. A right waste of the taxpayer's money if you ask me."

"Not a waste," I said. "I fucking loved that cat. But enough of the bollocks, I have something to say." All eyes were on me. "To you." I moved closer to Tricky Ricky.

Norman frowned. "Maybe that's not such a good idea, know what I mean, son?" Then to Ricky, "The lad doesn't have anything to say. He's confused. Truth be told, he's only caught up in this whole mess because of me. I made some dumb decisions. You know what I'm like, Ricky. But the boy shouldn't suffer. So, whatever the consequences, you punish me, not him. He'll stay out of this, and he'll keep quiet."

"I really *do* have something to say," I said.

Norman stamped a foot like a surly kid, then beneath his breath went, "Boy, I am helping you out here, but you have to keep that gob of yours shut."

"Last time you tried to help me out, Mickey Poole disappeared. I'll all right, thanks."

Norman went to argue, but I cut him off.

"So, Tricky Ricky …" I inched closer to him, feigning a confidence I didn't possess.

"Squire?"

And who in the name of Guy Fawkes said squire these days? Was this cunt fresh out of a Dickens novel?

"You took my girl," I said. "And I want her back."

Pat and Gary Knox began grinning as if this was the funniest thing. The laughter spread to Colin and Cummy Ian. Even Norman looked as if he was on the brink of a smirk. Like everyone knew the punchline to a joke but me.

Like *I* was the punchline.

Sickness rose in my stomach.

"I don't take anything that doesn't already belong to me," Tricky Ricky said calmly. "That wouldn't be very gentlemanly of me now, would it?"

"So then, you didn't take my girl?"

"*My* girl. Goodness, this fellow is awfully possessive," he said with derision, looking around the room at the rest of the lads.

"You don't know anything about the whereabouts of Amanda?"

He didn't answer.

I took my phone from my pocket, showed him the

photograph of Amanda and the text message I'd received earlier: *Don't need 2 cum 2 Kiddy. Kiddy cumming 2 U!*

"What do you say about this then?" I asked.

Tricky Ricky stared at me with a look that exhibited more contempt than Nigel Farage witnessing an illegal immigrant sailing into Dover.

Tricky Ricky cleared his throat. "I say, whoever sent it your way doesn't know how to spell come."

"Anything else?"

He paused, but I reckoned it was more for effect than consideration.

"The ropes are just for show. They aren't secured properly." He glanced at Pat, and I sensed a threat passing between them.

"So you didn't send the message?" I said.

"Come now. Don't insult me."

"And you didn't take the photo?"

"Do I strike you as a photographer, squire?"

"Where's Amanda? I want to know. I *need* to know."

"You're not in a position to be making demands."

"Tell me where Amanda is."

"He doesn't get it, does he?" He looked around at everyone else before turning back to me. "I can't say I know, squire. And even if I did, I'd have no reason to tell you. Not after what you and your father pulled."

"Amanda didn't do anything," I said. "She shouldn't be involved in this. So if you really are a gentleman, if you have just an ounce of integrity, you'll let her go."

His expression remained placid.

"That the kind of guy you are, Ricky? You enjoy harming women and children? Hurting people who haven't done a damn thing wrong? Marching around with your stupid cane and your phoney accent like some *Oliver Twist* street thug?"

Tricky Ricky remained calm.

"Harming innocent parties. You're no better than Fred and Rose West luring innocents to their—"

"Innocent," Tricky Ricky said. "Do you really think Amanda is innocent, squire? Goodness. You don't know the half of it."

"No? Then enlighten me."

Tricky Ricky tapped his cane on the ground. "I don't have to, you know? But your holier than thou attitude is … somewhat vexing. I trust you're acquainted with a gentleman by the name of Wild Bo. It just so happens he caught a couple of people snooping into my business. A particular irritant and geriatric by the name of Swain and your so-called woman, Amanda."

"I don't think so," I said.

"I don't *think* so either, squire. I *know* so."

"But what the hell would Amanda be doing with Swain? She doesn't know him. That doesn't make any sense."

"I neither know nor care. Either way, she will no longer be dealing with Swain as the situation has been successfully dealt with and concluded."

"The fuck is that supposed to mean?"

"Language, squire. There's no reason to get so heated."

"Wild Bo better not have laid a hand on my woman!"

Tricky Ricky sighed. "You're still a clingy old chap, but at least Amanda has progressed from your girl to your woman. If we keep talking like this, there's a chance you might show her some respect by the end of this little exchange."

"Fuck off. Stop it! Don't make me out to be the bad one when you're responsible for something happening to Amanda. Is she hurt? Worse? What the fuck have you done?"

"I haven't *done* anything, squire. Not personally."

I looked to Norman, hoping for help, but he was scratching his head vigorously and appraising the floor.

"Then Wild Bo. That piece-of-shit money-grabber. What has *he* done?" I said. "Give me specifics."

"I can't say there are many specifics to give. He did little more than transportation. Of course, he had to be firm in conveying the seriousness of the matter to ensure compliance. But my understanding is Amanda put up little resistance and understood the situation almost instantly. Unfortunately, the same can't be said for Mister Swain."

"Transportation," I said. "Where?"

"*Where* is of little concern. *Who* is a better question."

"Then who? For fuck's sake! Why are you doing this? Do you get off on it?"

"Wesker's Sister," Tricky Ricky said.

"The maniac with a sword!"

"I suppose you're right there. She does have somewhat of a liking for swords."

There was something sick and sinister in his words. Though it was the unexpressed words and looks from the others that caused the most discomfort.

"So, Amanda's with Wesker's Sister. Along with Swain. That's what you're telling me?" Sweat formed on my forehead under the pressure of it all.

Tricky Ricky sighed. "I mean, *with* Swain is stretching the definition of *with*. And indeed *Swain* for that matter. She *was* with Swain. To tell you the truth, Swain isn't with Swain anymore."

"That doesn't make any sense."

"It's a little complicated to explain through words alone. Gary, be a darling and show him, would you?"

Gary reached into his pocket. I flinched, expecting to meet with his knife again, but instead, he was on his phone and scrolling through images.

He held one up to Tricky Ricky. "This one good enough, boss?"

"Oh, yes. I'd say that one's rather splendid, darling."

Gary handed me the phone.

And what exactly was I looking at?

A grey bucket sat in a dank room, perhaps a garage. Sticking out of the bucket were what appeared to be great hunks of dissected animal. Skin and bones. Gnawed and sinewy. Blood red and gristle exposed.

When I saw the toenails, everything clicked into place, and it was as ugly as a staple gun to the testicles.

These were severed limbs.

Severed *human* limbs.

The red and white bloodstained dressing gown discarded a few metres north of the bucket confirmed the inevitable.

The severed limbs were Swain's.

34

I BOLTED from the hallway to the kitchen, and nobody tried to stop me.

I painted the kitchen sink with my stomach lining. Chunks of partially undigested sausages. Brown and yellow sludge. Stringy orange. Sweetcorn flecks.

I snorted, shooting sharp bile up my nose. I reached for a glass, then glugged back water. Acrid acid stung the back of my throat. When I staggered back to the hallway, Tricky Ricky was standing there. Unphased and patient. As if I'd returned from a quick piss.

"Amanda," I managed, "is she ..."

But I couldn't finish. Wouldn't finish. There was no way I was making this any more real. Words are powerful. Words have a habit of turning fiction into reality.

"She's with Wesker's Sister," Tricky Ricky said. "That's all you're getting."

"Where's Wesker's Sister?"

"That's all you're getting," he said, firmer and colder.

"Please ..."

"Pat, Gary, see that we finish what we came here for.

These two wasters aren't worth my time. Ian, be a darling and make a video or two. I'm going to relax in the car and listen to a little Vivaldi."

With that he exited the cottage and began the long walk down the driveway.

"You're gonna fuck off then, are you? Just like that? Get others to do your dirty work? You useless old man."

"Wentworth, please …" Norman said.

Tricky Ricky turned and winked at me. "So long, squire. Ian, the video please."

Tricky Ricky continued to confidently make his way towards the Merc parked outside.

Cummy Ian held up his mobile phone, a red Nokia with so many dents and scratches it looked like it had made it through a war zone and had stories to tell. "I put a new SD in especially. Just in case, like."

Ian looked proud. Gary side-eyed him with all the subtlety of a kick in the balls.

"It don't look much but the camera packs some power. I do all of Colin's videos for him, you know. The specs on this bad boy are enough to rival the latest iPhone," Ian said. "And it's got all sorts of modes from portrait to panoramic and even slo-mo. It's got a built-in editor, so I can make the vids black and white. Proper *Sin City* it, know what I mean?"

Gary clipped Ian round the back of the head, and he squealed like a cat getting its tail yanked.

"Quit screwing around," Gary said, then turned to me and Norman. "We're here to kill you. But I think you know that already."

Norman folded his arms but made no attempt to argue or reason with Gary.

"You don't have to do that," I said, sounding as pathetic as I felt.

"We kind of do. It's what Tricky Ricky wants," Gary said.

"So you're just gonna take orders from him?"

"Um, yeah. That's how this works …"

"Killing us seems a bit over the top."

"You dick-roids tried to steal Tricky Ricky's money!"

"Yeah, but we *didn't*."

"Because of your incompetence!"

"Doesn't matter. What matters is you still have your money."

"That's just a technicality," Gary said, his face getting progressively redder.

"No, it isn't! Without your money, you'd be fucked!"

"Exactly! That's my point," Gary said. "That's precisely the reason you have to die."

"But you have your money, so you aren't fucked. That's *my* point."

"Listen, pal, if you didn't want this to happen, you shouldn't have busted into Tricky Ricky's gaff. What the hell did you think was gonna happen? Planning a thing like that …"

"Technically I didn't plan anything. As far as I knew, I was just giving my dad a lift. As a matter of fact, I didn't even know he was my dad at the time."

Gary looked befuddled. "The fuck you on about, *didn't know he was your dad*? Are you retarded or something?"

Norman grimaced as the ugly words spilled out.

"I hadn't seen him since I was three years old," I said. "Anyway, if I'd have known what we were really doing, I'd never have agreed to—"

"Whoa! Whoa!" Norman interrupted. "Way to rat your own dad out."

"Yeah! That's right, Norm," Gary said, quickly changing sides and pointing a sweaty finger at me. "I hate the way you did that. I know Norm's a mega cunt but he's still your dad."

"Norm's MAGA, too?" Ian said, pointing to his Trump t-shirt and brightening up.

"*Mega* cunt not MAGA cunt. Fuck's sakes, boy, try using your ears once in a while," Gary said, then turned back to me. "You shouldn't hang your dad out to dry like an old towel just cos things are getting tough. Where the hell's the respect?"

"A bit rich coming from a guy who won't acknowledge his son." I looked to Cummy Ian, who was directing his banged-up phone in my direction. I had a feeling this was not the content Tricky Ricky had wanted him to capture.

Gary nodded to Ian. "That ain't my son."

"See?"

"Daaaaad!" Ian said in disbelief.

Gary's hands rolled into fists. "You're not. You can't be! It's an impossibility."

"You shot so much cum into his mum it started multiplying at a rapid rate. That's why he cums his pants so much," Colin said, then started laughing.

Ian looked hurt.

"Fuck off, Colin, you sweaty old cheesecloth," Gary said. "You're an even bigger embarrassment than Ian. Your videos only get pity views and likes. Nobody thinks you're any good at rapping but just like a car crash, it's impossible to look away."

Rather than object or stand up for his son, Pat silently nodded.

Gary looked at me. "I still think you should show some loyalty towards your old man."

"I've barely seen him in the past three decades!"

"Not my fault! Not my fault and you know it!" Norman shouted. "Don't you turn this around on me. Christ almighty, I had enough of that from your mother."

"The fuck's that meant to mean?" I shouted back. "Don't act like you're better than my mother. At least she was there for me."

"She took you from me, you little shit. I tried to be there, but she took you. Just like that wacko ex of yours took your dumb cat."

I was seconds away from charging at Norman when Pat cut above the noise. "All right, all right. Settle down, boys. We want to kill you ourselves. Don't go killing each other."

"How about nobody kills anybody and we sort this out another way?" I said.

Gary rolled his eyes. "Here we go again. Always with the *don't kill anyone* shit."

"Now, hold up," Pat said. "Let's hear what he has to say. You think there's another way to sort this? Well, consider my interest piqued. What is it you're suggesting? Cos I know you don't have any money. That much is obvious from how this all started."

Norman was breathing heavily, no doubt still vexed, but he saw me struggling and spoke softly. "You could give him your car."

That had not been the interjection I'd expected. "What are you going on about? How am I gonna get back to Kiddy if I don't have a car?"

"Same way I get around," Norman said. "You hitchhike."

"Hitchhiking's dangerous. I might get killed."

Norman looked around at the men, who were now circling in. Surrounding us. Hyenas ready to pounce.

"Boy, I dunno if you've noticed the severity of the situation here, but you're probably gonna get killed if you *don't* give him the car."

"I'm not giving him the car. It's sentimental."

"It's a bang-average Toyota Corolla!"

"My grandad gave it to me."

"He gave you a car? Bloody hell, boy," Norman said, taken aback for a moment. "Ask him to give you another. Think about it, if he gave you one, he'll give you another."

"That's not how it works."

"It's how it works with me."

"You give away cars?"

"What I give away once, I'll give away again."

"And what exactly do you give away?"

"Well, I don't give away much apart from arse kickings." He gave a big barrelling laugh and looked around the room for approval.

Nobody laughed.

"Know what I mean?" he said. "Know what I bloody mean?"

Still, nobody laughed.

"Well, anyway, it's worth a shot," Norman said. "You don't know if you don't ask. So next time you see him, ask your grandad for—"

"He's dead!"

The room descended into more silence than 11 am on 11th November at the community church.

Then Norman spoke, "I dunno, boy, first your mother, now your grandad. Is there anyone in your family who isn't dead?"

"You," I said.

He shrugged. "Anyway, the car—"

"It's really important to me ..."

"For fuck's sake," Pat said. "We don't want your piece-of-shit car, okay?"

Norman laughed. "He fucking told you, boy."

"Shut up, Norman."

"You shouldn't stand for it," Norman said. "He dissed your dead grandad's car. Fucking lamp him, my boy."

"Quit it," Pat said. "Just stop already. It's obvious you don't have any other way of settling this. And you have nothing of value here. Sod all you can offer. So a fight to the death it is."

"This is ridiculous," I said. "There's no reason we need to

go that far. If you want to see who the more dominant father-son team is, then something more proportionate like, I dunno … arm-wrestling, would surely do it."

"Ha!" Norman squawked. "You hear that? My boy says he's a much better arm-wrestler than the four of you nerds put together. He'll arm-wrestle the lot of you blindfolded and still come out on top."

"Norman!"

"We are not settling this with a poxy arm-wrestling match," Pat said.

"How about real wrestling?" I suggested.

"Wrestling isn't real," Pat said. "It's fake."

"You tell that to Brock Lesnar and see how fake you think it is then," Norman said.

Pat feigned looking around the room. "It doesn't appear he's here. And besides, he was in the UFC. Now that's real fighting. I love a bit of MMA."

"Me, too, like," Colin chirped up, but was soon quiet and sheepish again after a glare from Pat.

"So, what you're saying," I said, "is you want us to settle this through some MMA?"

"Some MMA," Pat scoffed, and I wasn't sure if he was mocking my wording or words. "What's your discipline?"

"Sorry?"

"What martial arts do you know?"

Knew of was more accurate. "I mean, I guess I don't."

"For fuck's sake, boy," Norman said. "If that's not reason enough why I should have had custody of you over your mother, I don't know what is. I'd have at least enrolled you in a taekwondo class or two."

"Why would you enrol him in two?" Gary piped up.

"So he'd be twice as good."

"That's not how it works. Just sounds like a waste of money. Like throwing your coins in an old wishing well and hoping your dreams will come true. It defies common sense."

"Sometimes it works, so who's laughing now?" Norman said. "Not you, pal. You won't be calling any of this a waste of money when you're peeling your face off the floor cos of my boy's taekwondo."

"But he doesn't know taekwondo. He said so himself!"

"We are fighting to the death and that's that," Pat shouted above the noise.

"No, no, no," I said. "There's a better way. There's a better way, I know it." I wracked my brain for something, for *anything*, listing things quicker than a child prodigy spitting out letters at a spelling bee. "Maximum push-ups. Scrabble. Punch-the-ball-sack. Soggy biscuit. Tables. Frozen sausages competitive eat-off—"

Norman checked his watch, then said, "Bloody hell, lads. *Naked Attraction's* on in five minutes. Why don't we take a breather? I'll grab us some tinnies from the fridge and we can watch the episode together. Then, when it's done, we can settle this once and for all."

Gary rubbed his hands together. "You know, that's not actually a bad idea. I was once a—"

"Yes, it *is* a fucking bad idea," Pat said. "About as bad as the time you decided to raw dog Cummy Ian's mother and look how that turned out."

"In fairness, she wasn't his mother at the time or I never would have gone there."

"Hold up," Norman said. "What were you saying Gaz?"

"Just that I have standards. I ain't putting my shooter in anyone capable of spawning that ugly load of human-shaped jizz."

"Not about that. About *Naked Attraction*. I was once a *what*?" Norman stared wide-eyed at Gary as if he were a priest capable of absolving him of all his sins.

"Oh, just that I was a contestant once."

"YOU BLOODY WHAT?" Norman screamed with a face that looked like he'd jizzed his pants, which was, coincidentally, the expression Cummy Ian wore most of the time. "No way. No *bloody* way. You have got to be joking me?"

"I'm not."

Norman gave a high-pitched scream and pushed Gary in the chest as if they were mates and he was not, in fact, threatening to shank him with a knife minutes earlier.

"This is a joke," Norman said. "This is an absolute wind-up. This is an April Fools'!"

"It isn't. I really was on *Naked Attraction*."

"Oh my god. OH MY GAAAAAWD!" He spun around in a circle, staring up at the ceiling. "Are there cameras? Is this a reality show? Am I being pranked?"

And from the way he was scouring for surveillance, he meant it.

"Ah! FUCK! This is incredible. This might be the best day of my life. One of my friends was on *Naked Attraction*." He turned to me. "Did you hear that? This lad right here, my good friend, Gary, was on *Naked Attraction*?"

"Friend? Fuck off. He literally wants to kill us."

But Norman didn't care. Couldn't have listened less if he was Helen Keller in an MRI scanner. More doped up than a recently admitted burns victim pumped full of morphine with a tab of acid on their tongue.

"Spunk in the bed and call me Richard Madeley, I think I'm gonna shit myself!" Norman said.

"Don't," Pat said. "We've already got a cunt who cums himself like clockwork. We don't need a perpetual pooper."

"You swear on your mum's life you're not bullshitting?" Norman said to Gary.

"I swear."

"Can't believe I haven't seen that episode … You swear on your dad's life, too?"

"Sure."

For a moment Norman was hyperventilating, but he

brought it back under control and between breaths said, "That's. My. Dream. Mate. Being on *Naked Attraction*."

"It was mine, too," Gary said, his voice now also an octave higher. Norman's giddy excitement was more infectious than an STD at a herd immunity orgy for gonorrhoea.

"Was it as good as you thought it would be?" Norman asked, lips trembling.

"Even better, mate," Gary said, voice feather soft. "Anna Richardson signed my stomach."

"Piss off, did she!"

"I got it tattooed the next day. Here, let me show you …" Gary tugged on his tight rugby top. Norman was practically salivating as he waited for the reveal.

A thunderous gunshot clapped around the room.

Colin screamed.

Gary let go of his top, and it snapped back to his belly.

Norman stumbled as if he'd been clobbered in the jaw.

And from the look of confusion coupled with euphoria upon his face, I think Cummy Ian might have performed his famed party move and delivered a protein shake in his tighty-whities.

Pat held a firearm high in the air.

"You actually brought a gun?" Norman said.

"Of course I did, you muppet. You didn't really think we'd only brought knives to a gunfight, did you?"

Colin grinned. "They didn't bring a gun to a gunfight though, did they, dad?"

"Only cos he left them at the range," Norman said, nodding to me.

"You didn't tell me to bring shit to shit. And besides, I left *you* with the guns, so who's really to blame?" I said. "And what happened to the gun from earlier? We sent them a photo."

"Replica, mate."

"For fuck's sake! Well, if we don't have guns, it isn't exactly a gunfight."

"Then why have I got a gun?" Pat said.

"Cos you're a nutter with a gun. That's why!"

The lads considered each other in silence.

A soft sneeze from upstairs broke the noiselessness.

Alex!

35

"Who the hell was that?" Pat said.

I kept my lips tightly prised together as if sewn shut. Alex had scarpered around the time the gang had arrived but had never left the cottage. And now the lads would soon be onto her unless she got the hell out of dodge or I came up with some incredible excuse as to why the upstairs floors periodically sneezed. I didn't think 'there's a ghost with seasonal allergies' was going to cut it.

"Are we not alone?" Pat said.

Norman began folding and unfolding his arms at a rapid rate.

"Sorry, am I a fucking mute?" Pat said. "Are all you useless cunts temporarily deaf? Is there someone else about or not?"

"No," I said.

Norman stopped moving his arms and shook his head at me. "Come on, son. He heard her. Old Pat's a son-of-a-bitch, but he ain't a bloody idiot. Can't just say 'no' like that and expect him to buy it."

"Her," Pat repeated. "Oh now I *know* we're gonna have

some fun. Maybe you don't have to die. It could be there's another way to settle things after all."

"No," I said, sounding more confident and surer of myself than I felt. "We fight to the death. It's the only way."

Norman raised an eyebrow and put his hands in the air in faux surrender. He was a grifter, a chancer, the kind of person who would worm his way out of any situation. He wanted no part of this.

Then something ignited in Norman, and he switched gears, saying, "Yeah, boy! You kick Cummy Ian's arse so hard there's jizz spraying out of every orifice. Turn that sperm-ball into a spunky sparkler on Bonfire Night!"

"Now, now!" Pat said, waving his gun in the air. "Like you said before, dying might be a little extreme. As you rightly pointed out, you only *tried* to steal from Tricky Ricky. Nothing was actually taken. And okay, you *did* damage his rug, but given what we found in your own entrance, shitting on the floor is just a thing you do."

"Yeah," Norman said, straightening. "They call me Shit-a-Brick—"

"Shut the fuck up!" Pat snapped. "Gary, go get the woman."

He rubbed his hands together, the kid who'd found the cookie jar. "Oh boy, I knew I smelt pussy the moment I—"

"You shut the fuck up, 'n' all," Pat said. "I said go get her. That's it. No funny business, you sick cunt."

"Right you are." Gary lowered his head, then skulked upstairs.

The room went quiet. The only sound, the whirring of an old boiler from the adjacent room.

We were moments away from chaos. That much was obvious. There was little left to lose. We were as good as dead. Alex, too. We needed something to change and fast.

"You know where Amanda is," I said to Pat.

"No."

"It wasn't a question. You *know*."

"I know as much as you. She's with Wesker's Sister just like Tricky Ricky told you."

"But you know where Wesker's Sister is, don't you?"

He didn't reply.

"I don't want anything happening to Amanda," I said. "You guarantee her safety and I'll do anything you want. *Anything.* I'll work for you for the rest of my life if that's what it takes."

Pat shook his head. "Believe me, based on what we've seen here today, and based on what I've seen over the years I've known your father, that is more burden than benefit."

"I'm not like my dad," I said. "I know how to do things. I can be of use to you. And anything I don't know, I can learn. So please, just tell me where Amanda is or at least make the call and set her free."

There seemed to be some understanding in Pat's eyes as if he was considering it.

Then there was a scream from above and Gary came stamping down the stairs, dragging Alex after him by her long mane of hair. He pushed her in front of Pat and she fell to her knees. Her oversized sunglasses almost tumbling from her face.

Pat punched Gary in the cheek who held his palm against the point of impact, wincing in pain.

Gary went to protest, but Pat spoke first. "The hell do you think you're doing, you stupid bastard? Pulling her around by her barnet like some bloody monster! You show her some respect. What did I tell you before? We ain't animals. Not like this brick-shitting punk."

"It's territorial," Norman said. "And manly."

Pat turned to Alex. "Go on. Up you get. No one's gonna hurt you here. They bloody well try and next time it will be a darn-sight more than my fist they feel." He looked to the gun in his hand, then put it in his pocket when he clocked her alarm. "It ain't for you. See?"

Alex rose to her feet, looking around warily.

"Who are you then?" Pat asked, speaking gently as if to a child.

"Alex."

"Pretty name. I wonder if you're as pretty as your namesake. Take those glasses off, would you? Let me get a good look at you."

"I'd rather not."

"And I'd rather you did."

Pat had saved her from Gary but to what end? So he could have his way with her himself? None of this was good. Far from it. But what the hell could I do? Pat had a gun and Gary a knife. Colin and Cummy Ian were there, too, and whilst they were about as threatening as a couple of toddlers with pound shop water pistols with the safety lock on, they still increased the numbers. This was two against four. Five if you included Tricky Ricky, who waited out the front in the car, armed with god knows what. For all I knew, Wesker's Sister was in the vicinity, too. Then there was Wild Bo, had he come along for the fun?

Jesus Christ, however you sliced it, we were outnumbered and overpowered. Which meant whatever Pat, Tricky Ricky, and the rest of the bunch of bastards wanted, they could get.

Alex removed her sunglasses, revealing bruises her makeup hadn't quite managed to patch up and cuts to match, red and raw.

"What happened there?" Pat said.

"Nothing."

"Nothing always means something," Pat said, taking his gun from his pocket once again and putting the lot of us on edge.

He held the gun by his side, but the threat was clear. Was

this utter loon gonna execute Alex if she didn't explain her bruises?

"These two limp dick excuses for men fucking with you?" Pat said, looking to me, then Norman. "You their play toy? Their bit of skirt on the side? You like a bit of father-son action but when you say the wrong thing, they show you the belt? You play the subservient daughter, they play the seventies daddy? That what we're dealing with here?"

She shook her head.

"But they're treating you wrong in some way? Bruises don't magic out of thin bloody air."

"That's not how it is," she said. "Wentworth was—"

"So it's the son who's the sick fuck. That what you're telling me?"

"No."

"He your lover?"

"No."

"You sure?"

"I think I would know," she said with a hint of sass.

"Cos I don't want to protect no lover boy."

She shook her head again: part-denial, part-exasperation, largest part-despair.

"Then who the hell is he to you?" Pat said.

"My neighbour ... and friend."

Pat nodded slowly but soon got up in my grill. "You bruise her up, kid? You like beating on women? Does it make you feel like a big man?"

"What? No. Obviously not."

"But you like to prey on those smaller than you?"

"No."

"Those weaker than you?"

I shook my head.

"It gets your dick hard, doesn't it?"

"Please," Norman said. "My boy ain't like that."

"No?" Pat said, stepping from me and towards Norman. "But you are, aren't you?"

Norman didn't respond.

"Oh yeah, you've got a right history, Norm. People talk. I know all about you and the things you've done, you fucking woman beater. Well, not anymore …"

Pat swung a right to Norman's stomach, connecting so hard in the gut, Norman looked like he was going to puke.

"Dad!" I said, and the word surprised me. Embarrassed me even, but it's how it came out.

"He ain't your dad," Pat said. "Biologically maybe. But this waster hasn't been a dad to any of his kids. Have you, Norm?"

"I have siblings?"

"Norm …" Pat laughed. "Your parents couldn't have got your name more wrong if they'd written *Not-A-Cunt* on your birth certificate. Though, just so we're crystal, if they had written *Not-A-Cunt* they would have been wrong on that count, too, because you, Norman, are an absolute monster cunt. You're the kind of cunt that eats other cunts for breakfast. Slurp, slurp, slurp."

Colin looked uncomfortable and confused. Gary was halfway between embarrassment and approval. Cummy Ian was glancing down at his own crotch.

"Norm," Pat said again. "There's nothing normal about you. You brick shitting freak! You used to wet your trousers in first school, didn't you?"

Cummy Ian looked up. "I'm not alone," he whispered, and gave a smile packed with such relief, I wondered if he'd actually jizzed himself.

"Shut up, Pat," Norman said.

"Make me."

Pat opened his arms wide, gun in one hand, the other a clenched fist, offering Norman a free shot.

"I said *make me*, you fucking coward!"

But Norman didn't do shit.

None of us did.

We all stood there like candles on a birthday cake without the light. How long was this going to go on for? Was there a point where Tricky Ricky would come hobbling back up the driveway and demand they hurry things along? And why was Cummy Ian no longer recording any of this? Had his new SD card run out of memory already or did he know more than the rest of us? Had he had a premonition? An inkling? A superpower that said, this ain't the moment Pat starts spilling lead?

Pat lowered his arms. "Just what I thought. You didn't do shit in school and you still won't do shit now. That's why I was always taking your women." He leant over to me. "Maybe he ain't even your biological dad. Maybe that's me."

"Piss off," Norman said. "You didn't even know his mother."

"You don't think I knew Kate?"

Norman froze worse than before.

"That one got you good, huh?" Pat said. "There's nothing in this world you can do that I can't. And there's no one in this world you can do that I can't."

Tears were forming in Norman's eyes, only it was worse than that—it was as if they were calcifying. Hardening his face. Spreading to the rest of his body and choking the life from him. Melancholia infecting his organs, his mind, his very soul at an accelerated rate until he would transform into nothing but concentrated sorrow. And if it got to that point, I didn't see a way back. Either he'd drop dead on the spot or remain paralysed in a coma of misery for eternity.

"*Naked Attraction*!" I screamed. "*Naked* fucking *Attraction*."

Everyone was looking at me as if I'd lost the plot.

"What?" Pat said, neither angry nor disagreeing, just puzzled.

"You said there's nothing in this world Norman can do

that you can't, but that isn't true," I said. "He'd make a better contestant on *Naked Attraction*."

Pat scoffed. "Piss off, would he."

"It's true. He'll get accepted one day, but you won't."

"Son, *Naked Attraction* is just a dream for many men."

"A dream?" Gary said. "You used to chastise me and take the piss out of me for what I did. But now, after all this time, you're telling me it's your dream, too? After everything you did to me?!"

"Calm the hell down and do something useful like fix your tampon. *Of course* it's my dream, but I couldn't stand to admit it at the time and grew to resent the show and Anna Richardson herself because you took what should have been my spot. You took everyone's spot in the Wyre Forest. So, the truth is, me and Norman, ain't neither one of us getting accepted."

"Agree to disagree," I said. "I know for a *fact* Norman would get accepted on *Naked Attraction*. Matter of fact, I reckon he already has."

Pat rolled his eyes. "You are so off your face, you're starting to sound like your old man in the nineties. Obviously I'd make a better *Naked Attraction* contestant than anyone in this room, but it's absolutely pointless because Gary—who was eliminated early, by the way—took everyone's place."

"Better than anyone in the room?" Colin said, his voice weaker than a pale glass of lemon squash. "I'm not sure that's true."

"Don't backtalk, boy."

"I'm with Colin," Gary said. "I beat off a lot of other guys to—"

Cummy Ian burst out laughing. "You did *what?*"

Gary frowned. "I had to beat off a lot of people to get on that show."

Norman put a hand to his mouth, also grinning.

"Gary, shut your mouth. You're embarrassing yourself," Pat said.

"There was some stiff competition!" Gary said to the amusement of everyone apart from Colin, who was preoccupied—tugging at his basketball shorts.

Pat glanced at Colin. "The hell are you doing?"

"What needs to be done."

"Get your hands out of your drawers, you creepy cunt."

"Doesn't anyone else get it? Can't you see what's happening here? Isn't what we have to do obvious?" Colin said, feverish excitement consuming him.

"The only thing we *have* to do is take care of these side-show goons for Tricky Ricky." Pat shook the gun towards Norman, then me.

"How many of us men are there here?" Colin said.

"This isn't a fucking maths test," Pat said.

"Six," Cummy Ian said. "There are six of us."

"You don't count as a man, you useless punnet of ..." Gary stopped himself, actually putting a hand to his mouth. "Oh *shit*! Oh SHIT! I get it now."

"Get *what?*" Pat said, so vexed there was visible sweat dripping from his forehead, sluicing down his cheeks.

"*Naked Attraction*," Gary said. "It's perfect. Absolutely perfect. Six of us. One of her. It was meant to be. This is what our entire lives have led up to. We don't wait for Anna Richardson to bring *Naked Attraction* to Kiddy. We bring Kiddy to *Naked Attraction*."

"We're not even in Kidderminster!" I said.

Gary put his hand on his heart. "Kidderminster lives in my heart. I carry it everywhere I go."

Cummy Ian nodded. "It's a state of mind, mate."

"Piss off, Cummy!" Gary said. "I don't fucking need you backing me up. I've got a tattoo of the Horse Fair on my back for fuck's sake."

"Let's just do this!" Colin said.

And with that, he dropped his boxers.

36

COLIN REVEALED his anaemic-coloured bean sprout of a penis and stared at Alex dementedly. "What do you think, love? Any questions?"

She did not speak.

"Jesus Christ," Cummy Ian said. "The last time I saw a penis that small it was on a kid."

"Nonce," Norman said.

Cummy Ian put his hands up in the air. "Not like that. It was at a swimming pool."

"That's even worse. Why were you looking at children's penises at the pool?"

"I wasn't looking, it was just there. If anything, it was the other way round. The penis was looking at me, okay?"

Norman shook his head. "Isn't anything *okay* that just came out of your mouth. It's about as sick as Colin's penis. Looks like the poor thing needs to be put on life support."

"Pull your pants up, boy," Pat said. "You're embarrassing yourself."

"It isn't that bad."

"It *is* that bloody bad."

"Dad, don't be like—"

"Dad? Dad?! Don't call me that after the shit you just pulled. For the first time in my life, I understand where Gary's coming from. Plainly speaking, I don't want to admit you're my son right now."

"Cummy Ian isn't my son," Gary said.

"Pull your bloody pants up!" Pat shouted at Colin.

"No! You pull yours down. Let's do this. I'm serious."

Nobody made to move.

Colin let out a sigh, then started working his hand up and down his colourless bean sprout.

"Stop that! Stop it! For heaven's sake, boy!" Pat said.

"*Please.* It's a grower not a shower. I *need* you to see it. I need you *all* to see it. To know what I'm about."

"That doesn't make any sense. Now put it away!"

"It's a grower, Dad. It's a *grower!*" Tears started streaming down Colin's face as he violently whacked off his weasel with no change to its size whatsoever. "Shit," he said. "I really don't work well under pressure. Performance anxiety." He shuffled towards Alex, boxers round his ankles. "Please just say something about it. Anything. Don't let this have all been for nothing."

Alex swallowed. "I mean, I don't know what to …"

"Anything!"

"We can't host a *Naked Attraction* competition," Alex said.

"Of course we can," Colin said. "There's six men and a bird."

"You're one short."

He shook his head, using his fingers to count. "Me, Cummy Ian, Pat, Gary, and those two dick-bursts, Norman and Wankworth."

"Wentworth," I corrected.

"You're still one short," she said. "There's no *Naked Attraction* without Anna Richardson."

Norman snapped his fingers. "She's right, you know. I guess the competition's off."

"It was never on!" Pat said.

"No. No. We can do this. I know we can do this." Colin was properly blubbering, and I swear, in his distress, his dick was actually shrinking, something that minutes previous I'd have thought impossible. "We'll get someone to play Anna Richardson. We just need time. Tricky Ricky's in the car, maybe he could—"

Norman held his hand up in objection. "I can't wank to him. Which means he can't play Anna Richardson. It would require too much imagination."

"You have a good imagination," Gary said. "You jacked off to Andi Peters for fuck's sake!"

"I was off my face! Right now I'm stone cold sober."

"You haven't been stone cold sober in over thirty years."

"Yeah, well, I'm just saying … The Andi Peters era, it was a different time. Don't act like you weren't at it, too. I bet you were. I bet you had a tug to John Fashanu 'n' all. He was well good in *Gladiators*. And not bad at the Villa either."

"*Naked Attraction*! Let's do this!" Cummy Ian screamed, and with that he unzipped his flies and huffed out the thickest slab of prime hog I had ever seen in my life.

It's impossible to describe Cummy Ian's penis and do it the justice it deserves but, suffice it to say, we were all ogling it with a mixture of envy and genuine awe. It hadn't flopped out of his pants but rather it had roared, commanding respect and attention from all who stood in its presence. It was the Kobe beef of dicks. A proper premium cut of penis. A genuine work of art.

I looked up first. All eyes, save for Alex's, were still on Cummy Ian's man sausage as if hypnotised.

We were dicknotised: the act of being so utterly fixated on a beefy dong you are temporarily paralysed.

"THAT'S A MEATY HOG!" Norman shouted, snapping us all out of our dicknosis. "What?" Norman said. "It's what you were all thinking. Someone had to say it. Why not me?"

Colin hiked up his boxers and shorts. "That's that then. Guess it's all over. No one can compete with *that*."

Gary nodded. "Perhaps Cummy Ian could be my son after —Wait a minute ..." He pointed, drawing everyone's attention to the crusty floater in Ian's black boxers. It sloshed around like a chunk of partially dried rice pudding in the bottom of a black bin bag. "By god, the boy's jizzed his pants." Gary added, his finger still directed towards the soiling.

Awe soon turned to disgust. Normality restored.

Pat grinned, swimming in more smugness and superiority than there was cum in Ian's underwear. And, for absolute clarity, there was *a lot* of cum. If you'd have wrung his boxers, you'd have heard them squelch. He'd shot the kind of load you could still smell in the room 24 hours post-release and after a hearty airing with all the windows open.

"As I was saying," Pat said. "Ain't nobody around here getting on *Naked Attraction*. Not even you, Ian. Though, by the state of your briefs, you might get a job working in the special effects department on a new *Ghostbusters* film cos you know how to make a lot of slime."

"You're wrong," I said.

"How much slime do you bloody want? That wasn't single serve spunk. That was an industrial vat of—"

"I'm talking about *Naked Attraction*."

"If you think you or your old man are featuring on that show, you're dumber than a box of rocks in a Woolworth's warehouse."

I pulled out the stack of envelopes I'd stuffed in my back pocket earlier and rummaged through them until I got to the one with the *Naked Attraction* logo emblazoned on the front and held it up in the air as if it was the golden ticket to Willy Wonka's Chocolate Factory, which to these guys, it was as good as. "Then what's this I found earlier with Norman's name on it?"

Norman gasped.

There was a squelch as Ian adjusted his trousers, apparently having pulled everything back up without attending to the mess in his drawers.

"What's going on here?" Alex said.

But nobody else paid her any interest. As captivated by the envelope as they had been by Ian's pork truncheon.

Pat took in the pink and yellow *Naked Attraction* branding and looked to Gary, who nodded as if to confirm this was the real deal.

"You ever got one of these before?" I asked Norman.

"Never," he rasped, coming out of his trance.

"But you've applied many times?"

"I sure have."

"How about you, Pat? You ever got one of these?"

He shook his head.

"Gary?"

"Just the once."

I grinned. "So it's gonna be an acceptance then, isn't it?"

"Go on, boy," Norman said, his voice shaking. "Open it. Let's see what we're dealing with here."

Before I could so much as rip a corner of the envelope, Pat intercepted, snatching it from me, and stuffing it into his own pocket with so little care he creased the edges. "Fuck this letter. And fuck *Naked Attraction*."

"DON'T SAY THAT!" Norman screamed. "NEVER FUCKING SAY THAT!"

Pat grabbed Alex, wrapping his arm around her shoulder, pulling her tightly against his body, and pointing the gun at her head.

Alex shrieked, eyes wide, lips trembling.

"This woman is yours," Pat said to Norman. "Now it's time I make her mine."

"I'm not his!" Alex said, slapping at Pat. But he tightened his grip, digging his fingernails into and pinching her skin.

"Stop struggling, you dopey cow. I've got a gun for fuck's sake."

"I'm not his!" Alex said, her struggle muted, staring straight at Norman.

"Then what in the sweet fuck are you even doing here?"

"I'm … it's … You see …"

"Speak up, bitch."

"I'm the neighbour. I was getting some air, okay?"

"Getting some air by staying *inside* your neighbour's place? That don't make no sense. How stupid do you think I am?"

"Things got tense with my … with my husband." She looked sheepish, reluctant to admit it.

"So *he* did this to you?"

She shook her head more frantically than a pre-schooler refusing broccoli. "Whatever you're thinking, it's wrong."

Pat grinned, but there was no joy in it. "What I'm thinking is you're married to a wife-beating cunt."

"No!"

"Hey, Gary, perhaps you should pop next door and drag her loser husband over here, so we can show him what happens to wife beaters back in Kiddy."

"You cannot do that," Alex said. "I swear to god, you can't."

"Can't? *CAN'T?* Little lady, I'm sorry, but that word isn't in my vocabulary."

"Please. Do not bring my husband into this. You can have me if you want, but don't bring him into this." Alex wrestled one of her hands free enough to squeeze Pat's own hand, resting it there. "Do with me what you will. Do anything you want. But do not bring him into this."

Pat eyed Alex's hand for a moment then pulled away, letting go of Alex but keeping the gun directed towards her. "You move, I shoot." He turned to Gary. "Go get this bitch's husband."

Gary stuffed his hands in his pockets.

An electronic sound bleated from the side of the hallway. I glanced over to see Cummy Ian filming, a grin of pride on his face as he directed the Nokia towards the action. Had he just started recording again or had he been capturing events for a while?

"Gary, what the fuck are you waiting for? Do you suddenly not speak English or something? I said get her bloody husband."

"I know but … I mean, she said we can do *anything* we want with her. There's a lot of possibilities. Could be there's more fun to be had than just beating on her husband if you know what I mean?"

"Gary, if I ask you to do something, you bloody well do it. When Ricky ain't here, you answer to me, and don't forget it. You're getting awfully cocky for someone who was practically picking up shit with his mouth less than an hour ago."

Gary glared.

"Save the anger for someone who gives a fuck," Pat said.

"She gave us her permission to do *anything* we—"

"Permission! We don't need her bloody permission. You trying to tell me everything we've ever done with a woman has been because we got a little permission slip?"

"I guess not."

"We're god damn men. We take what we want."

"I'm just saying it feels better if they want it, too."

Pat shook his head. "You're growing soft, lad."

"I agree with Uncle Gary," Colin mumbled.

Pat looked more repulsed by Colin than he had the brick in the centre of the room earlier. He went to berate his boy but must have decided he wasn't worth the effort because he turned his attention back to Gary. "Go get the husband."

Gary was barely a few steps forward when there was a thud from next door that shook the lot of us.

Shouting followed.

Indecipherable words. Tone full of fury and louder than a Motörhead gig.

"That your husband?" Pat said.

Alex nodded.

"And who might he be talking to?"

Alex looked down.

"Well?"

"Sorry, it's just difficult to talk to you when you're pointing a gun at me."

"You managed that sentence okay," Pat said. "So I have faith in you to come up with others."

Alex appeared on the verge of tears.

"Oh for fuck's sake," Pat said, putting the gun back in his pocket—and honestly, he was taking his gun in and out of his pocket more often than a referee reaches for yellow cards in a local derby. "Better?"

Alex said nothing.

"Please don't tell me he's one of those loons who has arguments with himself?"

Another bang and more angry words.

"He seems so measured and calm," Pat said, eyeing the direction of Alex's cottage. "It would be a right miscarriage of justice if we were to give him a beatdown."

Colin started counting fingers on his right hand, then went. "Noise from next door; can't ignore. Tension's on fire, we all shook. Cut him with my little finger, Captain Hook."

"Would you quit that?" Pat said. "This is not the time for one of your so-called raps. The lyrics don't even make sense."

"It's a work in progress. I had to come up with it quickly."

"You didn't *have* to come up with anything, you idiot."

"I liked the Captain Hook bit," Cummy Ian said from behind his phone. "It's got potential."

"GET BACK HERE! GET THE BLOODY HELL BACK HERE!" Richard said from next door.

Pat eyed Alex. "Seriously, who's he talking to?"

"No one."

"Screw it. I've had enough of this. Gary, stop standing there and do as you were told. Go get the cunt."

"Right you are."

This time Gary got further. Alex moved to block his path, but Pat grabbed her waist from behind, wrenching her out the way. "I don't think so, little lady."

Alex thrashed her feet about, attempting to break free, but Pat lifted her off the floor as Gary walked past the two of them and out the doorless front of the cottage.

"Get your hands off me. Let go! Let fucking go!" Alex screamed. "Wentworth, for the love of god, do something."

"Shut the fuck up, bitch," Pat said then headbutted her from behind, driving his skull into the back of hers. Alex's body fell limp in his hands.

Fuck it!

I lunged for Pat but before I got close, Cummy Ian, still recording with his phone, intercepted with a left hook to the jaw that stabbed like a bee sting. I fell into the wall, sliding down to the floor to the laughter of some of the men.

As I was recuperating, I caught Norman out of the corner of my eye, running for Cummy Ian, brandishing a kitchen knife, but before Norman could stick Ian with it, the lad known for cumming his pants, delivered a roundhouse kick that knocked Norman to the ground and out for the count. He may have looked as ferocious as an out-of-date Dairylea cheese triangle, but he was moving like someone fresh out of the UFC's octagon and still managing to record everything on his battered-to-shit phone.

Cummy Ian bent over Norman, retrieving the knife from the floor. He laughed, spit spilling out of his mouth like water, then stuffed the knife into his back pocket.

Ian flipped the phone so the camera faced him, and said, "One taken care of, boss."

Alex groaned from the floor. "What's going on?"

Before anyone could answer, Gary returned to the room, a fresh cut above his eyebrow and a much bloodier, beat-up Richard struggling to stand by his side.

Gary held a baseball bat towards Richard, gesturing for him to join his wife on the floor.

Richard quickly stumbled over in compliance.

"Good work," Pat said, slapping Gary on the back. "Now watch them closely and keep that bat on them at all times."

Gary nodded.

"Where'd you get it from anyway?"

"The bat?"

"Yes, Gary. Obviously the fucking bat."

"It was just sitting there outside the house. Waiting for me."

Pat laughed, then turned to Richard. "So, you must be the husband. The fucking wife beater, huh?"

"No," Richard said, his breathing laboured and voice ailing.

"Sock him, Gary. Below the neck, this time."

Gary swung the bat into Richard's stomach. He let out a grunt. It was obvious the big man was trying to hold it together and not react, but his eyes were watering under the pain of it all.

"You really don't hit your wife?" Pat said.

Richard shook his head, though even that slight movement seemed to bring him pain.

"Then why's she look like that?" Pat asked.

"It's not me. I swear."

"Again," Pat said to Gary. This time he drove the bat into Richard's ribs with a sickly crunch.

Alex screamed. "It's not him. It's not him, okay? Leave him alone, you monsters. He's innocent."

"He's a big bastard of a man who beats up those smaller than him, is what he is."

"No!" Alex screamed. "Just no! He's a gentle giant. He wouldn't hurt anyone deliberately."

"Deliberately," Pat scoffed. "You hear this fucking shit? He's got the little lady believing each punch is an accident. What you think happened, bitch? He reached for a bottle of water, tripped, and smacked you in the face? That how you think all this happened?"

"It wasn't him! His fist never touched me."

"Guess she's never been fisted," Colin said, laughing to himself.

"Neither have you, you fucking spaz," Gary said. "Haven't been fisted. Haven't fisted. You don't know the simple joys of a—"

"Shut up!" Pat said. "No more interjections, you big bunch of twats. You!" Pat pointed a doughy finger at Richard. "Just tell me why you beat your wife and if I think it's justified, I might go easy on you."

Richard tilted his head up towards Pat. "I don't."

"Gary," Pat said.

Gary launched the bat into Richard's back. He fell flat on his face.

"Next time it'll be the kisser," Pat said. "We've played nice but like Gary's hairline, my patience is running thin."

"You can hit me as much as you like," Richard said. "But it won't change the facts. I haven't laid a finger on my wife."

"I'd finger his wife," Colin said, grinning and searching the room for a reaction that wasn't forthcoming.

Even Cummy Ian shot Colin a disapproving glare.

"He's a stubborn cunt, ain't he?" Pat said to the room. "Change of tack then. Here's what's gonna happen. I'm gonna show you just how you should go about loving your wife. I want you to watch every detail. Every intimate little movement. Take it in. Learn. Then, once we're done, I'm gonna beat the bejesus out of you. A preview as to what will happen should you touch the little lady again. After which, I think our business here is concluded, at least for now. My nephew's already seen to it that those two dweebs have had a receipt for their bullshit, ain't that right?"

Ian nodded. "Was just doing my job. And I got it all on my Nokia so we can watch it as many times as we want on the way back."

"I can hit them, too, if you want, Dad?" Colin said.

"No, thanks, son. I think we've made our point. As long as they don't try to interfere with what we're about to do then we're all square." He turned his attention to me. "But if you *do* interfere. If you so much as raise a single objection, then we'll gut the lot of you, including that bird of yours, Amanda."

Adrenaline fired through my body. "So you *do* know where Amanda is. Please ..."

"Silence!"

"It's okay," Alex said. "Everything is going to be okay. We all need to remain calm. Let's just do what they want."

Norman started to stir on the floor.

"You see?" Pat said, clapping his hands together. "The little lady gets it. Smart as well as sexy."

Pat ran a weathered hand through Alex's hair. She shivered with repulsion.

"No!" Richard said. "I can't let them do this."

"Darling, please ..." Alex said. "You have to. Think about what's at stake here. Think about *everything* that's at stake."

"She's right," Gary said. "If you want a shot at being on *Naked Attraction*, you've got to stay alive."

Richard looked at Gary, utterly confused as to why this inane man with *his* baseball bat was talking about Channel 4's surrealist attempt at a dating show.

Gary took the look for permission to give a fuller explanation. "It's a reality show in which—"

"No! You stop that right now. Shut the fuck up about *Naked Attraction*," Pat said.

Norman sat up, rubbing rheum out of his eyes. I wouldn't be surprised if mentioning *Naked Attraction* was the most effective way to wake him from a coma.

"All you need to do is sit there like an obedient little puppy," Pat said to Richard, who was still in front of Gary, drenched in more blood than a metalhead at a Watain concert. "Watch and learn. Take some notes as I show you how to make love to your wife the right way."

Richard pressed his hands into the ground, ready to rise, but Gary stroked the baseball bat against his neck in warning.

"You want me to get him a pen and paper to take notes like?" Colin asked.

"Not literally, you dumb cunt."

Pat took the knife from his pocket once more and stroked the blade across the top of Alex's bosom. "This is going to be a lot of fun. I'm getting a semi just thinking about it."

Richard let out a guttural scream. So primordial, so booming, it seemed to rock not just the house but the foundations on which it was built. The fabric of Mona itself.

Then there was a serene stillness.

As if the scream had the power to stop time.

Alex brushed the knife away from her breasts and took a single step away from Pat and towards Richard.

Her face was a ghost but it wasn't her own.

She wore the expression of the innocents who had died before her and, in that moment, I understood the grief and the unspoken secrets she carried. Her face was both a premonition and a warning. A tale of past and future horrors.

Then there came a rumbling in the adjacent cottage. We all heard the front door of the neighbouring cottage creak open and a rapid skittering advance towards us.

Alex reached for Richard, and he reached back for her.

Their hands touched for a moment until Gary pulled Richard back. But Richard was no longer concerned with Gary. Gary was a speck of spit in the vast ocean of life.

Alex and Richard stayed connected. Through eyes and understanding. Through dark secrets and repressed guilt.

The skittering grew closer.

Almost upon us.

"Oh, Richard, honey," Alex said, face full of fear. "Why did you have to unleash him like that?"

"He's a daddy's boy," Richard said. "He'll save us."

The skittering stopped, and we all looked towards the cottage entrance.

Richard cackled mad laughter. "He's here."

37

WHAT FOLLOWED WAS quick and chaotic. Colin stood closest to the broken front door, frantically counting syllables on his fingers as he attempted to compose another bar.

But it was the rhyme that was never meant to be.

A shadow of skin and hair scurried into the house on all fours like a human-sized arachnid. Screeching with such ear-splitting savagery, it made Richard's primordial scream resemble a soothing lullaby.

The amalgamation of flesh and fur launched itself at Colin, Thesz press-style. But instead of fists, Colin was met with a rusted hunting knife that slashed in swift succession as if slicing a crisp lettuce.

I darted into the living room. Hiding behind the sofa.

Pat reached for his gun, but suddenly Richard was on his feet, booting the firearm out of Pat's hand with a hefty Timberland.

Pat yelped, examining his newly dislocated index and middle fingers. Alex took advantage of the temporary distraction, fleeing into the kitchen.

Crawling on the floor, Pat scrambled for the gun. His buckled fingers were inches from it when Richard stomped his boot onto Pat's already injured hand, culminating in a branch-like snap.

Colin's body—still and stiff and smothered in shades of sickly red—was flung out through the front of the house. It flopped lifelessly onto the front lawn—a scrap of meat discarded for dogs. His treasured basketball shirt, shredded and frayed, drenched in crimson. Brown slush seeping out the bottom of his shorts, splashes of blood and nut-speckled muck catching on his leg hairs.

Then the amalgam of flesh and fur arched its back slowly, standing fully.

Elementary school student tall. Battered and weathered.

A boy?

Stunted and underdeveloped.

Wild and untamed.

Savage and feral.

Wiry chest hair covered his nipples. Dirt coated his body like clothing. The only actual garment, a raggedy pair of once white soiled briefs.

Cummy Ian ran over and delivered a devastating roundhouse kick to the boy's head. He connected perfectly, but the boy barely moved as if his skull was made of metal and he was the bionic-fucking-man.

Cummy Ian was already halfway to celebrating, hands triumphantly raised in the air, when this undomesticated beast of a boy, this feral, stunted male, jumped in the air as if a flying squirrel and stuck Ian in the neck with the hunting knife.

Ian staggered on the spot. Crimson gushed out of his nape like a hole in a water hose before he collapsed where Norman once baked his infamous brick.

A clap of gunfire. Then another. Pat was on his feet, taking potshots at the beast boy. But Beast Boy was too fast, jumping and dodging, screeching and squealing, darting around like a coked-up chimpanzee. It didn't help that Pat was using his uninjured left hand and his aim was as good as Stevie Wonder playing darts.

Norman got to his feet just in time to take one of Pat's rogue bullets. It kneecapped Norman, and he fell back towards the ground. As he was falling, a second bullet scraped his stomach and he yowled.

Pat limped over to Norman, ready to finish him. But I wasn't going to let that happen.

I leapt over the sofa and smacked the gun out of Pat's fist. Quickly, I wrenched at his wounded hand, putting him in an armbar on the floor. I jerked his arm back with all my might, pulling and twisting at the socket.

Norman, who was bleeding out, began chuckling. "Yeah, boy! Thought you didn't know taekwondo."

"I don't. But I did a bit of jiu-jitsu."

"Well, why didn't you say?" Norman grimaced, each word taking significant effort.

"Stop talking. You're hurt."

"You should have said something about your judo jitsu. I'm your father."

"Sometimes you have to hold things *back*," I said, slamming all my weight back against the floor, tightening my grip on Pat's arm, and breaking the fucking thing with a socket-wrenching snap.

Norman shook his head in disbelief. "I thought you were a dry fanny, but you've got some moves, lad. That's my boy, that is!"

"Stop talking. *Please*."

I pushed myself up from the floor. Pat was screaming. His eyes watering. His trousers stained piss-wet at the crotch.

When I turned my attention from Pat, I found myself standing face-to-face with Beast Boy.

We locked eyes and he actually fucking snarled.

If you find yourself face-to-face with a bear, you shouldn't make any sudden movements. You should stand your ground. Make yourself tall. Wave your arms and intimidate the grizzly fucker. Then back away slowly.

I wasn't sure if the same rules would apply with Beast Boy, but it was worth a shot. I raised my hands above my head as if I was the pro wrestler Kane, gearing up to bring the fire.

But instead, the fire came to me with a ferocious roar and soon I was covered in a wet and mulchy substance.

I turned around to see Gary, close enough to slap, clutching the baseball bat.

Before I could react, half his face was shot off into a tapestry of whites and reds. Dripping and wet.

Behind Gary stood Richard. He held the gun Pat had brought to the party.

Gary slunk to the floor, dropping the baseball bat. The loud ring of metal hit the ground and pinched at my ears.

Beast Boy let out a scream and switched to an all-fours stance, reverting to his primal nature.

Richard stuffed the gun into his back pocket, then dashed between us, facing Beast Boy. "It's okay, son. Daddy's here."

Beast Boy remained on all-fours but let out a whimper.

"Come to Daddy," Richard said. "It's all over now. Nobody here's gonna hurt you."

I jumped at a hand on my forearm from behind.

Alex.

She led me a few steps backwards. We slowly edged towards the kitchen where she'd been hiding.

"Richard won't let him hurt you," she whispered. "He does it all for Richard."

"What the fuck? Are you saying the boy is the one who …"

"Shh," Alex said. "He's a good kid. With a keen sense of right and wrong. It's difficult to explain."

I remembered the Mickey Mouse handkerchief and the

child's bloodied vest jacket with the rabbit ears. There was nothing right about murdering a child like that, only wrong.

"Come on, boy. Easy does it now." Richard crouched in front of Beast Boy, holding his arms out. Ready to embrace.

Beast Boy didn't move.

Richard inched forward, still crouched. He touched a hand against Beast Boy's hair and the kid softened, going from all fours to a squat position as he let his father pet him.

"Such a good boy. Such a sweet daddy's boy," Richard said, stroking his hair.

Out of the corner of my eye, I glimpsed Pat sliding on the floor towards the two of them. Before I could do a damn thing, he was tugging at the gun in Richard's pocket, but Richard was fixated on his boy.

It was as if Richard couldn't feel it.

As if nothing other than his boy existed in the world.

Then Pat got a hold of the gun, using the last of his strength to squeeze the trigger and drive a bullet cleanly through Richard's head.

Beast Boy wailed as his father fell to the floor.

Love filled fatherly eyes stared up at the ceiling in adoration for his boy.

Dead before he hit the ground.

He probably hadn't registered the bullet.

But Pat sure as shit registered what happened next.

Beast Boy sprung to action. Faster and more chaotic than before. Beast Boy's hands clasped around Pat's neck, choking the oxygen from him as he sputtered for air and thrashed around. Hopelessly trying to push the untamed boy from him. But Beast Boy was determined and powerful. Fuelled by hatred and grief and despair at not being able to protect his father.

Pat's eyes soon turned red and bloodshot. His face gained a pinkish hue.

The gun dropped from Pat's hand and Beast Boy removed his own hands from around Pat's neck.

Pat wheezed great gulps of air through his mouth. Greedily guzzling as if a child who'd found the secret stash of fizzy drinks. Pat's eyes displayed something bordering on gratitude for the boy. But it was short-lived. Beast Boy picked up the gun and started striking Pat with the rear. Pat made a hell of a noise at first—wheezing and yawping with such intensity he likely ruptured something. But as the boy drove the end of the gun into Pat's forehead again-and-again, Pat's protests faded, then silenced.

Only when the boy had borne a scarlet hole in the centre of Pat's skull, jam-like gunk leaking out of his new orifice, did Beast Boy stop.

But the boy wasn't done.

He dug his sharp, yellowed at the edges, fingernails into Pat's cheeks and began scratching his skin with cat-like sharpness. Only *scratch* wasn't right. He was using his strength. Pinching and clawing. Ripping and prizing wattles of flesh from both sides of Pat's face. Peeling open his sun-weathered skin like an overripe orange. Searching for the fruit inside, but only uncovering rot.

Beast Boy took a slab of newly removed face flesh and popped it into his mouth. He chewed loudly, then beetle-scuttled over to his dead father, curling up on his lap like a house cat.

The boy continued to chomp, then spat the masticated face flesh to the ground. It rolled under a tattered chair.

38

THE COTTAGE STOOD STILL.

And if it hadn't been for the carnage inside—more shades of red than a low budget giallo set—you might even have said it was serene.

Norman held his wounded stomach. Blood oozing between his fingers. Face growing paler and more pained.

Cummy Ian lay dead on his back in the front doorway. Hunting knife still sticking out of his neck.

Colin's ragged carcass was sprawled outside and out of sight after Beast Boy had violently discarded him for the elements to consume.

Gary was flat on his front in the hallway. His blood spatter on the floors and walls. If you sucked in enough air, you could taste the lad.

Still holding onto my arm, shaking more than an over-caffeinated junkie on a bucking bronco, was Alex.

Beast Boy began to wail. The pain of his father's death consuming his reality. All threat of violence now as absent as Norman had been for the first thirty years of my life.

Then the sobering realisation they still had Amanda hit

me harder than a drunken stepfather back from a night on the lash.

I pulled myself up from the floor. Alex kept hold of my arm for a moment before letting go.

"It's not over," I said, pins and needles sending my balance off as I staggered for the door.

But before I could get there, my path was blocked.

"You're bloody right it's not over, squire. You just keep getting yourself into a pickle now, don't you?"

Tricky Ricky stood in my way. Extravagant cane in hand, supporting his weight.

He was a man of wealth and power. Of influence and persuasion. But his cronies were dead on the floor. And an abundance of weapons were scattered around them.

Cummy Ian's head lay at my feet. I ripped the rust-covered hunting knife from his neck to a spurt of blood, then held it out in front of me.

"You tell me where Amanda is right now. I don't want to have to hurt you. But I will if that's what it takes."

Tricky Ricky guffawed with laughter. "Oh, squire, I think it will take a little more than that poxy knife."

"Can't say I agree with you there. I think this knife is gonna do more than enough to slice up your liver-spotted skin ... *squire*."

He grinned. "Quite the attitude. And, in normal circumstances, you might well be right. But you're not just up against me. Not really up against me at all."

There'd been far too much bloodshed for me to decipher codes.

"Stop spitting philosophy and talk to me plainly," I said.

He bowed to me, then stepped aside.

Behind him stood Wesker's Sister. She wore a black tank top, jeans, and combat boots. Samurai sword in hand. Up close, the weapon looked much bigger than it had from the comfort of the car.

"What a bloody mess. Look at what's happened to my men," Tricky Ricky said with thickened confidence now he had Wesker's Sister there to protect him. "And all because of this mutt." He gestured to Beast Boy, still softly mewling on his father's lap. "I know what he did here. And I know what he did before today, too. He might be able to evade the police, but he can't get anything past me. Nobody can. I have ears everywhere. Nobody can pull anything off without my knowing, you understand?"

Wesker's Sister nodded. A silent bodyguard reenforcing her master's words.

"For every action, there is a price to pay. The boy's had a good run of it, but it's now time to put the animal down."

"No," Alex said from behind me. "You can't—"

"There is no *can't* when it comes to me, love," Tricky Ricky said, then turned to Wesker's Sister. "Show them why you're called the Slicer. Put the animal down."

Wesker's Sister stepped into the cottage. I stood my ground, keeping the old hunting knife pointed towards them as protection. Though, in truth, my hunting knife to Wesker's Sister's samurai sword was the equivalent of holding a BB gun to defend against a rocket launcher.

"Please don't do this," I said, a tremble to my voice and hands.

"Get out of the way," Tricky Ricky said, "and there's a possibility you'll live."

But I didn't.

I couldn't.

"And if you live," Tricky Ricky said, slowly stepping into the cottage, a safe distance behind Wesker's Sister, "then you might just see Amanda."

He had to be messing with me. Mentioning the one person I would sacrifice anything for.

Would sacrifice *anyone* for.

I'd inadvertently let Rory get away. I could even admit I'd

wronged Amy before. And if I was being honest, I hadn't shown up properly for Amanda either.

Which was why I couldn't let anything happen to her now.

There wasn't a damn thing I could do about my past actions.

But I was better than them.

And I could affect the present.

I glanced behind me at Beast Boy, Alex now next to him. Stroking his hair as he nestled into his slain father.

Innocent.

That's what Alex had called Beast Boy. But it was so far removed from reality.

And Alex wasn't innocent either. Whatever she had or hadn't done, she'd enabled him.

Which meant she was complicit.

Amanda, though, she really was innocent.

I should get out of the way then.

Should let whatever was going to happen, happen.

For Amanda.

For justice.

And yet I continued to physically stand my ground whilst my mental resolve faltered.

"Put the animal down," Tricky Ricky repeated.

But Wesker's Sister stood as still as me. And for what? Did she realise I was an innocent in this situation, too? That there was no sense in killing me? Or was this a power thing? She expected me to comply due to intimidation alone. A refusal to use force when her mere presence could accomplish just as much if not more.

Well, not this time.

I didn't budge. I refused to be bullied.

"Put the animal down," Tricky Ricky said again, his cool front beginning to waver. "Put the animal down. What's the matter with you?" He prodded Wesker's Sister from behind. "You know who I am. You know what I can do. So get to it. Why are you still standing there?"

Wesker's Sister remained stuck in position. She looked through me. Towards Beast Boy. As if I was a ghost. Or perhaps worse.

Like I didn't exist.

Like I never had.

And perhaps that was true. For what had I really achieved in the past three decades? What the fuck had I amounted to?

If I was dying today, I could hardly say I'd made the world a better place.

Truth be told, I'd contributed more pain than pleasure, which made me an abject failure. But if I was given another chance, another day, I could make amends and rewrite my current trajectory.

"Put the animal down," Tricky Ricky said again, face reddening, sweat dripping down his forehead, his temperament taking a turn for the worse. "You're a daddy's girl," he said. "And daddy's girls do what daddies say."

"A daddy's girl," Wesker's Sister repeated, still looking dead ahead, her back to her father. "You finally admit it then."

Tricky Ricky adjusted his stance, trying to stand tall, but suddenly looking very old and frail.

"I *was* a daddy's girl," Wesker's Sister said. "But you weren't a girl's daddy."

"What are you talking about?"

"*Wesker's Sister*," she said, spitting the words out with utter revulsion. "My name is Ellie. But you stopped calling me that after Wesker passed. Because as far as you were concerned, the wrong child died."

"Please just be a daddy's girl and put the animal down. Come now."

"You weren't a girl's daddy!" she said and there was urgency mixed in with the anger because, after all these years, he still didn't get it. "You weren't anybody's anything. These men—*your* men—are dead on the floor because of you. They were all so loyal to you. They fucking loved you. And I did, too. But you never reciprocated. Ever."

"Put the animal down, darling."

"No."

"Put the animal down."

"I said no. For once in my life, I said no."

"Put the animal down. Put the animal down. PUT THE FUCKING ANIMAL DOWN."

Tricky Ricky's rage and fire scorched flames inside Wesker's Sister. A blaze of betrayal, of gaslighting, of abuse, of years of pent-up anger and injustice.

Wesker's Sister, Ellie, raised the samurai sword and spun around. Knuckles whitening and muscles flexing under the force of her grip.

With a quick, swift diagonal strike, she sliced cleanly through Tricky Ricky from shoulder to hip.

There was a moment where Tricky Ricky stood there, split in half.

Then he fell in two opposing directions, spilling blood and guts on Norman's entrance floor. An entrance that now resembled and smelt closer to an abattoir than a family cottage.

I looked up at the photograph of Norman's mother, above the kitchen entrance, gazing out towards the front of the property. The matriarch watching over everything. A placid expression of utter indifference upon her face as if she'd seen it all before. Given she was the mother of Norman, I reckoned she'd seen a lot, but I doubted she'd seen a pissed-off daughter sever her father in half with a samurai sword.

Wesker's Sister stared down at Tricky Ricky.

Cleanly carved in two with machine-like precision.

She stayed motionless, and the rest of us followed suit. Norman wasn't physically capable of going anywhere in his state and neither Alex nor I were dumb enough to pick a fight with a woman holding a sword dripping with her father's blood.

Beast Boy perked up, staring curiously towards Tricky Ricky's slain body, but there must have been something inside the kid that told him to stay away.

Then the neighbour's cat, Rufus, wandered in. Tale held high like he was above the lot of us.

My heart quickened when Rufus lingered next to Tricky Ricky's corpse, giving it a bit of a sniff. Wesker's Sister's entire body was tensed tighter than a welded straitjacket. I imagined her lashing out at the moggy with her samurai sword, but she remained passive, letting the cat do his thing before the animal jumped up the stairs to roam the rest of the gaff.

Wesker's Sister looked up, staring right at me.

"I'm sorry," I said.

There was recognition between us. An understanding that this apology was about more than what I'd done.

Matter of fact, it wasn't really about me at all.

I took a chance. "I see you, Ellie."

She stared at me. Pulled a pair of car keys from her pocket and threw them towards me. I caught them clumsily.

"Your girl's in the back of the Merc," she said.

I blinked. "You're telling me she's been here all this time?"

"I never touched her. Nobody did. I only hurt them if they deserve it."

I swallowed. "So, the photos of Swain ... they were faked?"

She shook her head. "He got what was coming to him. They always do. There's a reason he fell out with my father when I was little."

She walked past me, past the fallen bodies, her samurai

sword scraping the floor behind her as though she now lacked the energy or will to carry it.

When she reached the backdoor, she kept walking towards the woods.

"Wait," I said. "Where are you going? What about your cars? What am I supposed to—"

She looked back at me. "Keep them. Burn them. Do what you will. We're done here."

With that, Ellie walked into the forest.

I looked at the Mercedes key in my hand. The literal key to Amanda. Just a few seconds away, out the front of the cottage.

Norman muttered something on the floor. His condition fast diminishing. I had to do something for him, too. I got my phone out of my pocket, glanced at the *"Pay me my fucking rent money or you're fucking out"* text from Harry. All niceties removed. But he was small fry now.

"What are you doing?" Alex said, still seated next to Beast Boy.

He neither resembled beast nor monster anymore.

Just a shaken child.

And how was it possible this was the same person who had ripped a man's face open like a bag of crisps?

"We need an ambulance," I said. "And the police."

A massive understatement given the place was coated in more blood than a Cannibal Corpse album cover.

"You can't," she said. "They'll take my boy away."

"What he did to Pat was practically self-defence," I said.

She shook her head.

"He did it to protect you," I said. "And Richard. That's why he did *everything*, right?"

But she wasn't buying into my bullshit. There was no sincerity in my voice, just fear as I regurgitated her own lines.

"He's a good kid," Alex said, and did she honestly believe that? "But it's not the way the police will see it."

"But my dad needs treatment," I said. "We should have

called an ambulance half an hour ago. But we didn't. I have to call now. What other choice do I have?"

"She's right," Norman said. "The cops are all bent bastards. You ring the police and that kid's in jail for the rest of his life or worse."

"My sweet baby boy," Alex whined.

And Christ, why did Norman have to fuck up everything? Even whilst dying!

Of course the police weren't going to take pity on this murderer, but how could Norman be too dense to see I was just playing along for his sake?

"Norman, you need an ambulance," I said firmly.

"Look at me, boy. Take a proper good look. At the rate I'm bleeding, I doubt I've got more than ten minutes in me. No ambulance is getting here in that time, not when we're so out in the sticks."

"We should at least try."

He shook his head. "Go to your girl and get the fuck out of here."

"But …"

"Or stay here with us," Alex said, getting up off the ground and walking over to me. "I think it could work." There was wild excitement in her voice. Excitement bordering on insanity from the look in her eyes. "We've always had a connection, haven't we, Wentworth? From the moment we saw each other, we knew there was something bringing us together, right?"

That wasn't true at all. I'd just been intrigued and slightly perplexed by her cat. Especially the whole walking the cat on a lead thing. Plus, the moggy had reminded me of Rory. It was nothing more than that.

And Christ, why the fuck was this happening? Amanda needed me! I could just run out of the place and go to her.

Perhaps I should.

"My boy was so protective of us," Alex said. "Especially

of his daddy. But you know that. You know that's how this all started, don't you? He protected us, so we protected him. That's what having a family is all about. If only Richard hadn't got involved with Leah, none of this would have happened." Alex tutted, which seemed incredibly understated given what she was talking about. "He just wanted to protect Richard and me. To keep the whole family together. Problem is, anytime he saw anyone who so much as resembled Leah … Well, let's just say the poor boy was traumatised. His brain got scrambled by everything. There was a time I wanted to go to the police. But Richard talked me around. Families stay together, Wentworth. No matter what. They protect each other."

Beast Boy reached his arm up towards his mother, but instead of gripping Alex's hand, he grabbed mine. His hand was warm and worn. Calloused beyond his years.

"He likes you," Alex said. "And I like you, too. You can stay here. We can be a family now."

I pulled away from the boy and distanced myself from Alex. Sick and overwhelmed.

"This is ridiculous," I said. "Your husband just died. You're not thinking straight. His body is literally there."

"I'll handle it," she said, glancing at her dead husband's corpse. "I know what I'm doing."

"It's not just about getting rid of it. It's about grieving. You're in shock."

"I've never been clearer."

"And me neither," I said, making to call the emergency services.

The sound of a gun cocking.

Then a shot.

A bullet rapidly raced past my head and pierced the wall.

Alex stood there, pointing the gun at me.

How many bullets did this fucking thing have and how many times was it gonna be used to threaten someone? And, most importantly, why hadn't I pocketed the bloody thing after Beast Boy had finished pummelling Pat?

"Let that shot be a warning," Alex said. "But know this: you're staying here. Dead or alive. And assuming alive, you're looking after us. I'd hoped you would come willingly, but there's always a plan B. So here's what we're going to do."

But before Alex could finish her sentence, there was a swift wind-like gust and a blade cut her in half from shoulder to hip.

She dropped to the floor, revealing Wesker's Sister.

Beast Boy let out a hellish scream and charged for Wesker's Sister but before he could get to her, I had the gun in my hands and shot the little cunt in the back of the head. There was no honour in it, but it was effective. I stopped the bastard dead on the spot.

"You really can shoot!" Norman croaked from the floor, then coughed up blood.

Ellie and I looked at each other.

"I thought you went," I said.

"I had a bad feeling about that bitch," Ellie said. "And a sneaking suspicion you'd get soft and wouldn't do what needed to be done. I reckon I was right on both counts, no?"

I couldn't argue with that.

"And I told you," Ellie said, "they always get what's coming to them. But this time, I'm going for real. Say goodbye to your deadbeat dad and get the fuck out of here with your girl. Next time you find yourself in the shit, I won't be here to bail you out. So make sure there isn't a next time."

With that she traipsed back through the bodies, out of the door, and into the forest.

I never saw her again.

I tucked Pat's gun into my pocket, then looked to Norman. I'd been to open casket funerals with corpses more alive than him. His skin and eyes were fast approaching Prince Philip's final years levels.

"I guess I can call that ambulance now," I said.

"Don't be a dickhead." Norman grinned, wincing as the laugh caused him pain. "They ain't got a shot at saving me at this point."

"I dunno, you've been brought back to life eleven times already. If there's one person who can be saved, it's you."

"Not this time," Norman said. "Cats have nine lives and I have twelve. At any rate, this life is so bloody exhausting and I'm in too much pain. I'd rather just be done with it all. I had a good run of it, or maybe I didn't, but this is the end of the road for me. Besides, the way my mum's will was written, with me dead and Timothy out of the picture, I reckon this place will fall to you."

"Timothy? Your rich brother? What do you mean he's out the—"

"We don't have the luxury of time and you ain't a priest. Point is, if you want the cottage, it's yours."

"After what's gone down here today, I think I'll pass."

"I promised you a million pounds for an easy job. The cottage is worth at least that."

"Easy job …"

"I guess it got a little messy, huh?"

"Norman, I really don't know what to say."

"Say you'll take the cottage. Could make a nice little spot for you to set up a family."

Rufus walked downstairs, tail high and proud.

"Speaking of which …" Norman winked. "There's a sweet cat for the taking, too."

"There's no way I'm living here. I don't ever want to set foot in Mona again. No offense."

Norman shrugged. "You might not have a choice once the place is legally yours. But whether you keep it or sell it, you'll get your money. It's only taken me my entire life but I've finally made good on a promise. Dunno whether to be proud or embarrassed."

"I've got to get to Amanda," I said, holding up the keys to the Mercedes.

"Pass me your phone," Norman said. "I've got a guy who can give the Merc a paint job and get a fresh set of plates on her."

"I don't want your help anymore. You've done enough."

He went quiet for a moment, then said, "Yeah. I suppose that's fair."

"I'm sorry we didn't really get to know each other," I said.

"Oh, but we did. You came through for me, boy. Think about what went down today. Think about everything we've experienced since the day I approached you outside NatWest. We've gone through more in a week than most fathers and sons have in a lifetime. If I could do it all again, I wouldn't change a single thing."

"You have got to be shitting me ..."

"We bonded. We watched *Naked Attraction*. We shot guns in the woods. We ate frozen sausages. We almost had a wank together. Hell, I watched you break a grown man's arm. That's all a father could ever ask for." He took a moment to vigorously cough into the hand that wasn't placed against the wound in his abdomen—when he'd finished, his hand was dotted with blood. "I love you, son."

He stared at me.

An awkward pause as a dying man waited for me to say "I love you" back.

But it wasn't true. And I wouldn't lie to him like that, even if it would have helped him go easier. Too much of his life had been built on lies and half-truths. He'd lived like that, but I refused to facilitate him going out like that.

"Well then," Norman said, "you do Daddy proud. You've got your own family now."

"Excuse me?"

"Amanda. And that bastard cat over there. Plus, you've as good as got this cottage. I know you said you didn't want it, and I get that you're feeling that way right now, after all we've been through, but given some time, a lick of reasonably priced paint from B&Q, and a new front door, I reckon you'll be back here. Working the docks and living the good life," Norman said. "But whether you're here or not, you make a proper woman out of Amanda, okay? Don't make the mistakes I did. You treat her right. Do everything I taught you down below; the ice cream, the white-water rapids, the angry Jeremy Corbyn. You do them every night. You get all the juice out of her. Don't stop until she's got nothing left to give. Leave her dryer than the Sahara. You hear me, boy?"

I nodded because it was what he wanted and he was fading out of consciousness, but as per usual, I reckoned what he was saying and what he wanted to say was somewhat different. If he'd been performing until his women were sandpaper dry, he wasn't the prolific stud he talked himself up to be.

"Treat her good!" he shouted with more energy than he had any right to have.

"I really should go to her now," I said.

"You're right there, kid. But you've got to do me a favour. A dying man's wishes, yeah?"

I went to say "anything" but given who I was dealing with and his track record, I held back.

"The *Naked Attraction* letter," he said. "Get it out of the cunt's pocket, would you?"

I crept over to Pat nervously. There was a part of me that expected him to leap up the moment I got close, to wrap his hands around my throat and choke me until I was as lifeless as all those women Beast Boy had butchered. A nightmarish and unlikely imagining given I'd broken Pat's arm and Beast Boy had made a new hole in his head, bored out bits of his brain, as good as ripped his face off, and then ate bits of the cunt as if a hyena ravaging a body for scraps.

I had to roll Pat from his back to his front. There was a wet squelch as he went, something spilling from his body in the turning. I neglected to investigate further.

I retrieved the letter, tugging it from his pocket. There was no zombie-like movement from Pat. No hand-from-the-grave *Carrie*-style action. The dude was dead, but I felt no relief. Just unsettled and shaky from having to get so close to the bastard.

I rushed back to Norman, smoothing out the creased letter.

"Give us a look," Norman said, snatching the letter and squinting over its contents.

He sighed, agitated, which didn't make any sense.

"Damn vision's failing me," Norman said. "Words bouncing around more than Pamela Anderson's jubblies in *Baywatch*. What's it say, boy? Give me the skinny."

"It says you got in. They accepted you."

"Ha!" he said, high-pitched and excited, then proceeded to cough up more blood. "I knew it. I bloody knew it. I dunno if it was the application or the bribe, but whatever I did, it worked."

"The bribe?"

"No time to explain. You contact the producers and I'm sure they'll fill you in. Speaking of things I don't have time to explain, you check your grandmother's urn on the way out, yeah? It's on the windowsill in the kitchen, next to the Fairy Liquid. Now onto more important matters." He thrusted his mobile phone into my hand, then reached for his trouser zipper but couldn't quite get a purchase on it. "One last favour, yeah?"

And the way he was wrestling with his flies with increasing frustration, it became obvious what he wanted. A sex-obsessed loon until the end.

"I'm sorry, boy," he said, "I'm bleeding too much and the pain's stabbing in places I've never felt before. You're gonna have to do the honours. Unzip my jeans, yeah?"

"Jesus, Norman. You want me to beat you off?"

"Course I don't!" And for once, he sounded disgusted with me. "I'm losing enough fluid as it is, don't need to add cum to the mix. Although ..." He looked up at the ceiling, considering it. "It would be a pretty rock 'n' roll way to go. That's how Ozzy went, you know?"

"Ozzy isn't dead."

"Oh? Then I guess it was a dream. Or a premonition. Either way ..." He nodded to his crotch. "Get him out and take a snap. One last dick pic before I bow out."

"Jesus, what the—"

"Please, son."

There was desperation and vulnerability in him. As if he needed this more than anything. The way he'd called me son and not boy made me temporarily forget what he was actually asking. I was almost moved.

Almost.

"Whip out the old marrow snake, take a snap, and send it to Anna Richardson. Tell her I couldn't make it but I still wanted her to see this."

"You want me to send an unsolicited photo of my dead dad's dick to Anna Richardson?"

He shook his head. "You don't get it. This is a dying man's final wish. You can't refuse me. Them's the rules. This is practically the Make-A-Wish Foundation. They'd do it."

"I'm fairly sure the Make-A-Wish Foundation wouldn't allow a child to send an unsolicited dick pic to Anna Richardson."

"But I'm not a child," Norman said. "And it isn't unsolicited. That's what I'm saying. They accepted me. Which means Anna Richardson *wants* to see my dick. Please, son, I'm begging you here. If not for me, then do this for sweet Anna Richardson."

Go on. It's okay. Take the pic.

A voice that sounded like Alex's—or was it Amanda's—echoed inside of me. Encouraging me to take the photo.

I unsheathed my father's length. I'd never touched another man's dick before, but it felt cold and leathery in my hands, which I reckoned wasn't normal. My penis was mostly warm, but I figured there was a lack of blood pumping to Norman's as much of his blood painted the floor.

His dick lay there. Sluggish and slug-like.

"Pop back the lid," Norman said. "The foreskin, boy. Peel him back. It adds character."

But I shook my head and snapped the photo. Some final requests would have to go unfulfilled, and the old foreskin peel was one ask too many.

I showed Norman the photo, and he smiled approvingly. "Attaboy. You really are a daddy's boy after all."

With that Norman fell to his side, cock still peeping out of his wiry greying pubes, and died. A grin at the crease of his mouth.

He hadn't gone out with *Naked Attraction* playing in the background as he'd previously requested, but I'd wager this had been one better. I'd never seen so much contentment on a dead man's face.

After I'd found Rufus and secured him to a lead, I looked inside Norman's mother's urn, then raced out the front of the cottage.

Past the carnage. Past the worn-out Volvo. Towards the black Mercedes.

A click of a button on the key fob, a flash of light, and the doors were unlocked.

I pulled open the back passenger door.

Amanda sat there, impossibly still.

Black blindfold shielding her eyes, ropes wrapped thickly around her waist, seatbelt securing her in place.

I ripped the cover from her eyes.

"Amanda!"

She slumped to the side.

Her head almost conking the upholstery.

But then she course-corrected, struggling back up and opening her eyes. She looked towards me, though there was a grogginess there that made me doubt whether she'd really seen me or at least comprehended *who* she was seeing.

"I thought you were dead," I said, which for a moment I truly had.

I untied the ropes from her waist and unfastened the seatbelt, before helping her out of the car. Amanda's movements were shaky and uncertain.

I hugged her, then kissed her, and she kissed back.

"What happened?" she asked, her words jelly-like as if she was still coming to.

Perhaps she was.

I doubted she'd come with them voluntarily despite Wesker's Sister's insistence nobody had laid a hand on her.

"*Everything* happened," I said, taking her hand and walking back up the driveway towards my car. "It's a bloodbath in there."

"Then why are we going back?"

"We're not. We're going home."

"To the Midlands?"

I thought about Harry the landlord and the hostility in his last text. "I'm not sure there's a home there. Besides, home isn't a place. It's people."

I squeezed her hand. Amanda squeezed, too, then noticed the cat lead in my other hand.

"You got Rory back?"

"That ain't Rory. But looks a lot like him, huh?"

I popped open the old Toyota. The cat jumped up onto the backseat contentedly.

"Shouldn't he be in a cat cage or something? What if he does something crazy?"

"He can't do anything crazier than what I've seen these past twenty-four hours."

"You going to tell me about it?"

"In time."

I got in the driver's seat and Amanda took the passenger's seat up front, next to me.

"Why are you driving this when you had the keys to the Merc?" she asked.

"Because I'm starting afresh. Anything Norman would do, I don't want any part of."

"That sounds very virtuous of you, but how the hell are we going to start afresh with no jobs and no money?"

I pulled a stack of folded up notes from my trouser pocket and showed them to Amanda. "Got a little starter fund here. No ashes in Norman's mother's urn, just a thick wad of cash."

"Nothing Norman would do, huh?"

"Well, almost. Guess some things are in my blood."

"A daddy's boy after all then?" She patted her belly. "And soon a boy's daddy."

I turned to her. "You serious?"

She nodded. "Guess that explains the nausea, huh?"

This time we kissed properly.

I pulled away from the cottage. As it faded from view, I swore I saw grey billows of smoke encasing the place. Perhaps Norman had pulled off one final trick before death. Turning the house into one big incinerator and destroying much of the evidence of the evening's events.

It wasn't my problem anymore.

I was free.

At least until the will and insurance money caught up with me.

But for then, for now, it was just me, my pregnant girl, my cat, and the road.

A daddy's boy no longer.

Just a soon-to-be daddy.

A daddy who would be haunted by the demented nonsense words of his father for a long time to come.

Do the angry Jeremy Corbyn with Amanda and she'll never leave you.

I just might, Dad.

I just might.

ABOUT THE AUTHOR

Michael David Wilson is the founder of the popular horror website, podcast, and publisher, *This Is Horror*. In addition to *Daddy's Boy*, he is the author of *The Girl in the Video*, *They're Watching* (with Bob Pastorella), and *House of Bad Memories*. His work has appeared in various publications including *The NoSleep Podcast*, *Dim Shores*, and Hawk & Cleaver's *The Other Stories*. Michael lives in Gifu, Japan. You can connect with Michael on X @thisishorror.

For more information, including news and updates, please visit www.michaeldavidwilson.co.uk.

To support Michael David Wilson's fiction and get exclusive content such as live readings and Q&A sessions, please become a patron at www.patreon.com/michaeldavidwilson.

To support *This Is Horror Podcast* and get early access to episodes, and submit questions for guests, please become a patron at www.patreon.com/thisishorror.

Previous This Is Horror Podcast guests include Dean Koontz, Chuck Palahniuk, Charlaine Harris, Josh Malerman, Joe Hill, Jason Pargin, David Dastmalchian, and Caroline Kepnes.

ALSO BY MICHAEL DAVID WILSON